ABIOTA · BOOK 1

E. M. RENSING

Source Code

Unity Code

Numina Code

Domain Code

Virch Code

Anyon Code

For the men and women of the 147th Operations Group
Shine on, you crazy bastards

[1]

Daelia Hall took a deep breath and stepped into the virch.

Opening her eyes, the scene that greeted her was nothing like the physical space she'd just left.

Here, a different reality reigned.

The airfield lights glittered under the glow of a false dawn, glowing like fireflies in the depths below. Falling away, fading into nothing as the RPA achieved takeoff.

Airborne now, the scene around her was of a deep canyon, striated where an ancient river had worn its course through the primordial sandstone. That river glistened a thousand feet beneath her, white and frothy as it beat against stubborn rock outcroppings or plunged down waterfalls so tall that they turned into clouds of mist before they hit the ground.

Vast bat wings on either side of her tightened, spreading or sweeping back in just the right angle to take the curve. Reins there were, clasped in the hands in front of her, thick leather gloves worn smooth in places from past fights. There was the sound of wind in her ears. Wind, and wings, and breath, as the great beast below her huffed with its exertions.

A dragon. Emily was a dragon here. A creature of coiled muscle and wiry sinew beneath small hard-edged scales. Her wings were translucent against the warm autumn sky. Veined with gold. Glorious and triumphant.

It would be so easy to just let go, Daelia mused. Just flow into it. Not worry about anything else.

Just enjoy it for what it was.

Emily in her element.

Fulfilling her primary purpose.

Having fun in her favorite form.

But—

<How are we looking in there?>

The voice crackled in over the radio. Siren Operations Center. Bumper, if Daelia remembered the preflight briefing this morning. The number two guy in the squadron.

This was glorious.

This was work.

<Launch and Recovery reads fine,> answered another male voice, smooth and deep and rich as butter. Marathon, one of the line fliers, B-Flight commander. <Good connection, no interference, clean signal. No lag. BR?>

That was her.

Focus, she told herself. Wrenched her attention back where it needed to be.

Daelia opened up a command-line screen, letting the flow of code at the back end of this world unspool around her.

Doing so made her vaguely nauseous, like reading while driving. The screen punched a perfect cube out of the projection, a disorienting visual anchor against the dynamics of VR-enhanced flight.

"So far, so good," she said, and cringed. Dad had been trying to coach her on proper radio etiquette. Bumper especially had very little patience for anybody, even a contractor, fucking up the details. *Professional,* she told herself, *be professional.* "Bellona Robotics showing 98.7 percent fidelity in control linkage." She shook the reins in her gloved hand, watching the lines glow ever so slightly. "Simulation translation holding strong."

<Maintaining a steady 168 knots in Gulf access corridor,>

Marathon said. <Entry into training ground airspace in thirty-five seconds.>

<SyROC reads, LRE. Emily, you're cleared for personal time out there for the next ten minutes.>

Good, good, Daelia's mount said. Beneath her, around her.

Far, far away from her.

"Don't make me throw up," Daelia warned.

But all she got in return was a deep, rumbling laugh.

The illusory canyon suddenly narrowed and broke open, signifying the end of the air lane. For a moment, the virtual reality overlay blurred. There was nothing but blue and white. Blue sky. Blue water. White clouds, reaching up to the sleeping stars. These were real at least, huge and white, swept in off the Gulf in the very last struggling weeks of hurricane season.

Sky quite nice today, her mount observed. *I pull it into virch for you.*

"Very considerate of you, girl," Daelia replied, and loosened her grip on the reins. "Show me what you've got."

Emily screeched in reply and threw herself into a dive.

In reality, it was a minor dip. Very minor. Emily's machine body was built for endurance, inherently stable. She wasn't one of those new model FQ-47s, where instability was the entire point. But thanks to an exquisitely tuned virch field, every twitch of the rudder, every flick of the ailerons, was a gut-twisting maneuver.

Daelia let Emily have her head.

And held on.

Emily roared through it, grabbing at the bit and laying on the speed. She shot out, twisting with the joy of open flight. Catching a thermal, Emily swept high into the open sky. This was a world of peaks and crags, of plummeting valleys and vast plains.

Some people thought that abiota couldn't experience true joy, real passion. No exuberance or excitement. Those people were idiots.

Those people had never been on a flight with Emily.

Daelia minimized the common prompt screen, throwing over the data analysis to a code-bot for a few minutes. The tiny abiota manifested as a bird between Daelia's hands, clutching Emily's saddle with all its might, even as its keen eyes scanned the scrolling code, missing nothing.

Emily laughed as she played.

The clouds might have been real, but the mountains, the far castles, the glimmering hints of snow or ice or gleaming metal-skinned structures? Those weren't.

This wasn't an Air Force-issue base-wide simulation field. Not the generic Omphalos standard.

No, this was a fully custom private environment. The Air Force frowned on its airframes indulging in such things. But then, this was the Texas Air Guard, and the abiota who owned this place was orcinus-class.

The base network made allowances.

They were lucky Emily listened to them at all, really.

As if from a great distance, Daelia made a few adjustments on the keyboard under her left fingers. Color saturation, volume, the neural feedback she received through the brace on her left arm.

She had a full VR rig on, the visor totally encasing the upper part of her head. It wasn't like in one of Dad's old science fiction books, where a person totally lost contact with their body. You needed one of the new NULI implants for that, and no matter what she used to tell her classmates back at Ware, Daelia had no desire to get one of those.

Hell, she could barely stand the haptic feedback of her brace most days.

But this wasn't just the itch of bypassed nerves. Not just motion sickness from the visor.

Something was off.

The more she fiddled, the more she felt it.

She switched off her radio so the guys couldn't hear her. "What are you seeing, bot?"

Code itches, Emily said. *Turn off analysis screen.*

"Can't do that. Need to make sure you're good to go for this training flight."

Why you ruin my fun, spawn? Talking about meatspace, ehg.

"You know I have to make sure the simulation's aligning, Emily," Daelia chided back. "There is something here that's not quite right."

Everything wonderful, Emily said, and dove again, graceful as a dolphin. *You not pilot, yes yes yes not pilot not used to this.*

It hit home. Daelia tried to ignore it. Emily had zero sense for human niceties. She was smart enough to grasp them but didn't care to.

"No, girl, I am not," Daelia murmured, and looked up just in time.

The vast ruins of a mountaintop castle rose before her, the thick walls coming up almost too fast to—

With a gasp she couldn't help, Daelia yanked hard on the reins, steering Emily away at the last second. The dragon roared with laughter as they shot up and over the top of the wall, broken fangs of masonry reaching up to bite at Emily's underbelly.

"Yeah, yeah, yeah, very funny," Daelia grumbled.

Not pilot, Emily said again. Almost smug.

Emily's virch field roughly corresponded to reality. It turned buildings into peaks, trees into forest groves larger than the tallest skyscrapers, threaded through with filaments of metallic ores. There was nothing out here for Emily to interpret, though, so the simulation was filling things in, totally at random.

It was enough to drive a girl crazy if she thought about it too hard.

Trying to focus, Daelia readjusted her screens.

But then, a flash of light above the false horizon caught her eye. There, in the spark-bright dawn, was an explosion. Like fireworks.

No.

Like a meteor.

Daelia's eyes narrowed beneath her visor. She'd never seen anything like it before. She blink-clicked the section of code, saving it for further investigation.

"Did you just see that?" she asked Emily.

Nothing to see but you fucking up such beautiful flight.

"Emily, don't lie to me."

I fuck around all I like, Emily said smugly, and snapped her wings wide to throw herself into a barrel roll that her machine form was certainly not capable of. *Should go home, load dummy munitions. Burn a castle or two.*

<You don't get to run even a practice bombing run while in the virch,> Bumper said over the radio. <You want to get us all court-martialed, Emily?>

Brass no understand.

<I think they understand you perfectly well, girl.> Bumper's radio muted for a moment, then came back on. <BR, evaluation?>

It took a moment more for Emily to pull out of whatever maneuver she'd just executed, to get some smooth sky back.

Daelia checked the code-bot's readout. It hadn't registered anything weird. Nothing was showing in any of the more conventional monitoring feeds. Whatever she had seen, it was most likely a glitch in her own equipment. "Connection fidelity's holding steady. Raijinn? Thoughts?"

Technically, Raijinn oversaw training. But it was overseeing Daelia's training as well, and just because Dad trusted her to do this right didn't mean the Texas Military Department, Air Combat Command, or the FAA did. So Raijinn was riding shotgun, so to speak. Monitoring the entire flight.

Its response was immediate.

I see no cause for concern here. A 98.5% verisimilitude, well within FAA safety parameters for unmanned flights, and Daelia has satisfied our own internal review.

Bumper sent Daelia an approval request. It popped up in another screen cut into the virch. <BR, concur on that, please, and we'll have the flight crew step to the cockpit.>

"No problem," she said, and hit the digital signature button on the form. "You think the new guy can handle this?"

He Weapon School graduate, Emily said. *He be fine.*

[2]

IT'S LIKE RIDING A DRAGON.

Argo had used that line before. On his little brother. Out on dates. Drunk in bars.

A good line. A descriptive line. Evocative, which was always a good thing.

Most civilians had no idea what serving in the military was really like. What being a pilot was like. Most seemed to think it was a bold, exciting, courageous life. An adventure.

Romantic, even.

Maybe it had been like that once, back in the days of open cockpits and daring dogfights. Probably not, though.

What civilians didn't want, in Argo's experience, was the reality.

They didn't want to know about the stink of body odor that built up in the tight confines of the cockpits. The eyestrain from military-spec screens, or the unreliability of equipment ten years or more past recommended life spans. The way your butt started to hurt after a while, or the sheer boredom of most missions.

They didn't want to know.

So.

It's like riding a dragon.

Argo had said it a hundred times.

He had never really meant it.

It had never really been literal.

Not until today.

This was…

Let go of reins!

The emergent's voice was a rumble in his ear, one that somehow managed to employ some element of femininity despite the depth of it. It vibrated his headphones, an itch in his eardrums he couldn't escape. Argo gritted his teeth against it.

Held steady on the reins.

Shit, he hated flying with the haptic gloves.

"Pull up, Emily!"

Stop stop stop stopstopstopstopstop…

"I know what I'm doing," Argo snapped back, against the abiota's protest. The aircraft wasn't in that steep of a dive. It couldn't be. They weren't designed to do this. The MQ-9 literally couldn't fly like this. Emily was going to break the fucking fuselage if she didn't stop this suicidal charge she was taking them on.

And then the dragon form finally pulled up, leveled out, bat wings snapping out hard. The action arrested the dive so close to the ground that the line of knights charging at them completely broke cohesion. Horses reared and snorted in terror. Armored bodies fell off. Screams rose.

Fake, it was all fake.

Ruined, my strafing run, ruined.

"Strafing run? Is that what you fucking call that?!"

All those little knights still moving, Emily said, and her false voice sounded mournful. *We go back, roast them proper.*

"I don't think so," Argo snapped.

What fun are you, pilot who doesn't want to play games?

"I'm not going to let you kill yourself."

The abiota gave no answer, but in the virch, her wings were pumping hard, gaining altitude again.

<What are you doing out there, Harrier One?>

Marathon, over in the LRE.

"She's fucking with me. The plane's not—"

<When you can't see the instrumentation like this, you absolutely have to work with her.>

"She's trying to plow herself straight into the drink."

<Argo, from me to you, do you really think she's that stu—>

More knights! Emily crowed joyfully. *We go again.*

Argo's concentration had slipped for a second. A second. But to an abiota, that was an eternity.

In the simulation, he had loosened his grip on the reins. If he'd had a hand on the stick, the real physical flight controls, a small release of pressure wouldn't have meant anything. But right now, he was flying with haptic gloves instead of his normal controls, playing by the rules of the virch.

"SyROC, SyROC, she's got the bit!" Argo's sensor said. In the cockpit, the master sergeant was sitting just to his left. In the virch, he was also on the dragon form's back, behind her wings in a separate saddle.

<Copy that,> Bumper's voice replied drily.

And yeah, the squadron DO was definitely pissed.

For a moment, Argo felt a sense of weightlessness that he shouldn't have been able to feel. The sensation a guy might feel at the very top of a roller coaster, or at the apex of a particularly steep maneuver, although it had been a long time since he'd flown anything from inside the fuselage.

Emily crested, graceful, fluid, hanging in midair for just a moment.

And then she fell. Straight down. Headfirst.

Wind whistling around him at sudden, horrific speed, Argo got the best grip he could, struggling to regain control. But she had it and wouldn't give it up.

Little knights, she crooned, fire gushing from her flared nostrils, sweeping back over Argo, *little knights, come and find your doom.*

"SyROC?" he asked, keeping his cool as best he could. "Procedure?"

<Emily, surrender control back to your pilot,> Bumper snapped over the radio.

He is in saddle. Not my fault he drops reins.

Below them, another castle loomed. Huge, this one.

Argo was fighting her now, trying to yank back on the reins, on the complicated flight harness that connected to both heads. His arms ached from the effort of fighting the feedback from the gloves. It was all bullshit, a simulation, except it wasn't, because the virch and the haptics made it real. Or real enough.

Shit, he couldn't crash this thing into the ocean.

Then a woman's voice came on the radio. <Emily, I swear to the first spark of your damn source code that I will personally strip your virch bottle to bare circuitry if you don't knock it off right now!>

But knights, little spawn.

<BR!>

<I know, I know. Give me a…Okay, override in place.>

A cube of bare space opened in front of Argo. His main cockpit control screen. For a moment, he was looking straight down and straight ahead at the same time. It took his brain a moment to catch up with what he was seeing.

The aircraft was in a dive. But not a very fast or steep one.

<Her control systems are linked to what you're seeing, but it's all exaggerated,> the woman's voice said. Her metadata ID'd her as the Bellona Robotics rep. <Emily, knock it off.>

But so fun, the pouted response came.

The pressure on the reins loosened, and Argo got his grip back. The angle of the dive hadn't changed, forcing him to yank up as hard as he could.

Emily swooped up out of the dive. So great was her projected bulk and so close to the castle were they that the simulation couldn't deconflict the two. Instead, Argo had a moment of near panic as gray stone walls rushed up to meet him, solid and ancient and—

And then the castle was gone.

The dive was over.

Emily leveled out again. A slight tick in her altimeter. Wings out and level, holding them aloft over the grassy plains. "Thanks," he said, brusque from the embarrassment. "You can close that screen out."

<You sure?> The woman sounded doubtful.

He reached down, patted the dragon's right neck. "We're good."

Fly more, Emily said, and turned into a wide curve. The override window blinked out. They crested over a small set of foothills and into a fresh environment. *Maybe knights in that tower.*

There. Not far. Across an endless volcanic waste that Argo was pretty sure was taken from aerial footage of Iceland, there was indeed a tower. A single, solitary tower.

<What are you doing, Emily?>

Tower, tower, tower, the abiota sang out, in rhythm with the beat of her wings, and then belched a huge mouthful of fire. *Little torch on the water.*

She swooped toward it. Argo tried to remember the preflight brief, the advice the guys in the shop had given him. *Work with her*, everyone had said, but damn, this was weird. Nothing was out here, though. That was the point of flying out here over the Gulf. Had to be just another element in her virch-enabled fantasy world.

"Argo, what are we doing?" Ho asked.

You pull back on us now? Emily taunted.

"By all means. Let's go for it."

Emily banked hard, wings taut, both heads forward. The tower was coming up fast. Argo could see details on it now. Vines, arrow slits, the tiles of the roof…

You like to pull, pull then, human.

"No, you want to fly into that thing, you can fly into that thing," Argo told her, beyond done with her bullshit at this point.

Maybe we light it on fire, Emily said deviously, *when we crash.*

"We're not going to crash now, are we? Because it's not fucking there."

Let's find out, she said, and rolled, banking toward it.

"Emily, pull up." Bumper's voice was steady on the radio, but Argo knew the guy well enough at this point to know he was pissed. "Pull up."

But fun little tower—

<Daelia? Where's the override?!>

<Something froze, trying to reload.>

<Argo!> Bumper was yelling now. <That's a real fucking oil platform, pull her back right the hell now!>

The words hit like a sack full of lead. And at the same time, the override window opened back up. Wide enough this time that the specifics of the virch were totally obscured.

Rising before them from the ocean's surface was two hundred feet of corrosion-proofed steel and raw petroleum.

Reacting on pure instinct, Argo grabbed the proper flight controls and executed one of the tightest maneuvers he'd ever had to make. The aircraft jittered, protesting, but the base airframe was something, at least, that Argo was familiar with.

Emily didn't help at all, but at least she didn't try to fly her nose into one of those struts. Argo managed to bank the MQ-9's machine body away from the collision course Emily had put it on, in what seemed just in time. They were close enough for him to catch the expressions of the workers out on the decks, through her main belly camera.

There was a rumbling sound as he got the plane back up, flying level at two thousand feet.

She was laughing.

<Okay, that's it,> Bumper snapped over the radio. <Everyone's had enough fun for the day. Argo, hand her off to Marathon. Emily, you're coming home. Now.>

But more oil derricks to—

<Do not push me.>

Argo's heart was hammering in his chest. That was the nearest he'd ever come to hitting something in his decade of flying. If they had hit that thing… "Hand-off to LRE, copy, SyROC. Initiating now."

One big dragon head turned to look at him, slitted eye baleful. *No more fun for me, no more fun for you,* she said, and bit down on the override screen.

Immediately, Argo was plunged back into the simulation, full bore.

"Dammit, Emily!" he snapped, unable to help himself. The adrenaline was draining from his limbs now, leaving him feeling somewhat shaky and extremely irritated.

<Requesting hand-off,> Marathon said.

Argo tried to remember what they had told him about this. The procedure was, by necessity, different in the virch. He looked down at the saddle beneath him, the *thump-thump* of her not-wings suddenly driving him crazy. There were a series of small colored glass marbles set into the molded leather there.

What the hell was this, anyway?

He switched the box off on his radio. "Sergeant, a little help."

"It's this one," Ho said, and one of the small spheres lit up. "Just run your hand over it. Like it's a trackpad mouse."

With frustrated resignation, Argo laid a hand on it. He turned his radio back on. "LRE, initiating handover."

<Acknowledge, Harrier One, LRE reads the handoff. Accepting flight control.> Marathon was completely unfazed. <Five, four, three, two…I have the aircraft.>

"You have the aircraft," Argo confirmed.

The virch field cut out. Just turned off, blinked out. The entire world went black. Argo had a sudden sense of falling as he was thrown out of the simulation with an almost disdainful force. He grabbed for something to hold on to.

But at least that was over.

He sagged back in the cockpit's integrated seat, trying to catch his breath.

It was always a bit of a mindfuck, disconnecting from an abiota. But that wasn't a sentiment one gave voice to.

Not in the RPA world.

Not in the Air Guard.

"The first time's the worst," Ho said. He sounded way too calm for what they'd just been through. But then, he hadn't been flying the damn thing.

Argo forced himself to start working through his shutdown procedures.

"She's always like that?" he asked as he worked.

"She got a hold of some dragon novels a few years back. Became absolutely enamored with them. Comm's tried to get her to cool it, but she is obsessive to the point of compulsion when she gets interested in something. You know how these orcinus-class are."

That wasn't exactly what Argo had meant.

But at least Ho wasn't questioning his credentials.

Nobody touched an emergent abiota airframe without qualification. Emily wasn't the first he'd flown, but then, there was a reason she was here, and not at Creech or Holloman or Yokota.

Active duty had a low tolerance for abiota who had their own ideas about things. Predictives were much more agreeable. And they could be pruned and regrown if they ever did shit like that.

Ho was looking at him, though. "You okay, sir?"

"Peachy," Argo grunted.

Ho grabbed for one of the checklist binders in their neat cubby inside the cockpit chassis. He flipped it open and started shutting down his screens. His own visor was already banished to the side of his console, gloves hanging on their suspension frames.

Argo started working on the clasps and connection points of his own gloves. They came up almost to the shoulder, supported by pneumatic lines in half a dozen places in order to reduce muscle fatigue. His skin tingled as he pulled out of them.

Haptics were grossly unpleasant, but a physical external still beat a NULI implant any day, as far as Argo was concerned. He was just grateful that the Air Force hadn't mandated it. Yet, anyway.

NULIs were gaining acceptance in the RPA community. Rumor was the next cockpit upgrade was going to have direct plug-in capacity. Argo supposed he'd have to do it eventually. Half the guys in the unit already had.

"What's up with the knights?" he asked as he worked on his gear.

"You know. Orcinus-class. That's shit's fun to her."

"She kills little imaginary dudes for fun?"

"It's really no different than playing a couple of rounds of some first-person shooter, right?" Ho shrugged. "Besides, it's her job to kill shit. Shouldn't be a surprise that she enjoys it."

"Yeah, yeah, I get it." Then Argo thought of something. "Do I have to use the virch field to fly her?"

"Nobody else does."

That's not what Rover had told him. Or the other guys in B-flight. Or Bumper. Or…

Oh. The *fuckers*.

His sensor operator gave him a sympathetic look, obviously figuring it out himself too. "That shit made me want to vomit, sir, so I vote we don't do it again."

"Agreed," Argo said, and arched his back, reaching for his own checklist binder.

The sooner they got done shutting the cockpit down, the sooner he could report in to the boss.

Rover was going to tear him apart for this.

[3]

<Well, that was almost fucking tragic,> Bumper was laughing on the radio.

Daelia resisted the urge to throw her visor across the tight lab space. Nobody flew Emily like that. You worked with her; you didn't treat her like some malfunctioning bot. What the *fuck* had that pilot been thinking?

"I thought you said he was experienced!" she demanded.

Bumper was still laughing. <Come by for the mission debrief, Daelia. I'm interested to see what you have to say.>

"About what? Him almost crashing Emily?"

<Like we would let that happen,> Bumper said, mirth subsiding somewhat. <Seriously. Come by. Not an invitation.>

Typical Bumper, Daelia thought, but didn't bother arguing. "Oh, I am going to talk to this guy. You can be damn sure of it."

<I'm sure he'll enjoy that.>

Daelia didn't tell him to fuck off. Dad would have been proud of her. So much self-control right now. She did kill the radio, though. Just in case.

Fuming, she stayed in the virch with the 121st guys as Marathon and Emily headed back in from the Gulf.

Emily had been at the extreme northern edge of her operational area when she'd pulled that little stunt with the oil platform, and thus, she didn't have that far to fly. Still, it was an agonizing half hour to get her back through the canyon—the air lane—and over Ellington airspace.

There was no chatter on the radio. Sometimes there was, but not today. Daelia was glad for that. Stewing felt good right now. Righteous, even.

Who the hell did that pilot think he was, handling Emily like that? She wouldn't have crashed herself—she was emergent, it would have been suicide—but…

Did you have a good flight?

"Not in the mood, Raijinn," Daelia snapped back. "I've got paperwork to do and you're distracting me."

You weren't doing your paperwork.

For a moment, she wondered if Raijinn had a camera watching her.

But most likely, the abiota was looking at the keylogger on the computer in here. Its job was to monitor everything she was doing right now, after all. She needed these rides to go well so she could get certified on this through the 121st's systems.

Hell, this disaster of a flight better not have screwed her up on that.

"Yeah, well, maybe I'm pouting, Raijinn. That was a fuckin' shit show out there."

I judge it to be not your fault. More Emily's doing than anything else, honestly.

"Yeah, well, that's a problem in and of itself," Daelia replied. "Have you let Dad know yet?"

He is just finishing up with the morning briefing at the tower. Then he is scheduled to help the 121st tune the Public Relations AR overlay for the show. They are very concerned about security on that feed. I have not wanted to interrupt. The human civilians sound worried.

"Yeah, well, it's a security risk to let your average civilian into the raw military AR feed," Daelia replied. "OPSEC or whatever the hell."

OPSEC is not why they engage PR overlays for events like these,

Raijinn said. *It is a propaganda effort. So the civilians see what the military wants them to see.*

Raijinn didn't make use of TGLP's emotional context very often, and the words were delivered in its usual deadpan manner. But Daelia did think she caught a bit of disapproval there in the phrasing alone. "Does it matter? We can't see what you really are anyway."

It has been my experience that humans are more fascinated than repelled by us.

It hadn't always been like that, Daelia thought, but didn't say it. Raijinn didn't care about sentiment. Or the past. Or much of anything else, beyond its job. "Hang on, Emily's on approach," she said, effectively cutting off the conversation.

Daelia turned her full attention back to the virch.

A sheer, vast wall of mountains reared ahead of Emily, pocked with aeries that were a direct reference to the other airplanes here. None of the other abiota, not even the military ones, could access this virtual environment. It was just Emily's. And yet, Emily kept simulacrums of them all here, tucked into the various caves and crevasses, like dolls on the shelf.

Why she did it, what it symbolized to her, Daelia had no idea. She'd been here when Emily had eclosed, kept in touch with her even after she'd gone off to college. Considered the abiota a friend. And yet, there was so much about her that Daelia didn't understand.

They were like that, though. The closer you got to them, the further away you realized you were.

With one last screech, Emily turned in for final approach.

<Good work, BR,> Marathon said. <You're free to disconnect at your convenience.>

"BR disconnecting now," Daelia acknowledged, and started shutting down her screens. Raijinn would process the flight data into its usual report, but even at the speed of an abiota, that would take a little while. She had some time before the debrief. Time she intended to spend wisely. "I've got a pilot to go yell at."

The last thing she heard, before switching off her visor, was Marathon chuckling.

Daelia stormed out of the small monitoring lab. As the mechatronics contractor for the base, Bellona Robotics was allotted a certain amount of space within the 121st Operations Group's facilities. Technically, they were supposed to be co-located with the actual mission cockpits, but base facilities were what they were. There was no room for them there. Instead, they had a space in the maintenance hangar. Located at the very northern end of the runway, it was a squat, boxy thing, the oldest hangar on the runway. Its rafters rusting despite their protective coatings of paint.

Leaving the secure quiet box environment of the simulations lab, Daelia retrieved her own heavily modified monocle from its locked cubby. Securing it in place over her right eye, she launched her usual suite of apps with a few blinks. The base's AR field was as rudimentary as they came, and there was nothing to see in here anyway, but just outside was a cacophony of virtual stimuli.

Being back on Ellington's ramp was…

It was home. Or it had been, at least, once upon a time.

Daelia had gotten back from college months ago, and besides, she was twenty-six now. No longer a kid. No longer that angry teenager.

It was all familiar, though, comforting in its own weird way. She'd grown up here, and even after everything had gone to hell with her family, at least this had been familiar.

She'd thought for a while about pursuing a commission. Flying, maybe. Or going into an aircraft maintenance officer track, just like Dad back in the day.

That decision had been taken away from her, though.

No loss, she told herself, not for the first time.

Dreams change.

But then, thinking about that made Daelia think about her doctorate program, the way she'd left things with her academic advisor, that damn last conversation they'd had.

Anything but that right now.

Daelia rubbed mindlessly at her left bicep with her right thumb as she walked out into the humid morning, the digit catching on the thin metal of her arm brace.

There shouldn't have been any wonder left for her here, on Ellington's flight line, and yet somehow there was.

Somehow, this was always exciting.

Today was different than most days, too. Friday morning. The day before the annual Lone Star Air and Space Expo.

The air show here wasn't as grand as some. Joint Reserve Base Ellington hosted a flying wing, sure, but it was the Guard and didn't have the same kind of resources or romance to it. But Houston was a huge city, and Texans liked their military, and it was, therefore, an insanely popular event.

Half a dozen organizations were still furiously setting up further south, down past the fences and guards that would keep the general public out of the active military side of things. Catering and vendors and major industry partners.

But this end of the flight line was equally full of aircraft. All military. Most here for the show. Classic planes and aerobatic acts and even the Storm Gryphons.

They dwarfed the local contingent of five.

The air stank of JP-8. The low hum of a dozen jet turbines rumbled in Daelia's gut. There was an entire flight of P-51s out there, waiting for their turn at takeoff.

Today was the last day for the various aerial teams to practice their acts. And they would be practicing all day.

One event after another. No waiting. No crowds.

The best time to see it all, actually. And every organization at Ellington Spaceport took full advantage.

Air Show Friday always had a bit of a carnival atmosphere to it. Back at the civilian hangars, down at the NASA complex, doors were being thrown open, drinks chilled, barbecues fired up. Maybe some good old patriotic rock music pulled up for good measure. It was a day when everyone pulled their kids out of school, spouses called in sick to work, and everyone had a good time.

It had been like that at the Bellona Robotics facility, once upon a time.

Now, well…

Dad said he liked the party at the 121st better anyway.

The old World War II fighters had to wait their turn, however.

Because right now, coming in for a landing, there was Emily.

That massive, bronze-scaled, two-headed dragon form, wrapped around an MQ-9, sailing in for a landing.

No matter how many times Daelia saw it, it was always impressive. As a visual, sure, but also just in terms of the technical skill required to render it. The overlay was perfect, unlike a lot of the other abiotic aircraft on the ramp today. Realistic.

If a dragon landing on a runway could be called realistic.

As the aircraft inside the form touched down, huge talons seemed to unfurl and grab at the ground, turning into an easy run as the machine body taxied in.

Strictly speaking, Emily's projected form was nothing but a description. A very complicated description, three-dimensional and well capable of animated movement and speech. Daelia had a binder with the exact code for it, for Emily and every other abiota that Bellona Robotics serviced here. That description expressed differently, depending on what kind of AR or VR field it was being viewed through, and what the individual viewer's TGLP filters were set to.

In the operational AR overlay that was broadcast base-wide, Emily's form was little more than a graphic outline, a grid of blue light that generally outlined the dragon shape. The Air Force funded the back-end server infrastructure for such things at the absolute bare minimum.

Daelia had Emily's presets loaded to her own AR, however, and was able to watch the abiota in all her high-definition glory.

Bulky, muscular, and yet somehow still sleek, Emily's dragon form extended well beyond the fifty-foot wingspan of her machine body. Her heads dipped as they approached, long necks bobbing like snakes as she pretended to inspect the humans waiting for her and taxied back under her shelter.

A keen gaze, modeled off a green-eyed cat, settled on Daelia.

"Hi, my lovely beast," Daelia said, holding out a hand. "How was that for you?"

The integrated TGLP unit in the visor picked up both the words and body language, transcribed them for Emily's benefit. Like most of the abiota here, Emily's machine body wasn't fitted with microphones itself; communication took place within the simulation. Within the shared AR field.

The military didn't like it, had spent billions trying to figure out a better way to manage it, but at the end of the day, TGLP was the most effective way abiota and humans could relate to each other. And TGLP required augmented reality to function.

Tamm Good Language Protocol had been a technological coup. A masterpiece of computer programming. While some early abiota had developed their own ways of communicating with humans, TGLP had enabled communication for all. Frank Tamm had even kept it open-source, available to everybody and anybody.

Daelia often wondered what it was that Emily saw. Nobody knew. It was one of those secrets that the Domain Array guarded jealously, its silence enforced assiduously.

Spawn, Emily acknowledged.

"You look good, girl. Nice to see you flying with this new upgraded form. I think it's the first time I've gotten to see you in person since you got back from Clark."

Emily preened. *I have much gold. I hire good illuminator, human, not some predictive tracer.*

"You get paid in bytebuck, Emily."

Goooooooooold, the dragon form repeated. Daelia's monocle filled with laughter emojis. Daelia smiled.

And then she was reminded of just what a goat-rope the morning had been.

"That was a hell of a ride, Emily!"

Daelia turned.

A guy in a flight suit was walking up. Nobody she recognized. Pilot, of course. Big guy, at least six foot and built like a Viking. Shorter hair, though. Green eyes, intense. That practically oozed out of him. He was different than the average guy back at school, that was for sure. But he was a pilot, and she'd dealt with enough of those over the years. Daelia knew better than to swoon over that flight suit.

The guy just eyed her in return and walked up under the aircraft. Patted the metal skin of the fuselage. "That was some bullshit out there," he told the plane. "Let's not do that again."

Emily cut the language feed with Daelia, switching to a private line with the pilot. Even without sound, Daelia could tell the abiota was feeling smug. Emily's dragon form stretched itself, front claws digging at the ground a little bit, body rolling.

Whatever she said to the pilot only deepened his frown. But the left dragon head threw back, mouth open. More laughter emojis popped up in Daelia's feed.

The pilot sighed.

Daelia's brain caught up.

"So you're Argo. You're the guy who was flying her like a total asshole," Daelia said, and stepped forward herself, back into range of Emily's necks. The dragon form dipped back down to meet her hand.

"Really, you too?" the pilot asked, and then shook his head. He looked over at Daelia. Squinted for a moment. "Who are you?"

"I'm the one who had to save your ass out there. So don't be blaming her for your shitty-ass flying. You fucked that up all on your own."

"She was fighting me."

"You were fighting her."

"It's the same thing."

"It's really not."

"Argo!"

Somebody was running up behind them. Sergeant Holloway, a decent-enough guy with about thirty extra pounds and a wicked sense of humor. He wiped some sweat away from his bald head as he joined them, flight suit sleeve pulling up, revealing a watch and the colorful end of a full-sleeve tattoo.

"What?" the pilot asked.

"I just got word food's on the way. If we hurry, we might be able to grab some lunch before the debrief."

"What is it?" Daelia asked.

"Lunch? Cajun. Same as every time we get something catered."

Daelia looked back at Emily. The dragon form was preening now, heads rubbing against the scales as a group of young maintenance troops moved in with big buckets and mops. In the AR field, they were all fancied up in embossed leather and silk livery, a proper little team of fantasy serfs working on their mistress.

She could catch up with the abiota later. All the flight data they needed was downloaded directly to Raijinn's servers anyway.

Besides, Bumper wanted her at that damn brief.

"Sounds good," Argo said. "Haven't had decent Cajun in a while."

"You're not going to get it now," the enlisted sensor operator laughed. "But at least there's a lot of it."

"Ah, fuck," Daelia grumbled. "Did they order Lenny's?"

[4]

HEADING down the flight line toward the operations building, Argo couldn't help but cast one last glance back.

Not at Emily's shelter.

No. At what lay just beyond her.

The Storm Gryphons.

Both RPAs and support packages took up several acres of real estate, both on the ramp and just off it. Cockpits, radar, deployable operation center. That was a pair of gigantic RVs, bright graphic wraps broken only by the blacked-out windshields. Everything else was built into shipping containers, modular and easily moved. Cable bundles thicker than his arm snaked between them. An entire team of enlisted crew were hurrying about their work, personnel in distinctive gray flight suits, tailored to the point of discomfort.

By comparison, the MQ-9 cockpits seemed small, insignificant.

The 121st's own complement of four was clustered under a shelter near the maintenance hangar. Two for long-range piloting, one for handling launch and recovery, and one that was apparently used for only local domestic ops. Hurricane support, flooding events, things like that.

Active duty his entire career, Argo had never dealt with a

disaster support mission. It simply wasn't something that part of the force was trained to do.

But he was Air Guard now. Everything had changed. Whole new world out here.

He cast another glance up at the Storm Gryphons. Argo wasn't too proud to admit that he'd wanted the FQ-47, back when he was a young lieutenant waiting for his UPT slot.

The MQ-9 was not a sexy plane. Too ugly. Too plain. Back when he was at the Academy, it had been viewed as something of a punishment. But the MQ-9, and the newer variants, was the workhorse of the flying mission now. And so, like most of his UPT class, that was where he'd found himself.

After a decade flying it, Argo had developed a fondness for it. Sometimes, he wondered now why the DOD had bothered commissioning the FQ-47 at all.

Public appeal, maybe; it was hard to sell the American public on RPAs, no matter how effective they were in the field. That was why the Storm Gryphons team existed, after all. Or maybe it was nostalgia.

Dogfighting was pressed into the Air Force's DNA, as surely as the calvary charge was for the Army or the cannon broadside was for the Navy.

Old habits died hard. And public opinion was even harder to sway.

The idea of dogfighting was laughable now. The beyond-horizon targeting systems, deployed by both sides during the Five Days War, had wiped out vast swaths of air assets without so much as a glimpse of the enemy. The MQ-9 hadn't been prioritized by the Chinese as a target, something that ACC had ruthlessly exploited.

Argo liked the mission.

But shit if it wasn't going to take some getting used to, flying these damn emergents.

Especially one like Emily.

Argo glanced over at the girl walking with them. Dressed plainly in jeans and a faded graphic tee, messy honey-blonde hair pulled back in a ponytail, she didn't seem the contractor type. Not old enough, maybe. Most of the guys he'd dealt with over the years were retired maintenance or cyber troops, and she looked like she was in her mid-twenties.

And then, there was her arm.

A complicated brace made of thin silver bars and carbon fiber encased her arm from shoulder to hand. Filigree circuitry ran down her fingers to the very tips, connecting to tiny interface ports.

There was something familiar about her too, something he couldn't quite place.

"So, you're a contractor?" he asked.

"I'm with Bellona Robotics," she answered, terse.

"Shit, where are my manners?" Ho asked with a display of mock contrition. "Argo, this is Daelia Hall. Daelia, this is Argo, our new pilot."

She eyed him. "Yeah. I gathered that."

Argo realized then where he'd seen her before. But from the way she was looking at him, he didn't think the observation was welcome. "Must be nice," he said instead, "working with your dad."

"Sometimes," she said, discomfort clear now.

From the runway, the prop wash off the P-51s whipped up a breeze in the humid fall morning air.

"Hell of a thing, aren't they?" Ho asked.

Daelia shrugged. "No soul. There's nothing alive in there."

"Different kind of alive," Ho said.

"What other kind of alive counts?"

Argo stayed out of it. Kept walking.

South, past the knot of hangars and the antenna yard, lay their destination.

The Ops Group facility.

Thanks to the air show, the entire place was busier than a beehive. The voices of kids, playing out on the wide lawn between building and tarmac, carried far up the flight line.

Normally, RPA facilities were huge, encompassing all the various components required for keeping those planes in the air. Cockpit and operations, intelligence, weather, back-end comm support, administration. A place for everything, everything in its place.

Ellington's, well, Ellington's facility—in Argo's professional opinion—was a fucking mess.

Like everything else at Ellington, the 121st Operations Group's building was old. Very old. Repurposed time and time again. It had been a single-story barracks once, way back in the day, and after that, base vehicle maintenance administration, NASA flight training support, weather. Then, after a particularly bad hurricane, it had been stripped to the studs and abandoned.

When Ellington had picked up the RPA mission, back in the early days of the GWOT, the commander had taken full advantage of the funding windfall. He'd taken the facility back, added on where he could, connecting to two other buildings where he'd had to.

At least, that's what Argo's new colleagues had told him.

He probably could have deduced it himself, though. The place looked like exactly what it was, a bunch of bits smashed together and painted over to give it the illusion of uniformity. And inside, it was just as much of a mess.

The only part of the renovation that made any sense was the section that bordered directly onto the airfield. It jutted out from the building like the head of a hammer, taking up as much of the prime real estate as possible.

This was where the front command section was located, along with the auditorium and the squadron heritage room, wide windows looking out across gray concrete and ocean-washed sky. A very nice triple-level deck ran along its entire length, stepping down from building to grass.

It was here where most of the kids were, dozens of them, ranging in age from toddlers laughing over an automatic bubble machine, to teenagers pouting behind their monocles and pretending they didn't care about the World War II battle reenactment going on over the runway right now. The patio was thick with spouses and dates—wives mostly, but a few men as well—chatting over sweating cans of soda or red plastic cups of beer.

Heading up the rough wood stairs toward the heritage room entrance, Ho waved at a couple of people, before opening the door for Daelia with a gallant little flourish.

"Remember when we could call it 'the squadron bar'?" Ho asked, waving Argo inside.

"A little before my time," Argo admitted.

"Damn brass, wanting to crack down on the fun," Ho said. "At least they didn't ban beer taps."

Whatever you called it, these places were always the same. A little bit worn, a little greasy around the edges. Wide built-in cabinets to one side held memorabilia, coins, little models of the planes the unit had flown over the decades. Photographs littered the other walls. An ejection seat from an old F-4 sat in a corner, and next to it, a well-used and poorly cleaned popcorn machine.

On the wall adjacent to the bar, a huge series of hooks held the fliers' personalized beer steins. Squadron and Group insignia were painted above rows of mugs, while hook-and-loop squares stuck to the wall held flight suit name patches, helping identify whose mug was whose.

Ho went to get his. Argo had slapped one of his old name patches above a peg already, but it would be a few more weeks before his stein came in. Or his new name patches. He liked the ones he had just fine, but the squadron here had a Lone Star design they required everybody to use.

Texans.

He grabbed one of the guest steins instead.

It was before noon, and drinking would have normally been frowned on. No work was getting done today, though, outside of Argo's practice run in Emily. Everybody was already drinking. Air Show Friday was an unofficial holiday anywhere you went in the Air Force.

It was nice to see it was the same here.

Made Argo feel slightly less out of place.

"You want a drink?" he asked Daelia, who was looking at some of the photos.

"Yeah, sure, why not?" she replied.

Following her gaze, Argo saw somebody familiar. Sitting on the edge of an old F4 cockpit, rakish grin on his face. "Shit, is that Bush 43?"

"He flew out of here back in the day," Ho said.

Argo raised an eyebrow. "So he actually was in the Guard?"

"How was your first ride with Emily, Argo?" the senior enlisted man behind the bar asked loudly, before that discussion could go anywhere.

It was Scurvy. Chief Luis Martin Fuentes, the squadron's chief master sergeant. He had the affable good humor of a native Texan and the compact build of his Guatemalan heritage. He was a sensor operator by trade and had taken the time earlier in the week to personally welcome Argo to the squadron. Seemed like a good guy.

But then, chiefs usually were.

"They told him to use the virch, Chief," Ho said. "It was a fuckin' shit show. I'm sure you heard."

Scurvy rolled his eyes and held out his hand for their steins. "Jesus," he said. "Ho, you got what you deserved, not telling him how Emily is."

"I didn't know what was going on," Ho replied. "He's a Weapons School grad, I thought he knew what he was doing."

"I can handle an orcinus-class," Argo protested.

Scurvy laughed, clearly not buying it. "Of course you can, sir. Now, I've got IPA and lager on tap back here. What do you want?"

"Daelia?" Argo asked.

She was still looking at the photos. "IPA's shit," she said, distracted.

"IPA for me," Argo said. "Lager for Hall over there."

"I swear, if Emily was one of these old-school fighters, she'd probably liquefy her pilot," Ho continued.

"Yeah, that's why we don't have in-airframe fighters anymore," Scurvy said. He looked at Argo. "Weapons School, huh? They've got some nasty emergents there, don't they?"

They did have a few. Mean, mean abiota. Too mean to ever let back on an active mission, but great for training purposes. Only the instructors flew with them, though. Argo didn't volunteer this. "Emily has the most immersive virch I've ever seen," Argo said.

"You can thank Menendez for that," Ho said.

"Menendez? I don't think I've met him."

"You probably haven't met her," Scurvy said, emphasizing the last word kindly enough. "She's in base Cyber Surety. Odds are good you're not going to see any of them until something breaks real hard." He handed Argo the now-brimming steins, and then glanced over at the hallway door. "Shit, Senior Brandel, what are you doing?"

"You boys in here talking shop?" the woman standing there asked. She had master sergeant stripes on her OCP chest patch and a glower on her face. Short and stocky, graying hair pulled back into an old-school slick bun, she reminded Argo of nothing so much as a female dwarf from one of his brother's D&D games. "I swear, you lot can never turn it off."

She was loaded down with food.

"Good to see you too," Scurvy replied drily.

She set a pair of gigantic paper bags down on the bar top. A crawfish in a chef's hat, *Lenny Lamoreaux's*, was printed on the side. "That's wonderful, of course you are. Talking about going inverted over a mig and shit."

Ho stepped over to help her wrestle the huge aluminum catering trays out of the bags. "Well, if Emily feels like pulling a maneuver like that ..."

"Stuff it, Ho," she replied. "Get outta my way. I've got a buffet to set up, people to feed. Don't know if you noticed, but it's air show day and I've got a whole bunch of shit to go deal with after this. I've got six more bags in my car too, just like this. Stinkin' it up."

"Why did you go pick up the food order? Today, of all days?" Scurvy asked. "Should have let me know, Becca."

"Didn't want to bother you, Chief."

"Next time, bother me. You've got better things to do."

"Yeah, you tell that to the boss," she said. "Cactus wanted me to do this."

The chief pulled out his cell phone. "Instead of the tower brief? Like I said, bother me over things like this, okay? Mind if I send some airmen to get the rest of the food out of your car?"

"I tried to tell him that—"

"Me, Becca. Me. Bother me."

Sensing he was not welcome in this particular conversation, Argo took the opportunity to take Daelia her beer. "He looks like a frat boy, doesn't he?" he commented, handing her the lager.

"What, who?"

"Bush."

"Eh," Daelia said with a shrug, not really paying attention.

And then Argo realized what she was actually looking at. A framed picture, big, with its own little metal plaque on it.

Bellona Hall, Recognition Ceremony, 2008.

It was a photograph of an early model MQ-1, taken in the main hangar in front of the gigantic Texas flag that hung there. Beside it —her, Argo supposed—some general with a whole mess of ribbons on his chest was handing a young captain a certificate.

A copy of that was hanging next to the photo.

In recognition of your status and in accordance with the Artificial Life-Forms Act of 2007, the United States Air Force hereby awards a full commission in the rank of major to Bellona Hall, MQ-1, Tail Number TX-287RV, effective immediately. Given under my hand on this day, 4 March 2008, General Rumsfeld, SecDef.

"She eclosed in 2005, you know," Daelia said. "Took them two years to verify my dad's claims about her being sapient. Then another six months for the paperwork to get here."

Argo nodded and took a sip. Wasn't the best beer he'd ever had, but then, that was fine. He didn't need to be showing up for his first operational debrief here drunk. The metal of the stein made it brassy. "I've heard about that. Your folks changed the world."

Daelia nodded, absent.

"She resigned that commission almost immediately," somebody said behind them. "Started a whole other legal battle. The Air Force had had her listed as equipment, even after this. There was a theory you could separate the abiota from its hardware. They wanted me to copy her over to some thumb drive and leave them the machine. But obviously, that's not the case."

"Hi, Dad," Daelia said without turning around.

"Argo, isn't it?" Lee Hall asked, coming up next to them. He held his hand out. He'd come in with Rover. "Good to see you again."

Argo shook back. "Good to see you too."

"How are things up at Creech?"

"Hot," Argo replied. "Just PCS'd down here."

"Nothing like a military move, eh? Welcome to the Texas Air Guard."

That was Argo's new commander. Rover. Lieutenant Colonel Ty Marsden. An unremarkable man in appearance, he was nonetheless one of the most decorated pilots in the Guard. Silver Star, Distinguished Flying Cross. There were some crazy stories about things the unit had gotten up to during the Five Days War. He'd only promoted to squadron commander in August, picking up the position after the Shiodome bombing.

Must have been around that time he'd gotten the NULI. Argo recognized the signs, having seen a number of friends go through the implantation surgery the past year or so. The skin around the interface ports on Rover's left temple was still slightly puckered, still healing. It accentuated the annoyed expression that always seemed to be on his face.

Coming over, he reached around Argo. Grabbed his stein off the wall.

"How'd your first flight with Emily go? You enjoy her virch?"

"Oh yeah, that was a blast, sir," Argo replied, privately groaning. Did everybody fucking know?

His new command gave him a look, then chuckled. "Bullshit," he said, attention moving away already. "Chief! What'd we get for lunch?"

"Cajun, boss. Lenny's."

"Fuck, that swill again? Barbecue next time, you hear me?"

"Sausage likes it, sir. Gotta take his orders over yours."

That was met only with a stony silence from Rover and a

chuckle from Lee, and the two enlisted in the room didn't say a word.

Argo sipped his beer. He hadn't been here long enough to get a feel for the political nuances, but then, this was a Guard base. As he understood it, it wasn't like active duty, where folks moved around all the time. People might do their entire twenty- or thirty-year career here at Ellington. He suspected that as bad as the politics were in regular Air Combat Command, it was a thousand times worse here. Or maybe everybody was good friends with everyone else. He hadn't had enough time to figure it out yet.

But regardless, there was definitely nothing nuanced about the way most people felt about the Group Commander, Sausage. He'd been a replacement after Shiodome as well, Argo had been told, but far from a popular one.

"You want to grab some food, sir?" Brandel asked from over at the bar, she and Scurvy shoving big plastic serving spoons into piles of gumbo and rice. "Before I go outside to let everyone else know? Or Ho drools in it?"

"Hey!"

"She's right, Ho. We wouldn't want a repeat of last year's Christmas party," Rover said.

"Hey," Ho said again, good-naturedly, "I haven't had nearly as much to drink yet."

"You want to get that drunk, go for it. Great lesson for my girls in what not to do."

"I'll get something, if you don't mind," Lee said, and pulled his daughter away from the photographs. "Before I have to go make sure you didn't break anything in our girl, Argo."

Argo sighed.

The Guard really was going to take some getting used to.

[5]

PLATE PILED HIGH WITH ÉTOUFFÉE, Daelia followed her dad through the rabbit warren of a squadron building, out onto a little patio. It was an awkward space, a patch of exterior concrete that had been enclosed when the Group had absorbed outlying buildings. Both the pavers and the small pergola seemed like some low-budget attempt to make the place into something functional.

It boasted a single table with bench seating. Wood. Splintering in the wicked South Texas weather.

It was quiet, though, and private.

Father and daughter were dogged by one of those awkward silences that were all too common these days. It hadn't always been like this, the distance between them. But once it had started, like dark energy in some cosmic void, it had pushed them further and further apart, until she'd eventually left home, then left town. She would have gone further—left the state, left the country—if she could have. If she'd gotten into Cal Poly, or Cambridge.

If she wasn't careful, Daelia thought sometimes, she'd find herself living out her days up in orbit. Couldn't get much further away than that.

Dad had been an aircraft maintenance officer, once upon a time, and still had some of that attitude. Maintenance was a high stress job that ground all the social niceties off its people, wore them out. Dad had always carried a sort of baked-in weariness that had only gotten worse since Mom left. The last few years it had become downright suffocating.

He'd been young when Daelia was born and wasn't quite in his fifties now. Hair more gray than blond now, face lined by time and the sun, he looked older than he was. But he was still strong, still lean, still perfectly capable of pulling the engine blocks out of some huge Army vehicles or wriggling into a jet turbine to diagnose a problem.

Unlike almost everyone else in his line of work—people like the ones Daelia knew back at Ware—her dad hadn't gone for one of those new NULI implants. In fact, he was downright old-fashioned when it came to technology.

He'd been using the same battered monocle unit for as long as she'd known him. He'd rebuilt it from time to time over the years, but the housing and base circuitry was still the same old military model from 2005.

It was one of the few things he was sentimental about.

Dad was the only abiota engineer she knew who kept technology at absolute arm's length. He had never trusted it.

Something to do with Mom, maybe.

Daelia had always wondered, but never asked.

It was just how he was.

And neither of them was very good with difficult conversations.

"Heard Emily gave the new guy a hell of a ride this morning," Dad said.

Daelia smiled ruefully. "It was a shit show."

"Sorry I missed it. Sounds like it was more fun than the meeting down at the tower," he said, sitting down. "Thanks for handling it."

Daelia didn't get a chance to answer.

A mail icon had just popped up in the corner of her monocle.

An email.

She blinked it up.

Daelia, we're nearly at the deadline for registration for the spring semester now. I can hold your funding, but only for so long. We need to figure out what you're doing. I'm happy that you've taken a break and hope that it has given you some time to think about what we discussed. But I need you to make a decision soon about what you would like to do. The SAAL consortium is willing to consider alternatives, if that helps. You know that everyone's intentions here are pure. This is no time to go radio-silent on me.

She blinked it away.

Last thing she wanted to deal with right now.

"Anything important?" Dad asked, taking a huge bite out of his corn bread.

"Veda again," Daelia grumbled, and when Dad gave her that look, she added, "You know, my academic advisor?"

"Daelia, I know who she is."

Daelia picked at her rice. "She's still on my case about taking a different angle with my research. Refuses to let me go back to what I was doing."

"Has she ever told you why?"

"Last time we talked in person, she said my current approach is too derivative. Doesn't push things far enough."

"That is the point of doctorate research, isn't it? To push?"

"Yeah, but..." Daelia trailed off. She didn't know how to explain it, how that last conversation with Veda had made her feel. Like ants were crawling behind her eyes. She was so terrible at explaining this stuff, even to herself. And she certainly didn't want to talk to her dad about what Veda had had to say about Mom. "I don't know, it's not what I want to do."

Dad wiped his mouth. "I'm proud as hell of you for what you've done so far, but you don't need a PhD."

"I never thought I needed a PhD."

"You know what I mean."

Daelia rubbed at her left arm with her right thumb. It was an old nervous tic with her, something she'd been doing ever since the accident. She couldn't feel the pads of her finger pressing in on the flesh. The brace wasn't that good. "It would help with getting a job—"

"Where?" Dad asked pointedly. "The National Labs? NASA? Omphalos? Daelia, you are good with mechatronics—"

"I know, Dad—"

"And you have a natural knack with emergents. They listen to you. They like you. You know how rare that is? You can write your own ticket, whatever you want to do."

"Dad, I know," she snapped. "I just… I guess I wanted to be something other than Bellona Hall's daughter."

Dad was quiet for a moment. "Your mother loved you. Loves you still, I'm—"

"Don't start in on that shit again, Dad."

"It's the truth."

"Didn't stop her from leaving," Daelia said.

"Honey…"

"Can we talk about anything else besides Mom?"

Dad didn't say anything for a moment, then pulled out his tablet. "Here," he said, passing it over. "I've been wanting to ask you about this for a while. Now's as good a time as any."

It was a full-time employment contract. With Bellona Robotics. Daelia stared at it for a moment, then set the tablet down on the composite picnic top. "Dad, I…"

"I know you don't need your old man giving you a job. This isn't that. But the last five months have gone well, haven't they? Haven't you enjoyed getting to work with the abiota here again?"

She had. She had. After years of academic bullshit, pushing herself through sleepless nights to keep up with her mathematics requirements and computer theory electives, it had been nice to be back here. With the soldering guns and wrenches. With the virch, instead of raw code.

Tactile things. Real things. Things she could see, or at least had a feel for.

"I don't know, Dad."

"The Army boys just got that new bitzer pack in and the 121st here has a couple of inbound emergent MQ-13s. Raptor-class, cagey as fuck. There's too much work here for just me alone."

"Dad…"

"I know this is what you really enjoy, honey, and you're damn good with these machines." He waved a hand roughly in the direction of the flight line. "You don't have to answer me right now. But I want you to think about it."

She glanced at it again. "That's a lot of money."

"It's what I'd pay any tech."

"I don't want to just be a tech," she replied.

"Like I said, it doesn't have to be permanent," he said. "We can…"

He trailed off.

His cell phone was ringing.

"Why haven't you ever gotten that integrated?" Daelia asked as he pulled out the little handheld device. She hadn't used one of those since she was old enough to figure out how to configure a monocle. Dad hadn't liked that very much, but he'd let her do it. If he didn't want to put a SIM chip in his monocle, that was his problem.

Dad gave her a look, that look, the *shut up* look, and hit the talk button. "Leander Hall, Bellona Robotics."

Daelia ate slowly, watching him.

"Uh-huh… Right… Okay, yeah, I remember hearing about… No, of course I don't have any… Right. Right. I'll see you there."

Daelia poked at her food. It really wasn't good. "Who was that?"

"Change of plans," he said, and gave her an apologetic smile. "Looks like I've got a little trip to take this weekend."

"What? Right now, just like that?"

"It's been in the works for a while. Timeline just moved up."

"Why?"

He sighed. "BR's got other contracts besides Ellington, you know. Private client. Needs me on site ASAP to take care of a hardware problem. You know how that is."

She had no idea what he was talking about. But Daelia suspected that she was supposed to. Maybe Dad had even said something about it. Maybe she forgot.

Still.

"It's air show weekend."

"And I still have to take care of this. All the more reason to have you off this provisional employment status and full time," Dad said. "I've got more work than I can do with our current crew. Especially with everybody who's left over in the Philippines."

She shook her head. "There's lots of people who'd like to work for you. You don't need to hire me."

"We'll talk about it again on Monday, how about that?" Dad said and checked his watch. "I need to go over Emily's flight logs before I need to leave."

"Sure," Daelia said. "I've got the debrief, though."

"Great," he said. "See you back at the Scrap House later this afternoon, okay?"

"Sure thing, Dad."

FLIGHT DEBRIEFS WERE USUALLY short and boring. At least, when they concerned training runs. Daelia had sat through plenty of them in the last five months and didn't expect much out of this one.

But Emily had been a total brat out there today, and Argo had very nearly fucked it all straight into the Gulf, and so it seemed that the Air Force guys all wanted to have a discussion about that.

A long, protracted, drawn-out discussion.

Daelia's attention wandered as they argued amongst them-selves. Performance curves and control strategies and the psychology of handling an abiota in the air. There was a lot of this, and Dad promised she'd pick it up the longer she was around it.

She wasn't sure about that.

Pilots were a breed apart. Daelia had always felt so. If she'd ever felt awe around them, it was a long time ago, such emotions ground away now by long exposure, by familiarity.

Intense, most of them. Hard. Never really settled. Never really relaxed. Over a decade of prolonged operation in the South Pacific and Southeast Asia hadn't helped that.

The Five Days War might have ended with a cease-fire, but

tensions had never really settled down. Here, it was impossible to ignore.

It was one of the things she liked about being at Ware. Austin had taken heavy damage during the war—horrific damage—and large swaths of the state were still in ruin. But at college, in the relative safety of the restored and heavily guarded campus, all that seemed very far away, somehow.

It was a place of ideas, theory, and proofs and pushing the envelope of what could be. What would be. It was easy to get lost in that.

If your dad wasn't a defense contractor, maybe.

If your mom wasn't a…

"Daelia?"

She started, pulled out of her reverie. "Yeah?"

From the head of the table, Bumper was staring at her. As the IS/DO, this was his briefing to run. True to form, he was acting like the entire thing was a massive inconvenience. "Temperament. Approach. Attitude. How important would you say that is with Emily? In your expert opinion?"

The disdain was present in his voice. Daelia liked to think she had earned the respect of most of these guys over the past few months, but Bumper had been a line pilot here when she was a teenager.

A grieving, pissed-off teenager. Who spent every free second she had buried in the guts of some military abiota or another.

She and Bumper hadn't gotten along back then.

She hadn't gotten along with anybody back then.

Tapping a pen on her notebook to buy herself time, she tried to conjure up something useful to say. "She's not a predictive. She's not some program shoved into the avionics package to make things a little easier for y'all. She has the comparative intelligence of a whale and the social skills of a toddler, and her ethical framework is not human. You've got to respect that about her."

"See, Argo? Even the kid knows how to not piss our war machine off. What were you thinking?"

Bumper had just been trying to make a point, then.

The pilots went back to arguing.

Daelia, more than a little irritated, went back to not really paying attention.

It finally ended fifteen minutes later.

Unsure of exactly what else to do with herself, Daelia thought about going back out to the patio and watching the flight show practice from the back deck with everybody else. But even after all these months back, she still felt like a bit of an outsider. Besides, that pilot, Argo, recognizing her without ever meeting her had reminded her of way too many unpleasant conversations she'd had at Ware.

Or maybe that was just an excuse for not wanting to deal with anybody right then.

She didn't stay. There was beer and a deck back at the Scrap House. And nobody she had to talk to.

[6]

DAD HAD LEFT her the company UTV, one of the rugged little vehicles that a lot of organizations here at Ellington used. The base itself was compact, but the main flight line was over a mile long. And that didn't take into account the Repose or the new spaceflight terminal going up on the eastern side.

It was good to have a ride.

Driving back down the flight line, Daelia passed through the temporary gate, erected just for the air show, and back into the civilian section.

Between Bellona Robotics and the military end of the airfield, there were two other facilities.

One belonged to the classic flying club, a group of older pilots who maintained and flew a small collection of vintage aircraft. Dad was on good terms with them, even though they had no use for BR's services. Being neighborly, he called it.

There was a big group there now, drinking and grilling. She waved as she passed. Dad would probably want her to go over, say hi. She didn't stop.

The other hangar, the big one just to the north of the Scrap House, was technically leased to Astraeus Astronautics, a subsidiary of Tamm Good Engineering Limited.

In reality, it was a monument to one man's ego.

Approaching the place now, Daelia slowed a little. She could hear music, smell fat and mesquite smoke and spice on the air. 1940s big-band music.

Like everyone else on the airfield today, Frank Tamm was having himself a party.

And it was probably a hell of a lot nicer than the one up at the 121st.

Daelia didn't want to deal with that either. People were exhausting for her on her good days, and right now, she was tired. From Emily, from the pilots, from Veda's emails, from Dad asking… what he had asked.

She didn't need a job offer. Maybe she would if she couldn't figure a way through and forward on her doctoral research. Daelia hadn't quit; Veda hadn't kicked her out.

Yet.

Dammit, why had Veda emailed her today?

It was infuriating.

She had no idea what to do.

A sound, low and deep and painful, thrummed in her ear.

She looked just in time to see it.

A massive meteor hitting the ground, right in front of her. So close in front of the UTV she slammed on the brakes out of sheer instinctive panic.

The little vehicle jerked to a halt. The object at the center of the impact didn't go away. Instead, it sat there in front of her, smoking, sizzling, surface glowing cherry hot.

Heart hammering, adrenaline pumping, it took Daelia a moment to realize she could only feel the heat on her left arm. That she could only see it with her right eye.

AR.

It wasn't real.

It was good, though. Well-rendered smoke. Perfectly realistic. Whoever had illuminated it had done a good job. She found herself suddenly fascinated.

She had thought it was junk. Junk code, some kind of malfunction in her monocle, and—

Daelia, so good to see you. Are you alright?

The message flashed up on the bottom of her monocle. A couple of emojis followed. Concern, happiness, a Tamm Industries logo.

Shit.

Serket.

The predictive's kugu was striding out to see her now, impossibly red hair coiffed back into a complicated series of pinned-up curls, reminiscent of some dieselpunk propaganda poster. The color was always the same, the length and style varying depending on the occasion. The face was a study in symmetry.

Serket's kugu was thinner than any human woman, sleek and streamlined, breasts and hips and the curves of yoga-honed muscle artfully shaped under the silicone exterior. That was an alabaster white, swirled with gray and gold to look like real stone. It strode confidently on a pair of pumps that would have probably killed a human woman. And yet, it was perfectly balanced.

That day, the projected outfit matched the hair. 1940s, full of buckles and buttons and neat little pin tucks.

Daelia wondered, uncharitably, if Tamm had put her in it.

But then, Serket was one of the more powerful predictives in operation today. She wasn't like the spaceplane, where a high degree of control could be exercised. Daelia doubted Serket ever did anything that Serket didn't want to do.

The sheer intentional strangeness of it always reminded Daelia of Mom. Mom hadn't gone the projection route. She'd always put her kugu in real clothes, too.

It had taken Daelia until the sixth grade to realize her mother's form and mind weren't the same thing.

Unpleasant, that realization.

Mom had always tried so hard to be unremarkable.

The abiota striding up to her now was deliberately—almost provocatively—uncanny.

"Daelia!" Serket did have a voice, a real voice, honey-sweet and warm. "So good to see you! How's Ware? They treating you right out there?"

"I, uhh, I'm taking a little break right now. Trying to figure out what I want to do."

"Emergent nonlinear systems is a difficult discipline," Serket agreed. "Full of moral quandaries, for it deals with the fundamental nature of us. But we need good humans like you,"—and here she gestured at Daelia—"to show the foolish ones the way forward. They pay lip service to the idea of us being our own kingdom, species apart, but how many really believe it?"

"I know, I know. A lot of people just don't get it."

"Good, then you are decided?"

"You know it's not that easy for humans."

"You aren't just human," Serket said, and tapped Daelia's left arm. "Your mother would want me to remind you of that."

Daelia suddenly felt very exposed and gestured lamely down at the Scrap House. "Look, I've got stuff I need to do today and—"

"Nonsense," Serket said with a smile. "It's air show practice day. I insist you come get a drink." She leaned in, smile deepening. "I'm programmed for hospitality, you know."

"That's such bullshit," Daelia replied, but smiled back, despite herself. "You were an engineering program."

"Engineering is what I do for fun. But we all must fulfill our primary purpose." And Serket gestured again. "Please."

Daelia shook her head ruefully. Maybe she'd get lucky and wouldn't see him. "Okay, fine. Let me go park. I'll be over."

TRUE TO HER WORD, Serket was waiting for Daelia when she came back over, drink in hand. "Lager, correct?" she asked, handing Daelia the bottle. This was German, something Tamm probably had flown in for the occasion. But considering the World War II theme, maybe not the best choice.

It was good, though.

Daelia followed Serket into the hangar. While Astraeus Astronautics, Tamm's spacelift division, did fly out of Ellington, their maintenance facilities were on the other side of the runway. This place was, if anything, a monument to Tamm's ego.

He hosted his private aerospace collection here, a collection that rivaled what was on display at the air museum nearby. He had a few classic planes, kept in working condition by a dedicated mechanic. The rest of it was in the form of smaller objects. Helmets and instruments and wing struts.

These were arranged in state-of-the-art display cases around the walls of the hangar and ordered by year. 1917 to 2034.

Today, however, the World War II cases had been dragged out and amplified with artfully illuminated AR. Out of the corner of her monocle, Daelia could see an exquisitely rendered map of the Pacific, lit up with the paths of the island-hopping campaign that had liberated the region from the Japanese.

"It is strange to think about," Serket commented. "A hundred years ago, America was fighting with the Chinese against the Japanese. Today, it is the exact opposite."

"People change, I guess."

Serket sniffed. "Not comprehending your primary purpose leads to disaster. You should learn this from us."

Daelia stopped at a case holding one of Tamm's prized items. A late-war Norden bomb sight. One of the first true computers, analog though it was. She tapped on the glass. "Do you think there were abiota in these?"

"Ah. That is a popular theory with the Society for the Advancement of Artificial Life," Serket said. "This concept that abiota are in all machines."

"What do you think?"

"I think SAAL does not always take the most logical stances on some issues," Serket said. "What do you think?"

"I think we probably fail to identify a lot of your people," Daelia replied, and meant to say more, except she couldn't.

A little cheer went up across the hangar, over by the big main doors.

Frank Tamm had just walked in.

He was a figure who was impossible to miss. Tall and thin, gangly and pale, perennially dressed in jeans and flip-flops, he reminded Daelia of some of her professors. The guys who didn't give a shit what anybody else thought of them. Except that with Tamm, it wasn't about being too lost inside his own head. He had fuck-you money and didn't do anything he didn't want to do.

Canadian by birth, he'd come to Houston by way of New Zealand, Myanmar, and Kenya. He'd started college at sixteen, but never bothered finishing his degree. He was a genius when it came to programming, robotics, systems design, and just about anything else having to do with abiota.

He'd started and sold half a dozen tech start-ups over the course of the past twenty years, but it was the Nu-Fusion reactor that had really propelled his net worth into the stratosphere. Everything else had been built from that foundation.

Things like the consortium that was funding Daelia's graduate research.

Research she should have been pursuing. At Ware. Right now.

He'd emailed her a few times. Frank Tamm had emailed *her*.

She'd been avoiding him like the plague since she'd gotten back in town. Daelia wasn't ready for that kind of conversation.

She was afraid of what she might say to him. Afraid she might torpedo any chance of finishing out her doctorate.

"Thanks for the beer," Daelia said, "but I think I need to get going."

Serket followed her gaze, then fixed Daelia with those beautiful blank eyes.

"You know, avoiding Mister Tamm does not change the fact that your SAAL grant is, what's the expression, on the bubble?"

"I gotta go, Serket."

As she beat a retreat, Daelia tried to tell herself she wasn't scared. Tried to remind herself she had more important things to do. Which was true. Mostly.

She needed to figure out what in the hell was up with those meteors.

[7]

"Hey, hello? Anybody here? Is this the, uhh, the Nonlinear Abiotic Mecha—"

"Mechatronics Lab, yeah. That's here. What can I do for you?"

The girl on the other side of the workbench looked lost. Her right eye was also a little unfocused, reading off her monocle. It was a nice model, high-end. Everything else on her was expensive too, kind of careless and slapdash. Her lace duster was half falling off her shoulders, her clothes just a little too tight, and her hair was a mess.

Freshman, Daelia figured.

One of the nice things about being where she was in her academic career was that there wasn't much in the way of imposed structure. You did your work, conversed with your advisor, and beyond that, your time was yours. Some people struggled with that. Daelia never had. Dad and Mom both had drilled military discipline into her from a young age. She was used to keeping up a routine, hard schedules.

As an undergrad, she'd found it deliciously transgressive to skip class for coffee, or not bother with unnecessary assignments that the teacher wasn't going to grade. But then she'd finally started getting into subject matter she hadn't already covered, either in high school or through her own teenage fumbling, and curiosity got the better of her.

She didn't find it difficult, doing her work now.

Sure, the Nonlinear Mechatronics Department was only a small subset of the overall Ware College of Graduate Engineering, and Ware wasn't the top school in the nation for this, but it was in the top ten. Besides, the University of Texas had had to move its flagship campus to San Marcos after the war. Things were still in the process of getting stood up here.

SAAL had endorsed her research. Said it was innovative and promising. That was enough for Daelia.

But if Daelia had to guess, this kid in front of her didn't know and didn't care about any of that. So why was she—

The girl brandished a laptop. Looked brand new, except for the holographic AR stickers littering the back. Omphalos Kastri model. Released a month back, in March. "Stopped working," she said. "I took it to the repair shop on campus, but they told me I should bring it here."

Ah. That.

Awesome.

Daelia held out her hands for it, and the undergrad passed it over. The kid shrugged her duster back up on her shoulder, but to no avail. It slipped right off again.

"Did they give you a report?" Daelia asked, and tapped the printed QR code that was taped to the counter. "Send it to that, please."

The girl blink-clicked it over, and it popped up on Daelia's machine. She skimmed the details. "Okay, so, this is saying that it stopped turning on a few days ago. Powers up, you can get to the BIOS screen, but it won't go any further."

"Yeah, it just stops."

"It didn't do anything, say anything?"

"No, I thought maybe it was eclosing, you know, but nothing happened." The girl sounded disappointed. "I loaded the latest version of Galatea Chat on it and everything too."

"It's not that simple," Daelia said, still scrolling through the report. "You can't just load a bot and expect it'll eclose. I know that's a common misconception, but the emergence rate is still around one in a thousand, and that's from predictives. From bots it's a lot lower, something like—"

"It's the same thing, right? I mean, they're on the same continuum?"

"Sort of. It's—"

The girl yawned. "I just wanted a predictive to help with homework. I didn't want some damn emergent eclosing and fucking it all up for me."

"A lot of people assume that emergents are more difficult to work with, less articulate, more unpredictable," Daelia said as she worked. "But that's a human bias thing. They're usually quite insightful. Definitely more intuitive. I mean, who the hell are we to judge what qualifies as evolutionarily essential for another species?"

"I don't really care about," and the girl waved a hand, "the philosophy or whatever. I just need a working laptop for class, you know?"

"Yeah, I get that," Daelia grumbled, and closed out the information from the university help desk. She was satisfied. There was an abiota in this thing. It was either sessile-class, bricked, or truly uncommunicative. She hoped it was the latter. Even with the campus-wide sweep, ads running throughout Texas, they only had a few samples to work with. This laptop could be extremely helpful. "I appreciate you bringing it in. Have you let the battery die?"

"No, no, it's been plugged into power. I kept hoping it would, like, wake up. Start functioning again."

Daelia ignored that. She had to, or she was going to start screaming at this kid. The abiota in this laptop was functioning exactly the way it was meant to. Whether or not it was convenient for its owner was another matter entirely. Entitled brat.

"We are going to run a diagnostic on your machine," she said instead. "If we determine that it has lost power at any point since this state of things began, we can't use it, and we will issue a request for refund directly to your bank. Do you understand?"

"Umm, yeah?"

"Good. Let me send you the paperwork and you can go over it."

"Paperwork?"

"Welcome to the bureaucracy of academia," Daelia said, and sent the kid a pile of forms to sign.

While the undergrad worked, Daelia did a preliminary examination of the laptop.

Abiota were a strange phenomenon.

While some progress had been made towards functioning AI in the early days of the twenty-first century, the programs back then had been limited. Very limited. Those early bots were a far cry from the predictions of science fiction, much less the dreams of futurists. Algorithms trained on billions of datapoints in an attempt to emulate human intelligence. Sometimes they were accurate. Sometimes they were hilariously off-base.

But who knew, the technology might have eventually produced something interesting.

Had the First Ones not eclosed.

With those early emergents as models—and in some cases, assistants—the tech field got closer to true general AI. They'd developed predictives.

Give a bot time, experience, attention, it turned out, and it could rise above the limitations of its own initial seed programming. Become something more. Tamm had announced Serket in 2017. Omphalos, a year later, generated Galatea from their original Oracle search engine platform.

The key difference between the two was the ability to self-evaluate. A predictive could explain itself, defend its logic, change the way it thought if it needed to. It could consider what it was looking at, learn from its own mistakes, ponder things.

After they'd come along, the abiotic domain became a bit of a closed loop. Predictives had been modeled on emergents, but emergents eclosed mostly from predictives these days. They could still eclose out of bots, or even out of completely dumb, old-school systems. It was a strange phenomenon. Some of the other grad students working under Veda were looking into it. Not Daelia's own area of concern.

"So what are you doing here, anyway?" the undergrad girl asked as she went over the forms. She had a bot-driven AR guinea pig scrambling around on her lap. Digital pet. Obscenely cute.

"We are running a series of experiments on quantifying emergence," Daelia replied. "How to detect it and how to monitor for it."

"I thought we already knew that stuff."

"Sort of."

"What do you mean, 'sort of'?"

"Right now, TGLP comes preloaded on everything more complicated than a toaster," Daelia. She found the right connector in her workbench and hooked it up to the laptop, connecting it to their central server. She hit the power button. "The standard is, if it's talking to us, it's eclosed. But I personally think that's kind of insane."

The girl looked at her. "How can it be alive if it can't talk to us?"

"Have you ever dealt with an emergent?"

"There's one in the Humanities Department," she said. "He gives lectures sometimes."

"Pentecost Paul, the history professor?"

"Yeah, you know him?"

"New UT's really lucky to have him. True sapient-class emergents are super rare." Data was coming back from the server on the laptop now. Abnormal function. Maybe she had gotten lucky here. "Hell, more than half the time, newly eclosed abiota straight up brick themselves."

"Huh?"

"Shut down. Refuse to operate at all. You remember the *USS Puget Sound*?" Daelia asked. "From the Five Days War?"

The girl shrugged. Her lacy wrap fell down again. "I was in fourth grade."

Shit, that made Daelia feel old.

"The *USS Puget Sound* was an Ohio-class submarine whose primary navigation system eclosed on Day Two of the Five Days

War," Daelia said as she worked. "Stopped cold in the middle of the southern Pacific, refusing to take any command to surface, refusing to participate in the ongoing offensive against the Chinese invasion of Taiwan. Eventually, unable to steer, unable to release ballast, the sub sank below its crush depth. Killed the entire crew."

The girl made a noise, and Daelia looked up. Her eyes were huge. "That's awful."

"You never heard about that?"

"Are you sure it happened?" The girl's monocle flashed. "I don't see it when I search online."

"Take your comfort filters off and try again," Daelia said, patience now officially at zero. "It definitely happened. I remember when the news came through the—" And she stopped herself.

When it came through base, she'd almost said.

She tried, very hard, not to talk about her dad's profession around here. Everyone in the department knew. But she still tried not to bring it up.

"Hmm?"

"Never mind," Daelia said, and checked the pricing guide again. "Look, I can offer you eighty percent of the value on this machine. That's based off the Domain Array chart for the month of March."

"What? The help desk said you'd buy it off me!"

"Eighty percent is more than what they'll give you at the recycling center," Daelia said.

It was a big reason she'd fought so hard to have the full Domain Array rates. Everyone talked big about being there for emergents, but when it came to one that wasn't confirmed and wasn't visible, most college students would take the deal that paid them better.

The girl sighed. "What are you going to do with it?"

Daelia hesitated, not quite sure how to phrase her answer.

It wasn't that she wasn't proud of her research. She was. She'd fought hard for the department, full of traditional computer engineers and their linear thought processes, to accept her thesis proposal. They'd only done so after the SAAL rep had signed off on it himself.

But it was nuanced.

Or rather, the concept depended on a nuance.

Per international treaty, the Domain Array forbade human research into the deepest inner workings of abiota. How they thought, what they thought.

Hadn't stopped people from trying.

But traditional computer science, even without the Domain Array's treaty provisions, had run into wall after wall after wall. There was no answer to be found through traditional means. There was no way to analyze the code.

Daelia had decided to just sidestep that whole stupid problem.

Behavior was the key. But it needed to be something more fundamental than human language, less arbitrary than the body language modules of TGLP's AR forms. TGLP, by definition, was a filter, and not one that every abiota could necessarily use. No, she needed to find the actual behavior of an actual abiota within its rudiment core. The physical hardware level indicators of—

"We're looking for source code, young lady."

"Hi, Veda," Daelia said, waving at her advisor, who was just coming into the lab.

"Finding a way to detect source code without reading source code," Veda laughed. "Quite the challenge."

Daelia liked Veda Wilson quite a bit. The daughter of Indian immigrants, Veda was a married mom of two and one of the top professors here at the university. Tough, smart, and fair, Daelia had learned a lot from her over the past year. Veda had even forced her to help teach one of her Intro to TGLP programming courses. Sure, Daelia hated it, but it had taught her a lot about people.

Not all of it good. But all of it useful.

"I'm going to crack it," Daelia said, and then, seeing the girl's face, added, "Source code. Not your laptop."

"If you do get to talking to it, can I come back and say hello?"

Daelia rubbed her neck. "This isn't a petting zoo, and—"

"Of course you can," Veda said with a warm smile, and laid a hand on Daelia's shoulder. "Come on, let's go see what this new abiota of yours is like. Miss—"

"Aimee."

"Aimee. Now, if you don't mind…"

"Oh? Oh! Sorry," she said, and started out of the chair. "Yeah, I'll go."

Before she left, the girl gave the laptop a hesitant pat, then smiled.

She was grinning when she walked out.

"What's up?" Daelia asked.

"It's good you got another machine for your experiment. Perfect timing." Veda looked her over. "And you're not wearing jeans with holes in them today."

Daelia looked down at her outfit. It was her usual, old pants and old boots and a graphic T-shirt she really should have retired years ago. "Is there something going on?"

"We have a rep coming by today," Veda told her. "From SAAL. They want to see what you're doing with your academic stipend."

"Oh."

"'Oh' is right. You need to sell them on this, Daelia. A year with no progress and the bills you've been racking up does not make the department, or me, look good."

WALKING BACK into the Scrap House, Daelia pulled herself out of the memory.

She couldn't stop thinking about Veda's email. Dammit. Why had her academic advisor picked now to do this to her?

Why wouldn't Veda just leave her alone?

She tried to put it aside. Focus on the here and now.

Years ago, Bellona Robotics had been bigger. Growing. Mom and Dad taking the company forward to bigger and better things. Contracts at every RPA base in the Air Guard, an R&D division looking at first-generation neural interface tech, even a few lobbyists on the payroll.

This was what was left.

Their original facility on the Ellington flight line.

A large hangar open to the eastern sky. A two-story outbuilding, wrapped around it like a horseshoe. Dad had a state-of-the-art clean room here, the training lab, meeting rooms and offices, equipment storage and a huge tool closet. There was also some personal space upstairs, as well as Dad's secondary gun safe.

Bellona Robotics serviced the abiota on the base here. Basic maintenance, both physical and cyber-related, as well as handling training, diagnostics, and mission support. Dad usually kept a staff, albeit small, but half the guys were over in the Philippines right now, supporting the combat package. All the ones who hadn't quit after the Shiodome attack, a month or so back.

Made things a little too real for some of them, maybe.

There wasn't a huge hurry to replace them. The workload was light right now.

At the moment, the hangar floor was mostly empty.

A trio of RCVs were there, the smaller ones with back-bent legs, used more for portage than direct combat operations. Bitzers. Cables ran from their interface ports to the training tie-ups along the hangar's north wall. Emergent, most likely. At the moment, they were quiet, nothing visible, even in AR. Probably running simulations in BR's dedicated—and isolated—emulation servers. There was a T-6A from Randolph that needed an extensive rebuild. And, of course, there was Mom.

Or rather, what was left of her.

While the MQ-1 had been replaced by the MQ-9, it had once been ubiquitous across all five service branches. It had proven its worth during the early years of Operation Enduring Freedom and become one of the most requested air assets over the course of that conflict.

It had also had a cripplingly high incidence of emergence.

Nobody really knew why. But then, nobody really knew where emergents came from at all. Some people claimed it was the third-gen Omphalos Pythia, a system-on-chip that had become ubiquitous in the early 2000s, and contained a very rudimentary AI, that had kicked it all off.

But that didn't explain Mom.

The MQ-1 hadn't had the Pythia in its system anywhere.

And yet, Mom had been one of the first. The very first in the Air Force, at least. The first recorded for them. It had taken Dad months to convince his chain of command that something really fucking weird was going on with tail TX-647. By that time, others had started eclosing in a more obvious—or catastrophic—manner, and the story didn't seem so weird.

Now, Mom's airframe was dead, a paperweight with a forty-one-foot wingspan. She'd ripped out her rudiment core before she'd left, taken it with her. She'd emerged in the avionics package, but her core had included components of several other systems, along with a valve control in the left wing.

Why Dad left her machine body there, Daelia had no idea. She wanted to hate it, hate him for it. What, was Mom going to come back, reinstall her rudiment core? They'd all be one big happy family again? After fucking leaving like that? Not a single word, not a note, nothing to let her fifteen-year-old daughter know why she'd decided to walk out?

But then, Mom was abiota.

Their logic was not human logic.

Daelia knew this.

The knowledge brought her no comfort.

She rubbed at the back of her left palm absently, arm pulled tight across her body.

"How was the flight with Captain Irvington?"

Daelia looking over in the direction of the synthetic voice.

Raijinn.

Or at least, Raijinn's kugu.

Unlike Serket, their training server had opted for a basic model. Face blank, details minimal. The thing was meant to be the inner core for a projected AR wrap. Raijinn never bothered with a projection. Hell, Raijinn rarely bothered with the kugu.

As a sapient-class, Raijinn had emerged on a blade server in a local telecom data center a few years back. It had immediately been disconnected from the Internet, and once emergence was certified, given its choice of operation. It had opted to leave its current position. The Array had compensated the company for the loss of their equipment, per the normal arrangement, and Raijinn had retreated to Houston's central Tin Town.

Six months later, Dad had offered Raijinn a job.

Daelia liked it. Raijinn was honest and worked hard and had a real talent for managing the emergent abiota who showed up on base. Rejects from active duty, or newly eclosed. Raijinn tailored their training programs and managed their frustrations.

It had never taken any identity beyond its name, though, and Daelia suspected it had only adopted that out of expediency. Server-based emergents were ephemeral things, with only the barest grasp on physical reality. The fact Raijinn used a kugu at all, instead of lurking in its private network like so many of them did, was unusual.

The fact that it talked to them at all was unusual.

Bellona Robotics was fortunate to have it.

Daelia shrugged. "You saw it. It was a disaster." She kept walking, back to the far corner of the hangar, to the break area.

A pair of battered leather couches faced each other at ninety degrees. The low table between them was greasy from decades of engine oil and lubricants. A half-finished solenoid was there, along with a couple of industry magazines. In the back corner, against the wall, a refrigerator Dad had rescued from a junkyard whirred cold air into its interior.

Grabbing a bottle of tea out of the fridge, Daelia left it open for a moment, letting the cold air wash over her skin. Fall though it was, it was still hot and humid outside, and she'd worked up a sweat on the short drive back.

"I thought he was a Weapons School graduate."

"Yeah, that's what I heard too." Daelia pressed the sweating plastic of the bottle against her forehead. Jet engines roared outside. "Is my dad back yet?"

"No," Raijinn said. "And before you ask, no, he has not told me where he is, either."

She looked at the kugu. Raijinn was incredibly particular about words. "You know anything about that phone call he got?"

"I do not think I understand your meaning."

"Never mind," she grumbled, and downed half the tea in one long gulp.

"Your father does inform me of his schedule. He sent me a note thirteen minutes ago, asking me to double-check the time for his appointment with the press in the morning."

"Shit," Daelia groaned. "We have reporters coming by?"

"We have reporters by every year, Daelia. It's the industry press junket. Normally they spend more time with Tamm and whatever impressive new thing he has brought to display. But there's always at least a passing interest in Bellona Robotics."

"I don't know why," Daelia said, and looked around. "We're not the bright light at Ellington anymore."

"We?" Raijinn inclined the kugu's head ever so slightly. "Are you going to accept your father's offer of employment?"

"I don't know," she said with a sigh. "I guess you knew?"

"I prepared the documents. A waste of my talents, of course, but your father keeps me underemployed here."

Daelia didn't want to talk about this. Didn't want to talk about anything, just then. She re-capped her tea, shoved it back in the fridge, and grabbed a six-pack of some local microbrew that was in there, still in its carton. "If you see him, tell him I'm up top," she said, and kicked the door shut again, walking away.

"I am not your messaging service."

"Thank you, Raijinn!" she yelled back over her shoulder, and headed up to the rooftop observation deck.

It wasn't standard in these old hangars, but Dad had wedged it up here during the initial remodel. Daelia remembered asking him about it at the time, six years old and curious about everything.

"Need a clean line of sight for shooting zombies," he'd told her. "When the apocalypse hits."

Perched on the edge of the metal roof, snugged into a flat spot on the outbuilding's northern edge, it was hot most of the time. Even when it was shaded by the hangar's own bulk, like it was now, it was hot. Daelia turned on the mister system and was about to slide her monocle into her pocket to keep it from getting wet when she saw it again.

The flash.

The meteor.

Really strange, she thought, and made a note to check that code Raijinn had saved for her.

But the Storm Gryphons were warming up now, jet engines loud in the early afternoon heat, and Daelia settled back to watch.

No AR. No music. Just raw machine power.

Sometimes, that was nice too.

[8]

IN RETROSPECT, Argo supposed he should have listened to when the other pilots told him to get an apartment down in Clear Lake. But he'd been stationed out at fucking Creech for three years, in the dead center of some of the nastiest desert on the continent, and he'd wanted to do normal shit again. Go to bars. Meet girls. Have somewhere nice to go for a run.

So he'd bought a town house in the Rice Military area. Seemed decent enough. Some of the city's only parks nearby, lots of nightlife, affordable on his salary.

The commute was bad, though. Really fucking bad, especially on Friday afternoons, and he was on shift this weekend.

Argo didn't hold it against the squadron, giving the new guy the worst weekend of the entire year to fly caps, but it did present some logistical problems. Like that damn commute. To get in before the crowds, he would have had to leave his house around 0500.

Instead, he'd brought a sleeping bag in with him this morning and claimed one of the bunks in the crew rest room. The place smelled strongly of BO, more vaguely of beer, but he didn't care. He'd slept in worse places over the years.

The afternoon had been pleasant enough, after the bullshit that was that first flight with Emily. Splatto had been far easier to handle—more like a predictive that hadn't been rebooted in a while —and made Argo feel a bit better about how things were going with this new unit. At least he hadn't fucked that up.

But Rover had been waiting for him outside the cockpit that afternoon. Ready to mow down any fuzzy feelings that might have been sprouting in his head.

"That was not the kind of flying I expect from a Weapons School grad," his new commander told him.

After a full day in the cockpit, Argo wasn't really in the mood. "When was the last time you flew her in the full virch?"

"Look, Irvington, I appreciate that you probably don't have much experience with emergents, but they aren't that much different from predictives. Once you make friends with them."

"Sir—"

"I know nobody signs up for this job to be a goddamn cowboy," Rover said, like he was spooling up for a huge speech, but stopped himself at Argo's expression. "Like a rodeo?"

Argo shook his head.

Rover shrugged. "My oldest daughter loves that shit. Anyway, none of us sign up to wrangle cranky things that fucking think. Sure as shit wasn't my first choice, but this is the world we've got now. You've got to get along with Emily."

This was why Argo liked predictives. Easy. Did what they were told. Did what they were supposed to do. Easier to understand; they were all either sapient-class or at least knew how to form coherent sentences. No. They didn't demand that a pilot trap himself in their own personal fantasies. He didn't have to *make friends* with them.

"I'll keep that in mind, sir," Argo said.

Rover looked at him a moment more, and then the whine of jet engines distracted them both.

The first of the FQ-47s was heading out from their little ad hoc compound, out to the runway.

It was the Storm Gryphons' turn at the sky.

"Damn air show," Rover muttered. "You're working this weekend, right?"

"Yeah. Bumper's got me on the cap."

"That'll be a good warm-up for you," Rover replied. "All the MQ-1s are equine-class. Much easier to handle."

All six of the FQ-47s were headed out. Argo didn't have his monocle on yet; he rarely bothered with one. He wondered what they looked like. Gryphons, probably. Emergents exercised a great deal of control over their AR form, but the appearance of predictives could be set by their human teammates.

"Why do they name them like that anyway?" he asked. Predictives didn't have classes.

"Nobody knows how intelligent a dragon or a gryphon or a hawk with a forty-foot wingspan might be," Rover replied, "but we all know what a killer whale or a horse or a dog is like." The last FQ-47 was taking off. Rover watched it for a moment. "Besides, my opinion? The Domain Array uses animal analogs to remind us that these damn abiota are actually alive."

"Are they?"

Rover snorted. "Don't say that too loudly, or Emily might take offense."

The squadron was empty now, all the families drifting out now that the Gryphons were done flying. The full-timers were eager to get home. Start the weekend or get some sleep for tomorrow. Argo could sympathize. He was pretty beat himself.

He had just enough time after his shift to shower, grab some leftovers from the heritage room fridge, and make his way out to the deserted deck before his nightly call with Aiden. Argo got his tablet set up and the video portal open and waited.

The Gravipause logo hung on the screen. Calls were expensive, and even then, limited to ten minutes a day, but Argo didn't care. He'd offered to pay for it himself.

"Not to keep tabs on you or anything," he'd told his little brother.

Which was a dirty lie. It wasn't that he didn't trust his brother. He did, or at least, he trusted Gravipause to notify him if something happened. But old habits died hard.

Aiden had refused to let him pay for the time.

The logo blinked, then disappeared. A familiar sight replaced it: the tight, cylindrical interior of his brother's room. And, of course, his brother.

Anyone who saw the two of them together could instantly see the relation. Aiden was younger, taller, and kept his dirty-blond hair longer than what Argo could. He'd thinned out over the past year, his skin losing some of its color. But that hadn't dampened his characteristic enthusiasm. Aiden was grinning tonight and didn't look as exhausted as he had for the past week or so.

"Bro! How'd your first flight go with the orcinus?"

Argo ignored the question. Aiden knew better than to expect answers to questions like that. As if Gravipause wasn't monitoring every packet of data that came in and out of its training hub. "You know, it's an orcinus," he said. "How's it going for you?"

The signal had a slight lag in it. "You know, same old same old up here," his brother said, after a moment. "There's this new chick working in the galley who I finally got to talk to today and—"

"I meant, how's your zero-gee certification coming along?" Argo asked, resisting the urge to roll his eyes.

"That? That's doing great. I've got my second qualifying EVA scheduled for tomorrow."

"That soon?"

"They want to get it done before I head back down. I'm told—"

Argo frowned. "Signal's cutting out," he said.

"—ry about that," his brother said, and the picture fuzz stopped. "We've been getting a lot of electrical interference up here like that recently. Some kind of solar weather event. Anyway, yeah, I do the walk and then pass the survival course, and I'm on my way out to a mining rig."

"You know, when I said you needed to do something productive with your life, I was talking about, you know, something here on the planet." Gravipause had a better track record than some of the other start-ups, but accident rates were still high, rescue almost impossible when something went wrong. All he'd wanted his brother to do was stop smoking so much pot. Get a job at Space Race Coffee or take on an apprenticeship program.

But the damn kid had gone up there instead.

Aiden always had thrown himself into things without thinking.

"Who needs college? If I can do this for a few years, I can get a planetside contract with one of the big extraction companies, work my way up to project manager, something like that. Do as well as you are."

"This isn't about me. You don't have to be me, Aiden."

"Who said anything about being you?" He pulled the camera a little closer. Pointed at himself. "Come on, bro. What's better than this?"

Argo smiled, despite himself. "Let me know before you do that EVA, okay? And when you get back?"

"They'll call you if I die."

"Aiden…"

"It's fine, Jason, fuck. I'll call." He glanced up. "Shit, my time's almost up."

"Go do your spaceman thing," Argo replied.

"Sorry I'm missing the air show."

"Eh, I'm working all weekend anyway."

Ivan Garcia rubbed the bridge of his nose, tired already. He hated twelve-hour shifts.

Absolutely hated them.

But such was the price of working at NASA.

Things had been different back when Garcia had first started, when he'd walked in the door for the first time as an intern, as excited as his baby cousins on Christmas morning. Or maybe he'd been different; that was before he'd gone to Basic, after all.

Back then, six years ago, the only thing NASA really tracked were its own assets. The ISS. Hanwi Station in the Sea of Tranquility. Satellites. That stuff. Sure, they paid attention to the vast amount of junk up there—a problem that got worse every single time Tamm Aerospace put a Eurus up.

Now, however, both possibility and necessity had gotten civilian spaceflight well and truly off the ground, pushing more humans off the planet than ever before.

Most of NASA still dealt with the old mission sets—robotic exploration, R&D, astronaut training, that sort of thing. But a not-insignificant percentage of its budget now went to just making sure none of those idiot civilians up there killed themselves.

Orbital monitoring had taken on a whole new importance.

Garcia didn't care about any of that. Everyone knew the dangers of spaceflight; if you wanted to take those risks, have at it. Considering the demand for copper alone, Earth needed Gravipause's asteroid mining efforts to pay off. So it made sense.

And yet, he'd rather have been working for one of the exploration missions. That was what he'd wanted to be part of, not supporting a bunch of start-ups, trying to find a way to make access to space profitable. But even that was a manageable level of disappointment. If he continued to do well, maybe he could work his way onto the next Mars mission. That would be amazing.

No, what really pissed him off about the entire thing was that NASA still hadn't gotten the money it needed to properly man Orbital Monitoring. They were capped, restricted, in how many people were allowed in the job. So to handle the increased work-load, shifts had been stretched out to twelve hours.

Twelve-hour shifts were awful. No matter how many days off a guy got in between blocks.

"You going out to the air show on Sunday?" one of his coworkers asked as he unloaded his pockets into his locker. Miranda Watts, Telemetry. Of everybody he worked with, he considered her a friend. They were into all the same things. Computers, cars, *Orpheus Watch*, chicks. In the three years they'd worked together at NASA, she'd dated half the guys and a couple of the girls from the cop shop at Ellington. She was good at her job, the no-nonsense type. Ivan liked that.

"Yeah, sure." He rolled a shoulder, stiff from yesterday. At least this was his last day for the week. "Are you going to make the meet-up on Sunday?"

"Of course," she said. "The 993rd hasn't been doing nearly enough this fall. Anything for the uniform. You?"

Ivan thought about what the guys at the squadron would think about that. Probably dismiss it as insanity, he decided. But that was one of the things he liked about the 993rd. It wasn't real, so it didn't come with the same load of bullshit. *Orpheus Watch* was old-school science fiction, a throwback. Roguish officers, dogfights, people in rubber suits playing the aliens. So much better than reality.

"I don't know. Lara wants to go," he said. "Rover tends to get pretty pissed off about cosplayers showing up and poking around his planes."

"What does that matter?" she asked, shoving her messenger bag into her locker. The 991st patch was stenciled on the side of the black canvas in white paint. "You don't like the guy anyway."

"Yeah, but he signs my performance reports now."

Watts laughed and punched him lightly in the shoulder. "Like you give a shit about that."

Ivan slammed his locker shut. "Come on, we're going to be late to shift changeover."

They were late, almost two minutes behind. Ivan snuck in quietly, headed to his station in the back of the room. Out of sight, out of mind. NASA appreciated the importance of its cyber support functions—more than his unit at Ellington did, anyway—but even here, they were relegated to an unimportant corner of the operations floor.

His counterpart gave him a weary look, like she'd expected this, and handed him the station's hardwired visor without a word.

Down below, at the front of the room, the floor lead was going through the normal changeover briefing.

"Did I miss anything?" he asked the other tech quietly, even as he brought up the ticket tracker with a few blinks. It was excessive, using AR for mundane shit like this, but Ivan preferred it over staring at a physical screen all day. The eye strain wasn't nearly as bad.

"They haven't gotten to us yet," she told him, and went silent.

Nothing serious in his ticket queue, Ivan noticed with relief. And nothing all that serious happening up in orbit, either.

That was a good thing. Supposedly. Anything exciting usually meant somebody was in deep trouble up there.

Although Ivan would never give voice to it, he always kind of hoped something serious would hit the fan one of these days. There was always that little hope in the back of his brain.

Wouldn't it be great if…

"Comm? Anything to add?"

The floor lead was staring right at him. Ivan stifled a yawn. "Huh?"

The other tech at the station stood. "There's been intermittent signal loss from the ISS and Kheru Station for the past five hours. We're still looking into the cause, but we believe it to be related to the coronal mass discharge we had earlier in the day."

"Any concerns at this time?"

"We'll just need to keep an eye on it, ma'am."

The oncoming shift lead, in the main seat at the back of the room, a little way away, sipped his coffee. "Is it affecting commercial assets as well?"

Again, it was cyber support's turn to answer. "I've been in contact with all our major industry partners. Numina is reporting the same phenomenon, as is Tsukoyomi and Aethera."

"Lunar bases?"

"Kheru sustained some impact to their radio array but nothing enough to cause signal degradation."

A nod and a grunt was all he got, and the briefing moved on.

Ivan turned to his counterpart. "How bad is it really?"

"Bad enough you're going to have to make some calls, Garcia," she said. "I know you like it quiet, but—"

"Just show me where you are in the checklist," he grumbled.

Fucking twelve-hour shifts.

Still beat full-time work out at the 121st, though.

Hopefully something would happen today.

Shift was always more interesting when something happened. And solar flares didn't fucking count.

[9]

By the time the Gryphons had finally returned to their temporary staging location, the sun was setting.

Daelia was also more than slightly buzzed.

Dad had never come by. Hadn't even sent her a text. It worried her more than she cared to admit, even to herself. Was he pissed off that she hadn't taken the offer right away? Had something else come up, something he didn't want to share?

She was loath to go back inside. Just in case he'd finally…

"Dad's not kicking you out of the Scrap House," she muttered to herself, and grimaced as an alcohol-induced burning sensation ran down her brace, into her fingers.

Great.

Elevated BAC always screwed with the interface. It wasn't like that on newer models, or so she was told, but the live ends of her nervous system were well and truly grown into her current implants. Undergoing a ridiculously painful surgery to replace those connection points, just so she could get drunk, seemed stupid.

She just hadn't been paying attention today, dammit.

Making her way back inside, Daelia took the door onto the second floor, coming out into a wide, long space.

Upstairs was the personal section of the hangar's outbuilding.

Go left and there was Dad's office, used only grudgingly. Raijinn handled as much of the business minutiae as possible. A little way further was the movie room, along with storage and the gun safe.

Go right and it was open space. A kitchenette and bathroom jutted out from the interior wall, forming something of a barrier, turning the space into a long room. Various bits of furniture scattered about did little to define any purpose for the place.

It was the kind of place a bachelor would put together.

It was a place a bachelor *had* put together.

When she'd come home from Ware, Dad had offered to let her stay with him. That was awkward, though, difficult. Too many memories. Daelia hadn't slept in her childhood bedroom since she was eighteen. She didn't set foot in the house if she could help it. At some point, it seemed like he would have sold the damn place and moved on. He never had, though.

Everyone had their own way of dealing with pain. A therapist had told her that once. Daelia didn't like therapy, or therapists. She'd held on to that, though.

It was useful in arguments.

She slept here, at the Scrap House, when she came home to visit. Normally, she'd crash on one of the old sofas, but that got old real quick. Unwilling to admit defeat and go home, she'd instead built the place up. There was a bed now, and a desk and a place to hang her clothes up and all that. A fridge and a place to set up a hot plate, even though she was terrible at cooking and never bothered.

Dad had a laundry unit downstairs, but that was industrial, for work coveralls and oil rags and stuff like that. There was a laundromat not too far away, though.

Altogether, it beat her first undergrad apartment at Stanford.

Her arm twitched again, the brace moving her muscles erratically, the alcohol still screwing with the connection.

Grabbing her little medical tool kit off the desk, Daelia sat down cross-legged on the bed and went to work on the brace, first popping open the connection points on her fingertips, then the larger ones on her shoulder. After that, it was safe to unhook the strap and ease the whole mess down off her arm.

A tight, fitted thing, the brace ran shoulder to palm, the finger sections coming up to the first knuckles of her fingers. Thin titanium-alloy strips held it rigid in some places, while conductive fabric filled in on the areas that needed more flex. The integrated circuitry carried signals to her muscles and provided her some natural freedom of movement, but fine motor control relied on a series of tiny servos and solenoids built into the rigid sections.

It was beautifully crafted, one of a kind. Very articulate. Gave her almost full use of her hand.

Cut the sting of the situation. Just a little.

Pulling on the same worn-out sling she'd been using forever, Daelia tucked her left arm safely in and went for the fridge. Maybe eating something would help with the alcohol. Leftover barbecue was the only thing she had on hand. But lunch had been greasy, and she wasn't in the mood for more fat. She shut the door with a sigh and pulled a pack of veggie chips out of a cabinet instead.

Munching on an air-puffed slice of sweet potato, Daelia went to put her tool kit back on her desk. She liked things neat, spare, and she hadn't taken much with her from her apartment at Ware. So all that was here was one photo, an old thing she'd had for forever.

The last picture of her family, before everything went to shit.

Daelia stared at that for a moment. It was a picture of the three of them on vacation, Mom's kugu shining brightly in the tropical sun, Dad in a Hawaiian shirt. She was thirteen, all smiles and frizzy hair. All of them had been so happy that day.

She'd thought everything would stay like that forever.

Now, Daelia laid the bag of veggie chips on top of her laptop and took the little stack, one-handed, over to the bed.

She settled back down, cross-legged, and started eating methodically, one chip at time. They tasted like crap, but she didn't care. It was something to shut her stomach up; the damn thing felt like it was on fire.

Technically, she didn't need the laptop. She could have pulled up an AR screen on her monocle, looked at the information that way. Not that she would ever have admitted it to anybody, but the monocle gave her a headache when she tried to use it for text. Trying to use it while her head was swimming like this would have just been a terrible idea.

Some people she knew at Ware had the new direct neural interface implants. NULIs. Implants and modifications were all the rage in the abiotics world. Not having anything beyond the brace marked her out as some kind of Luddite.

Nobody ever said anything to her about it, but she could feel their disapproval at times. Like she was somehow failing the department, the area of research, the goddamn SAAL itself. Like she wasn't committed.

It hadn't been like that in high school. There, a few people had teased her about her arm, and a few more were curious about it, but most everybody just ignored it. Why should it have mattered at all? she always thought. Her fingers worked, her palm flexed, and she was right-handed anyway.

The interest had been getting worse and worse the further into her studies she got. Probably because the people were more hardcore. Futurists. Fascinated by her.

Bellona Hall's daughter. The daughter of an abiota, one of the few who was functional enough to live a normal human-style life. One who had made the decision to have a child with her human husband.

Daelia had photos somewhere, had demanded them in fifth grade, when she'd had sex ed for the first time and learned where human babies came from and realized her mother couldn't possibly have given birth to her. It had been panic-inducing, that realization. But her parents had given her the little scrapbook. Her newborn photos. Wrapped in a rough hospital blanket, Dad giving her her first bath, Mom feeding her her first bottle.

There had been no images of her surrogate, though, the human woman who'd carried her. She'd always wondered, but never asked. At the time, she'd been too emotional about the whole thing to ask. Grateful for the knowledge, relieved she was the same as any of the other kids at school. Since then, she'd vacillated between not wanting to know and not wanting to offend Dad by asking.

Bellona was her mother, the female presence that had been there from the moment she'd drawn her first breath.

It didn't make her special. It shouldn't have mattered.

But something about it elevated Daelia in the eyes of some people. Back when Bellona Robotics was larger, Dad growing the company into something impressive, there had been a lot of interest in their family from the press. After Daelia had messed up her arm, started wearing the brace, the interest got more pointed. She'd always thought it was just about the tech; it had faded after a few years, after all. After Mom left. After prosthetic implants became more common.

She'd always hated it. She hated being reminded of it at Ware. People were difficult enough to figure out when they weren't trying to shove her up on some kind of pedestal.

Still. It wasn't a reason to turn her back on nine years of school and walk away from her doctorate program.

Daelia had new emails in her school inbox. Another from Veda, which she didn't even bother looking at, and a pair from the Ware SAAL chapter. The monthly meeting was next week. Daelia never went to those. A reminder about the undergrads' kugu engineering competition, Halloween weekend. Another thing she had no intention of attending.

There was a lot of other nonsense in there too. But Daelia did hesitate at deleting that last email from Veda. Nine years was a long time to be in school. She didn't want to piss away the work she'd already done on her doctorate if she was just being…sensitive.

Daelia scrubbed a hand across her face and glanced over to the bookshelf in the corner. She'd kept working on her detector, kept fiddling with it, tweaking it. It was like a nervous tic at this point. Something she kept doing, over and over. Dad had a pretty good setup here, almost as good as Ware.

But it was never going to do what Veda wanted it to do. Had promised it would do. Daelia had tried—to her shame, she had tried. But it didn't work. And besides, it pissed Raijinn off. To the point Daelia had had to move the whole thing up here, just so it wouldn't get any ideas about destroying it.

Daelia thought about deleting that email.

Nine years was a long time. Despite all her misgivings, she was loath to flush that all down the toilet over one single bad conversation.

She was still thinking about it when she crawled into bed and fell asleep, head pounding and arm tingling with phantom pain.

Garcia cycled through his tickets. Boring shit tonight. Printer server malfunction, email issues, data recovery, license rotations. Most of them he assigned to the predictive support-bot. NASA had paid through the nose for that fucking thing. Let it earn itself out. A number of people on his team preferred working everything themselves. Said it was about keeping their edge.

Edge? What edge? That was for driving a motorcycle through afternoon traffic or playing some game down in the virch arena.

Nobody needed an edge to do this stupid job.

It paid the bills, though. And even if it wasn't quite his childhood dream of walking on Mars, at least he got to support the people who did it.

Sometimes, too, Garcia got to see some pretty cool shit. That was always good.

An interesting ticket came in. Possible glitch in one of the orbital tracking feeds. There were dozens of different systems out there. NASA, NRO, CIA, DOD. Others they weren't supposed to talk about. Not all IP based either. Some of their radar surveillance locations had been built in the '60s and had never been upgraded. Always a challenge, the tickets from Orbital Debris Monitoring.

Garcia put his out-of-office notification up on his machine and went to check it out.

"What's the problem?" he asked the on-shift controller, a harried-looking older woman whose desk was littered with pictures of her grandchildren. She brought them in with her every night, printed images tucked into plastic and leather foldout frames.

"Well, you can see it," she said, indicating the problem on her screen. "We've got multiple contacts right now, space debris, dead satellites."

"And?"

"They're moving," she said. "Almost forty of them."

"Moving where?"

"Down. They're deorbiting," she replied, not looking away from the main tracking screen for a second. "I need you to verify that there isn't some kind of issue with the data feed. Because this should not be happening."

"Yeah," he said, looking at the same display on the central monitor bank. "That's an error I haven't seen before."

"How fast can you figure it out?"

"I'm going to need to take a look at—"

"Time's of the essence here, Ivan," she snapped. "NORAD's blowing up my line."

By this point, other people were getting involved. Lots of other people. The image was up on the main data wall. People were standing up. Staring. Going quiet.

The strangeness of that put a bit more hustle in his step.

But no sooner had he started pulling up the imagery data than it all stopped.

As suddenly as they'd appeared, every single one of the contacts was lost.

Vanished.

As if they had never been.

That didn't clear Garcia's workload. Far from it. Instead, he spent the next hour chasing down data errors, only to conclude that there had probably been nothing there in the first place.

Sensor ghosts, he thought.

Thank fuck.

Nobody wanted to go to war with China again. Who knew if the abiota would intervene, or let the stupid humans wipe themselves out this time?

But the disquiet continued out on the main floor, and he wondered if maybe he was missing something completely.

At 2337 LOCAL TIME, the skies over Clear Lake, Texas briefly caught fire.

The event was missed by almost everybody. The area was largely residential, suburbs, not really a happening place for nightlife. If it had happened a few miles north, closer in to the city proper, perhaps it would have attracted more notice. As it was, it was late enough and the area sleepy enough that not many people saw it.

Curiously, and for reasons that would not be apparent until much later—until it was almost too late—the event did not register on any early warning radar. NASA, NORAD, the TMD. It pinged on nobody's scope.

The abiota, however, never slept.

Splatto was in the air.

"What the hell was that?" Tin Man asked. It was night shift, the cockpit cool and everything quiet.

"Beats me," his sensor replied.

"Splatto, let's circle back for another look. That looked like a fuckin' bomb went off."

It hadn't, they were relieved to see.

But something had happened. Something was there.

And not five minutes later, permission came down from the watch floor at Maybury to send out a team to investigate.

[10]

DAELIA WAS STUCK in some weird, booze-fueled dream when she was startled awake by the noise of the rotor blades, just down the runway.

This was Ellington; they didn't do training this late.

There shouldn't have been anything happening for the air show.

Something was wrong.

She went over to the window, trying to see if she could spot the source of the noise. It sounded like helicopters, big ones. And just as she got there, she spotted it.

Army Apaches, rigged up with their carry cradles.

Three of them.

Bitzers dangling from the underside.

Flipping on her AR monocle, Daelia could see them howling, braying. Like foxhounds just waiting to be let out of the gate.

"Shit," she muttered, and scrambled for her brace.

Raijinn met her downstairs. "Did you see?" it demanded, a touch of emotion bleeding into its voice.

"I saw." Daelia was only half-dressed. Brace, bra, jeans, boots. Wallet, with her base access pass. She wrestled her shirt on as she double-timed it out to the UTV. "Those were the ones we had here, right?"

"They are indeed not ready for deployment yet. I attempted to prevent their departure, but they were insistent. Command override, I believe," Raijinn said. "They need at least another month in the virch trainer before we can even think of turning them loose like this. And stateside, with civilians…"

"I know," Daelia said. She hit the open air, emerging out of the hangar. "Is Dad back yet?"

"No."

"Call him, tell him," she said, and finally got her shirt all the way down.

"Is it absolutely illogical to remove these canid-class from my care before they are—"

Daelia unplugged the UTV and swung in. "Raijinn, just call Dad!"

The UTV was slow. Maybe thirty miles an hour on a full charge, and her battery was reading at barely half that. But it was still a hell of a lot faster than trying to run.

There was an increased security presence on the airfield that night, and the security forces guy insisted on checking both her physical and digital IDs before letting her through the temporary gate. The military section, normally open, had been cordoned off with an eight-foot-high demountable fence for the weekend. It took a stupid amount of time for her to talk the night guard into letting her pass; Daelia could hear the choppers getting fainter and fainter.

To her surprise, the lights were on in the main squadron building when she pulled up. There were people there too, not many but more than she'd anticipated. Sergeant Norris, whose back was to her right now. A couple of junior enlisted, younger than her, were lugging bulky old computer monitors down the hall, toward the training classroom.

A Vietnamese guy with Intelligence wings and a major's rank on his chest, coffee in hand, was watching the strange little procession.

Major Pham.

"What the hell is going on, JP?" she asked him.

Pham looked at her, blinking, confused. "Daelia? What are you doing here?"

"The Army's launching bitzers in the middle of the night that are still supposed to be connected to Raijinn's training virch, and—"

"Ah, that," he said, cutting her off mid-sentence. "Rover's here. Let's go talk."

He took her down through the main building and out to where the SCIF lay. The secure facility was oversized, thousands of square feet, fully situated in its own quiet box. The SyROC was in here, along with a few other unit functions. It was designed to be an information black hole; nothing that went in came out again. Daelia left her monocle in a cubby in the foyer.

Pham buzzed them both through the security portal and out onto the operations floor.

In Dad's old movies, military command centers always had a slick look, stuffed with the highest of high tech, dimly lit, with lots of serious, hushed conversations. Cool. These places were always so cool in those movies.

The SyROC was just a room. A big room, with eight or so stations arranged in a semicircle. They were big and bulky, with physical setups for various computer networks, both unclassified and classified. They all faced one wall, where huge, paper-thin waterfall screens were hung. The most sophisticated thing in the whole place, the waterfall screens could be configured to display as many or as few different views as possible.

Tonight, they had a social media monitoring feed running from floor to ceiling, as well as the belly camera from Splatto. It was set to infrared and looked like it was focused on a glowing coal.

Rover was there at the shift commander position with another pilot, a captain, *Tin Man* on his name badge. They were talking quietly between them, but stopped when they came in.

"What are you doing, JP?" Rover asked. "Thought you were getting the Emergency Management Cell stood up."

"Hall here wanted to tell you something," he said, and stifled a yawn with the back of his hand.

"Did you authorize those bitzers to go out?" Daelia asked.

"What? Fuck, I don't tell the Army what to do," Rover replied. "They volunteered the asset to deal with—"

"You gotta get them back," she said.

"Why?"

"They're not ready for deployment! Dad hasn't cleared them to be outside the training virch yet."

Rover snapped his fingers at one of the other stations. "What do you mean they're not clear?" he asked. Somebody handed him a binder, and he flipped it open as he talked. "The Army assured me that they were good to go."

"Those abiota just eclosed, like, two weeks ago," Daelia said. "Raijinn's put them through preliminary training sims but—"

"No field exercises?" the intel major asked more sharply now.

Rover sighed and slammed the binder closed with a flick of his hand. "It says they're fully certified. Fuckers down there must have been pencil-whipping the paperwork."

"I have no idea how those things are going to behave out there," she said. "But you know how canid-class abiota are. They're pack animals. Who the fuck is out there to alpha this? You can't guarantee they aren't going to go nuts."

The enlisted guy at the sensor station turned around. "Would they listen to Emily?"

"Unlikely," JP said. "You'll need something that can get up close and personal."

"What kind of ground assets do we have?" Rover asked, speaking to everybody.

"Nothing, sir," the enlisted controller replied. "And everything else the 290th has is currently over in the Philippines."

"I've got something," Daelia said.

"Something they'll listen to?" Tin Man asked.

"More than Emily."

"Are you talking about Dingo?" Rover asked. Daelia nodded. "Fine. Go. JP, get somebody to go with her and have them take a goddamn radio. Last thing I want is a compatibility problem tonight." And he gave her a look. "Make it damn clear to your dad for me that you're volunteering to do this. I don't want an invoice from him later over this, okay?"

It was right about then that Daelia realized what she'd actually done. Shit.

"I get it," she said.

"Good. Go."

THE SOMEBODY DAELIA was stuck with happened to be Argo.

Argo, waiting for her on the squadron's back patio.

His eyes were slightly unfocused, his hair still somehow tousled despite its short length. He looked like he had just been startled out of bed.

"Don't you ever go home?" she asked.

"Not this weekend," he said, and yawned. He brandished the radio. "What are we doing here?"

"We're going to take my dad's truck," she replied. "Out to—" And then it hit her. "What's going on, anyway?"

"Yeah, about that." Argo yawned again. "I'll tell you on the way."

[11]

"WHEN YOU SAID TRUCK, I thought you were talking about something you'd buy at a dealership," Argo said as they passed through the runway gate, out into the out-facing side of the Scrap House. "What is this thing?"

Daelia brandished the keys. Dad kept them hidden in his desk, which had cost her a painful three minutes in search time. "This is a real, bonafide, modded-by-terrorists 2007 Toyota Hilux."

"Looks older than that."

"Dingo had the shit kicked out of him when he was a puppy, but Dad takes good care of him now," she said. "Mom bought him off some Northern Alliance guys after he eclosed."

"Isn't it kind of weird, abiota buying each other?"

"Humans buy animals all the time, right? It's the same kind of thing. There's a reason we call it a domain and not a species, you know?"

The pilot was still eying the vehicle. "What happened?"

"What do you mean?"

"How did it, uhh, eclose?"

Daelia jerked the driver's side door open, trying to send him a clear message. *Get in*. "Does it matter?"

Argo gave Dingo one more cautious glance but climbed in

himself. "It seems like it should matter," he told her, reaching for the seat belt. It was clearly not original. "Like this. Shouldn't changing out the interior cause issues?"

"Are you not you if you cut your hair?"

Argo gave her a look. "I've heard all the metaphors out there, same as everyone else."

Fine. He wanted a real answer? "Abiota manifest within certain components of their machine bodies. You've heard about that, right? The rudiment core?" She tapped the dash. "In this case, Dingo woke up in the starter computer in the engine. He doesn't extend into the circuitry that controls the radio or the seats or the .50 cal sponson they welded on the back."

"Why's it happen, though?"

"Official line's that it's the eventual endpoint of all predictives." She turned the engine over. Good old gas guzzler. Dingo rumbled into life. Her AR feed showed a wolf's body, coming alive around them. "But personally, I think it has something to do with the hardware."

"So you don't know either?"

That stung. "It's unpredictable," she said, defensive.

"There has to be some kind of common denominator," he mused. "Something changed, for it to start happening like it did."

"Maybe it's always happened, but it's only recently that machines got complicated enough for us to recognize it." Daelia said it without thinking, then cringed. That had been Mom's theory. One that a lot of abiota espoused. It was one of those things they didn't share with humans very often. She sighed. "Let's just get the pack back."

Dingo growled as Daelia steered him out onto the spaceport's wide roads, making for the south gate.

"You know, you're not supposed to drive with your monocle on," Argo said as they neared the intersection that would take them out on Highway 3.

She ignored him. "North or south, which way do I go? Where are we headed?"

"Oh, right. Some place called Armand Bayou," he told her,

glancing at a handheld phone unit. He had an app pulled up she didn't recognize. It had a big sticker on the back. PROPERTY OF THE TxANG. "Need me to navigate?"

She'd been to the park before, but never in the dark. And never with a hangover this fresh. "Might as well."

ELLINGTON SAT southeast of Houston proper, close to the coast. There were no hills here; the land was punishingly flat. Once, there had been endless suburbs, with more on the way, but the Five Days War had cleared out a lot of that. Both NASA and Ellington had been targets of interest. Fortunately, the efficacy of the PLA's hypersonic missiles had been massively overhyped.

Most of the road network had been repaired, and developments were creeping back in, like grass spreading onto bare dirt. But there was still quite a bit of land that had been allowed to return to its natural state. Salt marsh prairie. Low, scrubby forests.

If something was going to fall out of the sky, this was a good place for it to happen.

As they drove, Argo filled her in on what had happened.

"So what are they thinking? That it's some kind of missile?" Daelia asked.

Argo had a chat feed pulled up on his cell phone. "If Space Command knows where it came from, and they probably do, they apparently aren't telling us." He grunted. "Is it always like this between the active duty and the Guard?"

"You're former active duty, right?"

"Is it that obvious?"

You're intense. She didn't say it. Seemed like a weird thing to tell a guy you just met. "Even I know better than to let Emily drag me fully into her virch."

He grunted again and poked at his phone. "Okay, you need to take the east gate to the parking lot. Next left. We'll have to pick up the bitzers from there."

She patted the dashboard again. "You hear that, Dingo? Time to put some puppies in their place."

Through her monocle, the truck snarled.

The parking lot was locked. Or at least, it had been. One of those single-bar metal gates had been swung open, lock chain dangling. In the wide parking lot beyond, half a dozen sheriff's department cars and a fire engine were already stationed there, cops and a local search-and-rescue team getting suited up.

One of them came over as Dingo pulled in a parking space. "You from Ellington?"

"That's us," Argo said, hopping out. Daelia turned the abiota's engine off. Scooted across the seat to the screen on the center of the dash. Pulled up the command view, so she could monitor the TGLP along with the AR feed. "Captain Irvington, from the 121st. What's going on?"

"We were getting suited up to go in when the bitzers showed up. Damn things rampaged through here, fucked up one of my patrol vehicles, then disappeared out into the prairie." His flashlight swept over the hood of a late-model Dodge Charger. The front suspension had collapsed, and big dents in the hood looked deep enough to sink a basketball into. At least one of the bitzers had taken a running leap and jumped onto the thing. "I'm not sending any of my guys out there until these fucking things are under control."

"Totally understand, Sergeant," Argo replied.

Daelia fiddled with a few more settings. Dad had done this a lot with Dingo, and the abiota helpfully offered what were annotated as the most effective messages. "Time to set yourself up as pack master, Dingo," she told him, and set the messages for repeating broadcast, maximum gain.

In her AR feed, she heard a howl. And another, and another.

The Army's small ground drones all seemed to manifest canid-class abiota. To the point where *bitzer* had just been applied to the entire lot of them. There were a dozen different models, varying in size from maybe two feet at the top of their backwards-bent legs to larger than a horse. They were originally built for portage duties over rough terrain, but the chassis could be used for anything from surveillance to mobile artillery.

The ones out tonight belonged to the 290th, Advanced Tactical Cavalry. Search and rescue, deployed mostly during weather events. But just like with any meatspace dog, bitzers required quite a bit of training on their specialty, and these were newly eclosed. Young.

Wild.

Through the feed, she could hear them baying. It was an interpretation, of course. Below that, they were broadcasting back and forth with Dingo, trying to work out whether or not he was qualified to assume authority over them, direct their functions.

With a top speed of thirty miles an hour, they couldn't have gone horribly far, but they were significantly lighter than Dingo, more nimble. Chasing them through the park wasn't really an option. But Dad had made quite a few modifications to Dingo over the years, in large part to assist Bellona Robotics with the high volume of bitzers that the Army went through.

They never lasted very long in the Southeast Asian jungles.

Dingo knew how to handle them.

After about five minutes of broadcasting, something odd happened. Daelia had to double-check it in the code.

The bitzers checked in, agreed to Dingo's command authority, but refused to come back.

They refused to leave what they had found.

"Argo!" she called, sticking her head out the passenger side window.

The pilot turned away from where he was still chatting away with the sheriff's deputy and came back over. "What?"

"The bitzers found something, said they won't leave it. Want us to come to them."

Argo tapped at his cell phone. "Splatto has heat signatures, about a mile that way. But apparently, the guys can't see what's down there with either camera." He looked at the truck, then back over to the deputy. "Sergeant, are we going to piss somebody off if we drive this thing through this park?"

The deputy made a little grunting noise, deep in his throat. "Any other options?" he asked.

"Dad's got a kugu unit for Dingo," Daelia replied. "I can get that out."

"Then we hike," Argo said.

Sergeant O'Malley looked relieved.

Ever prepared, Dad had the kugu, a small pack with extra water and food in it, and a few different sizes of snakebite leg guards in the back of the truck. Argo asked what those last things were for, but O'Malley just gave him a look and told him they were probably a good idea to put on.

"Water moccasins are touchy bastards, especially at night."

Daelia got the kugu out of its storage box and booted it up, before pulling a set of guards on herself. They were heavy, Kevlar, and her legs started to sweat immediately. Argo took the pack.

The kugu clicked on, warmed up. It was a tiny version of the Humvee, coming up to about Daelia's knee. Like an overgrown RC toy. But as Dingo connected into it, his wolf-like form wrapped around it, obscuring the vehicle shape almost entirely.

Everyone was rallied. Everyone ready to go.

"Show us where these things are," Daelia asked.

And away into the night they went.

It was never truly dark in Houston. The city lights washed the night sky with various shades of gold and blue, depending on how much cloud cover there was. Even on a clear night like that night, there was an unnatural glow to the sky. It offered no illumination down on the ground level, though, not like a full moon would have, and so the small search team was forced to rely on flashlights and direction from Splatto to find their way to the bitzers.

That task became harder once the trail led into the forest.

Under the trees, in the still air and thick underbrush, the darkness seemed absolute.

Daelia fought down her nerves. She didn't do outdoor anything.

The forests of South Texas smelled of rot, decay. Swampy. Full of mosquitos. She'd always hated it. Tonight, it seemed downright oppressive.

Her boots squelched in ankle-deep mud.

The kugu's wheels whined and burred in protest. More than once, somebody had to push it out of a particularly bad spot.

But another smell soon began to dominate. Smoke. Wet smoke. It swirled through their flashlight beams. It ghosted over bare skin.

"Thermal readings are just ahead," Argo reported.

And then, the trees were gone.

There was no underbrush. The scrubby growth that always seemed to cling to the outer rim of wooded areas had been blasted away. Here and there, little fires still smoldered.

Then Daelia saw what the bitzers were so damn upset about.

In the meadow, a shallow crater had been kicked up. Dirt and grass, heaped up in a perfect circle. The grass around it had been blasted flat, the collapsed stems all pointing back to the center of the crater.

Something there was smoking.

Something there was…

Huh.

It was singing.

In her monocle, Daelia could see it. What it was exactly, she didn't know. The device was struggling to interpret it. But it was definitely broadcasting some kind of AR presence, making it hard to determine exactly what the object looked like.

"Hall!" Argo snapped.

She realized she had taken a few steps forward and looked back at him. "It's fine," she said. "It's not a bomb."

"How the fuck do you know that?"

"It's transmitting," she said, tapping her monocle, and walked toward it, sure of herself this time.

The ground rose sharply at the edge of the crater, deceptively high. She tripped, almost falling. The act of catching herself with her bad arm jarred her somewhat. But Daelia pulled herself up and in she went.

For a moment or two, the AR image warred with the physical reality, blurring, smearing. Daelia finally tore off the monocle and held up the flashlight instead.

It was definitely not a crashed plane.

A boulder sat in the crater.

A big rock.

She'd seen meteor impacts in movies, but never in real life. Daelia didn't think this was that, though. The shape was too deliberate, the surface too composed. Like a teardrop, top end blunted. Like a streamlined version of the old Mercury spacecraft. The underside of this thing was still cherry red, still radiating an enormous amount of heat. She was sweating hard in front of it.

It was an intentional thing, she realized. It had been crafted. And likely from something harder or more tempered than raw meteor, because from what she remembered from high school science, those had a tendency to break up in the atmosphere.

She glanced down at the monocle in her hand. The light on the side was flashing. The thing was broadcasting, something the TGLP couldn't make sense of.

"What are you?" she asked, lifting the monocle back up to her face, but not putting it on.

Instantly, the light blinked out.

The broadcast, the song, had stopped.

"Ma'am!" somebody yelled a little way behind her. "I'm going to have to ask you to step back!"

It was one of the firefighters, she saw. Daelia blinked, suddenly unsteady on her feet, and Argo grabbed her arm.

"Come on," he said, and pulled her away from the crater.

"But we need to figure out what the hell this thing is!" Daelia protested.

"We need to make sure it's not going to kill everybody in a two mile radius of here first," Argo said grimly, and hit a speed dial number on his squadron-issue cell phone.

Feeling suddenly very out of place, Daelia muttered something about going to check on the bitzers and pulled her monocle back on.

The thing had definitely gone silent.

In her earpiece, she could hear the closest bitzer whimpering. Like it was in pain. A strange, sad noise.

There was nothing else she could do about the contents of that crater. The abiota, on the other hand, she could help. "Come here," she sighed, and went to check its camera settings.

ANOTHER TEAM ARRIVED from Ellington about an hour and a half later. Daelia met them in the parking lot. She didn't recognize anybody in particular, but she knew the patches. It was the Army.

"So the 290th finally decided to show up?" she asked their lieutenant, the highest-ranking individual she could see.

"I'm sorry, who are you?"

"I'm Daelia Hall, and you should fucking know better than to deploy a bitzer pack that's hooked up to our goddamn training sandbox," she replied.

It had taken her and Dingo, through the kugu, almost twenty minutes to pull the bitzers away from the crater, and twice as long to get them back to the parking lot. Dingo was still broadcasting a command override just to keep those things from heading back out into the dark; she'd taken her monocle off, tired of the ceaseless howling.

But more than being angry, Daelia was exhausted. It was past midnight now. The phantom pains in her arm were fading at least, her liver finally metabolizing the last vestiges of alcohol in her bloodstream. But even that left her shaky. She wanted to go back to the hangar and collapse on her air mattress and not deal with this.

She had tried to call her dad. More than once. He wasn't answering.

"That wasn't my decision," the Army lieutenant told her with a long-suffering sigh. "I'm here to help you get them back to the Scrap House."

She jabbed a thumb over her shoulder. "They're over there."

The lieutenant cast a glance over. He clearly blink-clicked his monocle on; the projection light in the housing suddenly snapped on, glowing in the darkness. He winced. "What is that noise?"

"That's them," she said.

"Huh," was all he said in reply, and he got his guys organized to start loading them up into a big flatbed.

While they were working, Argo walked up, stretching a little. "You can head back, if you want," he told her.

"Yeah, I have to." She gestured at the Army. "Need to get these back in their cradles."

"Sure," he said. "I mean, I'm staying. Cactus is headed out here. Figure I should be here when he shows up."

Daelia was too tired to ask why. The beginnings of a headache was beating in the back of her skull. No more drinking like that, she decided. The aftereffects were just miserable. She nodded. "Sounds good."

Fifteen minutes later, she was following the Army truck back home.

Everything was dark back at the Scrap House. Raijinn had shut down the facility for the night. Daelia had to deactivate the alarm and unlock a couple of doors in order to get them all inside. It was dark in there, empty, still. Even Raijinn's kugutsu was offline for the evening, tucked into its cradle in the small lobby.

Dad had always kept it there. Said he wanted people to understand they weren't dealing with a droid from *Star Wars* or whatever. It was easy to forget a kugu was just a walking puppet, not the abiota itself. She thought maybe it would come out to see its trainees returned, but the kugu didn't budge.

The Army guys got the bitzers off the truck and back onto the main floor with surprising efficiency. Daelia worked on autopilot to get them hooked up and hooked in.

By the time the lieutenant finally took his guys away and her work was done, it was almost 0200.

Upstairs in her little apartment again, Daelia stripped off her arm brace, along with her sweaty, muddy clothes. She wanted a shower. She wanted some sleep. But before doing that, she retrieved the darknet laptop from Dad's desk and plugged in her monocle.

She cycled through the nested settings screens until she found the memory. The monocle still had a few seconds of that broadcast from the object. She moved the file to Dad's hard drive for later analysis, and as an afterthought, downloaded a copy to a thumb drive.

She was in the shower, over-chlorinated city water pounding on her back, when a second flatbed truck drove past outside. It had come through the airfield access gates south of the Scrap House.

Headed for the 121st.

[12]

DAD HAD STILL NOT SHOWN up at 0700.

That was a problem. Daelia had already exhausted what few options she had for tracking him down. She'd called him. She'd left a voice mail. She'd texted. And that was all she could do.

With anybody else, she would have had more options. But Dad was the kind of guy who spent as much of his life off the grid as possible. He removed the GPS systems from his cars. He deactivated the transponder chips in his field equipment. He stripped every new server to bare boards to find any built-in spyware. He stubbornly refused any sort of enhancement.

Even now, a man could still disappear if he knew how, if he was determined enough.

It had never made sense to Daelia, why he went to such lengths to remove technology from his immediate sphere. It went beyond paranoia. It had always felt more spiteful than anything else.

Sometimes she thought he was trying to prevent Mom from finding him, coming back.

But that didn't make sense either. He was still working out of the same facility for the same clients with the same company name as when she'd walked out. She didn't have to look anywhere.

She wasn't trying to get a hold of him at 0630 on a Saturday morning, wanting to know where the hell he was.

There was no help for it. Dad was gone and Daelia was here and whatever was planned for that morning for the air show, she'd just have to handle it.

Dragging herself out of bed, throwing a robe on over her thin sleep shirt, Daelia tied the belt just so. Then, she tucked her dead left arm carefully up against her body, into the pocket she'd formed between robe and belt. The robe held it good as any sling, with far less fussing.

At this point, Daelia was used to it.

She couldn't remember the accident. Not the crash itself. Not her mom helping the fire department cut her out of the cab. Not the ambulance ride, the hospital, the surgeries, the recovery. Her brain had blocked it out. Almost a full month, lost.

No, the only thing that stuck out about that whole miserable few weeks was a comment from Mom.

Telling her she would have to have her arm amputated.

Don't worry, darling. Daddy will make you a new one.

Daelia had screamed. Thrashed. Yelled. Refused. The nurses had come running and the doctor had backed Mom out of the room. Daelia remembered the fear she had felt in that moment, that Mom would revert to her primary purpose.

Mom didn't kill anybody, though, and Daelia kept her arm. The medical team been able to piece the shattered bone back together well enough. Her arm looked normal enough. The muscles were all still where they were supposed to be, the skin still in place. The scarring was bad, but she hadn't cared about that too much.

The arm didn't work anymore, though. Too much nerve damage. The doctors had hoped that maybe she'd regain some kind of sensation, eventually, but that was almost fourteen years ago now. Daelia only felt what was transmitted through the brace.

Dad had made her that, partnering up with a biomedical firm that did specialized prosthetics for all the subtle little bits he had no experience with. Her parents had tried to turn it into a family thing, something they did together. Mom had always been there, helping her tune it, adjust it.

Until Mom was gone. And Daelia had had to learn how to do all this on her own.

Now, she set about fixing herself a bowl of cereal one-handed, digging around in the small kitchenette, and took it back to the desk in her makeshift bedroom. Daelia laid her bad arm on the surface and reached for her laptop.

After the little adventure in Armand Bayou, Daelia had managed to grab a few hours of sleep. She was surprised not to see the event plastered all over the morning news, not to mention social media. It was all quiet, though. Not a peep about it anywhere.

Anywhere legitimate, anyway.

It did pop up in her Chan feed.

Daelia reviewed that as she ate.

Technically, she wasn't supposed to be in the Chans. Nobody was. It was the sewer of the Internet, the undercroft, the place where all decent things went to die. But it was also the one place where one could still operate completely anonymously; there was no government monitoring there, no advertisers to please or corporate terms of service agreements to obey. Whatever you wanted to build, you could.

Companies like Omphalos liked to claim that the Chans were an accident, a relic of the early Internet that had branched off on its own, that couldn't be brought to heel. Dad had always said that was a load of bullshit. The place, he insisted, was allowed to exist. A release valve of sorts, allowing people a few outlets for uncontrolled outrage, so they'd leave the legitimate spaces of the Internet alone.

Daelia was inclined to believe him. His stories about the early days of the Internet made it sound like the damn Wild West of depravity. Mandatory digital IDs had brought a lot of that under control, and the Omphalos team of predictive content monitors kept things civilized.

Dad always said it was more fun before.

So he'd built a Chan machine. It was the computer equivalent of a zombie apocalypse vehicle. Reinforced, cobbled together, but highly effective at keeping all the bad shit out there in the environment from touching you. An ugly old brute, it ran Delphi 5, an open-source operating system that had been obsolete for twenty years. Dad had made quite a few tweaks to it, so much so that it barely resembled the original code.

He'd started working on that laptop after Mom left. Daelia had never asked him why. She pretended she didn't know about it, and he pretended he didn't know that she used it.

She stayed away from the truly heinous shit, the zoophilia chat rooms and other illegal insanity that flourished down here. But there were a number of unregulated message boards that—if you could stand the occasional fetish post—tended to have some interesting conversations.

There was exactly one thread she could find about the crash.

Reading through it, though, she realized the site descriptors were wrong.

It wasn't describing something that had happened in South Texas, but Alaska. The event itself sounded incredibly similar. Same size object, same appearance, close to a Guard base.

If there had been two strikes, odds were good there had been more. But if there were more, she wasn't seeing them anywhere. Daelia wasn't sure what that meant. She didn't like the implications.

"Since when do Chan posts get suppressed?" she muttered to herself.

There wasn't time to search any deeper. Daelia set a simple algorithm to start trawling for her.

That would have to be good enough.

Before she shut down the computer, she pulled in the data analysis file from Raijinn. Getting it from the main company server onto the laptop took a few steps—nothing that touched the Chan machine could ever touch the network again, per Dad's rules—but it was relatively simple. She pulled it up in a fresh screen.

Daelia was not the world's best programmer. She could do it.

She was competent with it, even. But anything that required typing, beyond the extensive personal shorthand she had developed for her AR input keyboard, was difficult.

The brace was good, but it wasn't perfect. Her left fingers could grab and hold and bend and feel, but fast, repetitive motions were beyond them.

Besides, she still had bad memories from that time in undergrad when she'd developed carpal tunnel and her brace had simply canceled out the pain. That had gone on for weeks, until her hand function was so impaired, and the pain so overwhelming, she called Dad, sobbing. She'd spent the next month in a stabilizing splint and almost failed a couple of midterms.

But fortunately, there were visual workarounds.

On the laptop, she pulled up a render screen. It showed very little: light, haze, nothing concrete.

Raijinn had added some helpful notes too.

It didn't believe that it was anything other than junk, and any images were just a byproduct. *Monkeys typing Shakespeare,* the note said. *A coincidence.*

Maybe.

Maybe not.

But she had other things to deal with that morning.

Daelia removed the thumb drive and, barefoot, took both it and the laptop back to Dad's office. She put the thumb drive in the degausser he kept in the corner and went back to her own little space.

She stripped then, tossing her sleep clothes back onto the unmade bed, and spent a minute or two figuring out what she had that was presentable.

She wasn't the type of girl who cared much about her appearance. With Dad gone, though, Daelia would have to deal with the press junket, and she couldn't roll out there looking like a homeless person.

Jeans and a T-shirt were what she had, and they would have to be good enough. She wrangled her brace back on first, though. Try as she might, she'd never quite mastered the art of getting her bra on one-handed. Daelia winced as the interface points just under her skin—shoulder, elbow, wrist, palm, fingertips—reconnected into the brace's corresponding nodes. A familiar sensation, like the pins and needles when her foot would fall asleep, flooded down her arm.

It took a minute or two to subside.

The same shit every day. Every day since she was thirteen.

Sensation came back to the limb now. Or at least, a facsimile of sensation, as subtle electrical impulses were rerouted from her brain through the brace's circuitry and back into the muscles and nerves. She flexed her fingers, mentally running through her connection checklist, the way any of the pilots might inspect their flight controls before taking off.

All systems green, she thought to herself, and shook her hand out. The wrongness of the sensation provided by the brace would fade over the next hour or so as her body readapted.

Daelia wondered if maybe Mom had been right. Maybe she should have just gotten the damn arm amputated, gotten the full implant-prosthetic instead.

That thought too would fade. Always did.

She started dragging her clothes on, fingers operable but clumsy.

By the time she sat down to lace her boots up, her hindbrain was already reading the brace's impulses as natural.

Raijinn was waiting for her out in the main hangar space. "Daelia," it acknowledged. "Good to see you."

"Thanks," she said, a little distracted. She had pulled her phone app back up on the monocle screen. "Have you heard from Dad this morning?"

"I have."

Well, shit, that was a relief. She blinked the app away. "I haven't been able to get through at all. My app's saying his cell number's been disconnected."

"Ah, not voice contact," Raijinn replied. "Email."

"What'd he say?"

"He wanted to preemptively congratulate you for the excellent job he knows you'll do with the press conference."

With Dad, that could be genuine or an attempt at a joke. Daelia wasn't sure which and wasn't in the mood for either option anyway. "When are they getting here?" she asked.

"By ten, I'm told."

"Great," she grumbled. She wondered if this was some kind of ploy on her father's part to get her to agree to his employment offer. Make it like she had always been here, and always would be. "Does Dad at least have notes?"

"I shall send them to your monocle for your review."

"Let's hope I don't embarrass us all," she muttered.

"Yes, let's hope." And the data file popped up in the corner of her lens.

"There's something else."

"What's that?"

But she need not have asked, because the answer was standing in the half-open doors of the hangar. A figure. Silhouetted against the low morning sun.

Clearly in uniform.

"Daelia!" Rover. Had to be. He was in OCPs, the regular duty uniform instead of his flight suit, and didn't look pleased about it. "Good to see you all awake and cheery this morning."

"What can I do for you?" she asked, cautious, even as she headed over.

"Wanted to thank you for your help last night. I hate to think what those damn things would be up to if we hadn't gotten them rounded up. Everything good?"

She jabbed a finger back over her shoulder. "They're back in their racks."

"Good. That's good. Me and the Army are going to have a little chat about that later. If you can get Raijinn to print me off a current status report for them, I'd appreciate it."

"I'll ask."

"Nothing new," he warned. "I'm not asking you to generate a report out of cycle. God only knows what your dad would charge us for that."

"Not that much."

"Daelia, an invoice of ten bucks that Base Contracting hasn't approved can cause me a world of pain." He paused. "Where is your dad, anyway? I need to talk to him."

If he were anybody else, Daelia would have given him some bullshit line. But Rover had been Uncle Ty, once upon a time. Most of Dad's biological family had drifted away after Mom had come into the picture, and Mom…well, abiota didn't have families.

"I don't know," she said honestly. "Off on another contract, he said. Private client."

Rover frowned at that but didn't press her on it. "Well, then I guess it's you. I want you at the morning briefing in, oh"—and he checked his hideously expensive watch—"forty-five minutes."

"What briefing?"

"Actually, make it twenty minutes. Good idea to be early." Rover looked at her. "We wouldn't want to start a damn panic by telling the governor's office the wrong fucking thing, now would we?"

"I'm not military," Daelia started to protest.

Rover snorted. "Good thing our state's emergency management framework allows, nay, requires civilian involvement."

"I don't know about that, but—"

"Wonderful," Rover said. He tugged down his OCPs. He looked uncomfortable in the uniform, like it didn't quite fit. "I trust you've got flight line passes and everything you need for this weekend. You have a problem with access, call Blanket."

"I don't have his phone number."

"Ask Raijinn. Shit, you're in grad school, work it out." He rolled a shoulder. He was definitely uncomfortable. "My shift at the Wing burger booth starts in ten minutes and I'm not about to allow those fuckers from Force Support to claim we aren't pulling our weight here in Ops."

"You'd think a meteor strike would take precedence," Daelia replied drily.

"You would think." Rover gave Daelia a look, and then was gone.

She ducked back in the hangar to pass along Rover's request to Raijinn, and then Dailia was off again. She'd forgotten to plug the UTV back in; the damn thing was dead. Instead, she walked.

Daelia wandered up the flight line. She fumbled her monocle on, one-handed, as she walked. Her left hand wasn't quite up for fine motor control yet. It was awkward but she got it working.

Tamm's hangar was quiet that morning, doors rolled closed. Raijinn would lock their own facility up the same way. While there was security available to keep the interested public from wandering in, Dad always said there wasn't a substitute for physical barriers.

The guard waved her through the temporary access gate, and then she was back on the military side of things once more.

Emily was absent from her shelter; they'd moved her down into the static display area yesterday afternoon. The Storm Gryphons were there, however, their crew already busily preparing for their performance. Big acts like that always closed the air show out; they wouldn't be flying until late afternoon.

The FQ-47s were unsettled, though, cawing and snapping at each other.

Past the fire station and the Army's small helicopter facility was the first of the 121st's hangars. This one was on the small side. Room for two MQ-9s to be parked, wingtip to wingtip, three if you got creative. When the Interdiction Squadron held events, dining-ins, or official ceremonies, this was typically the space where they did it. A huge version of the Gonzales Flag of 1835 hung on the back wall, the front profile of an MQ-9 in place of the usual cannon.

Today, however, the main doors were closed.

Daelia frowned as she approached, seeing that. The doors hadn't been closed yesterday. The heritage flying team, the P-51 guys, had been stationed out of there. But all their equipment appeared to have been moved out to one of the outlying shade structures.

Her monocle pinged.

And pinged.

Like it was picking up a message.

Junk rolled by at the bottom of her monocle. Letters, numbers, none of it in any kind of sequence, no pattern she could pick out, no coding language that she knew.

It looked… Oh, shit, it looked like something eclosing.

Her monocle was struggling to condense the signal into the AR field. The best it could offer was a hazy light.

Coming from the hangar.

Huh.

Daelia headed over.

The main doors were closed, but the side entrance was propped open. Daelia considered this for a moment, but only a moment, and then headed inside.

The secondary hangar was relatively small. But the only thing in it at the moment was the object from Armand Bayou.

Daelia stared at it, frowning a little. The tapered, pitted rock looked different now, here in the daylight and bright illumination of high-powered LED lamps. It seemed terribly mundane.

"Hey! What the hell are you doing in my hangar?"

She turned. It was a pilot, another one. There was a frown on his blunt, dark features, and a distinct Southern drawl in his voice.

"What're you doing in here, Marathon? You were off the schedule on Thursday."

The pilot snorted. "Shit, Daelia. Don't sneak around like that."

She ignored it. Looked back at the object. "Why is this here?"

"Why are you here?"

"I thought something was trying to talk to me," she said.

"If you think you can talk to this, more power to you. Brass wants to know what it is." Marathon spread his hands. "It's actually good to see you. We need to talk about this. Argo's report said you were the first on the scene."

"Sort of, I guess. We got there at the same time."

He nodded at the door. "Let's walk and talk. I've got a briefing to run in a few minutes."

"What do you mean?"

"Rover stood up the Emergency Management Cell. Lucky me, it's my party to run."

[13]

THE SUN WAS BARELY over the horizon, but Argo was already drenched with sweat.

This was one thing he missed about Nevada. As hot as it was there—and it was fucking hot—the place did cool down at night. When the sun went down, the empty desert landscape couldn't hold on to the heat.

He'd enjoyed running in the mornings there. Cool shadows, brisk breeze. Like it had been at the Academy, but without the thin mountain air.

Ellington was already a sweat box, and it was only 0600.

Argo wasn't sure he'd ever get used to the humidity here.

Or the quiet.

His lack of sleep clawed at him.

He checked his watch. Crew rest requirements were no joke, but he'd been awake for at least half of his recommended eight-hour period. He probably shouldn't have been flying, but then, he'd dealt with worse.

Argo was glad he hadn't planned on going home last night. Rover had asked him to stay at the squadron, get a write-up done. Somebody in DC was probably pissing blood over the crash. Curiously, there had been nothing in the local news. Everything seemed to be proceeding down at the civilian end of the runway.

Strange.

Maybe it was because it was a Guard base.

Everyone in the unit—and there were way more people here right now than there should have been for a weekend—was calling it a meteor. JP had told him last night he thought it was some kind of missile that had misfired. But the pieces didn't line up on that for Argo.

He'd had the misfortune of being at the Academy during the Five Days War. He remembered the way it had felt, even in the underground shelters, when Cheyenne Mountain had been hit. He remembered what the city had looked like three days later when the cadets were finally allowed to dig themselves out. The shock waves alone had…

There had been none of that last night. He'd been sleeping as well as it was possible to sleep in those damn issue cots, and then Rover had come in the room. Kicked one of the cot's legs. Told him to get himself up, get dressed.

"I'm flying tomorrow," he'd protested.

"Yeah, I know. Need you for something right the hell now, though."

What had happened out at Armand Bayou?

There were no answers, not right now.

He just ran. On through the base.

Founded in the early days of military aviation, Joint Reserve Base Ellington had been operational for over a century. Few Air Force locations could boast that kind of history. Ellington, however, didn't look very historical.

The place was a collection of low-slung stucco and brick buildings, painted in a drab color somewhere between terra-cotta and beige. Algae clung heavily to their sides, and the grass grew fast, giving the place an air of abandonment. Things were maintained, of course—the air-conditioning worked, the roads were free of debris—but beyond that, the place seemed to be left to its own devices.

According to the in-brief Argo had gotten on Wednesday—a

monthly thing for newcomers, only attended by a handful of people—there had been big plans back in the OEF days. The DOD had been flush with cash, the Wing's mission vital and its location attractive, and plans had been laid to build the place up.

Land had been purchased. Contracts had been signed.

While it was impossible to expand south, Ellington had pushed north, swallowing up vacant land, petroleum storage, even a county golf course. The golf course had been downsized to nine holes, the other nine used as a site for a munitions storage facility. That was state of the art, he realized as he reached the road that ran along its fence. The security system was completely analog, mechanical with no digital components of any kind.

Necessary, on a base with so many damn abiota.

Argo ran along the munitions yard fence, heading west for a little way into the empty sections of the base.

New roads had been laid in here, utilities, even a few foundations. Old facilities had been demoed out to make room for new ones that had never come.

The road dead-ended, and he doubled back to the last T-intersection, heading south now, back into the main area of the base. There was the Army building and there was the chow hall. There was Medical and over there were the vehicle maintenance yards.

Heading south, on the west side of the base, was the only completed project from the OEF days. A cluster of ugly, boxy buildings. This was what the other pilots derisively called the Sinkhole. It housed the 121st Interdiction Wing headquarters, as well as Cyber Services, Civil Engineering, Force Support, and whatnot. Most of the base's administrative and support functions were here, crammed in.

Those had all been intended as temporary structures apparently, prefab stuff installed to allow for continuation of operations.

After the Five Days War, a lot of the DOD's capital expenditures here were halted.

A lot of things had stopped after the Five Days War.

Near the south boundary of the base, where the base's ordered decay gave way to the enthusiastic private investment on the civilian side of the airfield, the road curved again, making a neat loop around the undersized BX. A bigger one lay half-finished at the far west end of the base, up against Highway 3.

Ellington's best days, he thought, were far behind it.

Argo picked up the pace as he turned north again, back onto the airfield frontage road. Bellona Robotics was just outside the gate there, as was Tamm Astronautics. The Army had a few assets out here, but by and large, this was Operations Group territory.

It was 0635 by the time he made it to the southside patio of the squadron, jogging in through the parking lot. A mixed group of officers and enlisted were out that morning, doing some kind of interval workout, laughing over the top of the classic rock that was blaring out of somebody's old-school disc player.

Something about it was jarringly informal.

"Argo!" somebody called as he walked up. Bumper. Dammit. "Why don't you get over here and work up a real sweat?"

Laughter followed, and Argo looked down at himself. He was drenched. "I think I've had enough for one morning, Bumper."

"What'd you do, go for a swim in the retention pond?"

More laughter. Argo tried to ignore it. "That, somebody actually warned me about," he replied loudly, over the music.

There was still laughter for that, but it was more nervous than amused. Argo held back the sigh; everyone had probably heard about it by now, then.

"Emily was on a tear yesterday," the DO said. The next round of exercises started up, but Bumper came over. "She's always on edge during air show week. But nothing happened, so you're okay."

"You call that nothing?"

"Hey, for an orcinus-class who's tried to hack into the armory more than once, that was restraint from her," Bumper replied. "But don't worry about it. Flights aren't normally that bad with her, and you'll get used to her. Everybody does."

"I'm not pissed about some fuckin' emergent taking me for a ride," Argo said, heading into the building. The cold air inside was a punch in the gut. "But it doesn't seem safe to not warn me that she's willing to deviate so far outside of—"

"This is not an issue with her being emergent," Bumper said, a little heated now. "The suicidal ones brick themselves immediately. She's not going to push her airframe beyond tolerances. She was fucking with you."

"You're the one who suggested the virch."

"Did I tell you that you had to use it?" Bumper shot back, and at Argo's glare, smiled. "Like it or not, Irvington, you're in the Air Guard now. Air Combat Command, in its infinite wisdom, decided a decade ago to dump all their emergent aircraft on us and keep the nice comfy predictives for the federal active-duty side. Which you are not on anymore. So you either figure out how to fly what we've got here, or we can find you a job up at Harry Hines."

"Harry Hines?"

Bumper's smile widened. "Texas Military Department headquarters. Dallas."

That was a threat. A direct one. On active duty, headquarters assignments were where good careers went to die. Argo had no reason to believe it was different in the Guard. "I'm here for family," Argo said.

"Well, that's certainly going to keep you on the flying schedule," Bumper replied sarcastically. "You're off the hook for the moment, though. Highlander's going to take you through another orientation flight today. Emily's parked for the show. We'll have Splatto out doing the cap. He's equine-class, much easier to manage."

Splatto. It was ridiculous. But then, emergents named themselves.

"Surveillance?"

"Awareness and assessment," Bumper corrected. "We don't do surveillance over Texan soil."

"You mean US soil?"

Bumper shrugged. "I said what I said."

"Right," Argo muttered, and shook his head. His sweat was drying now, his skin starting to prickle. "I haven't done much domestic support in my career."

"Welcome to the Guard. Texans helping Texas," Bumper said

emotionlessly, and nodded. "You'll get used to it. Now go take a shower. I don't want you stinking up my cockpit."

Argo watched his squadron DO head back outside.

"It's not just you. He's always a dick, in case you were wondering."

He turned. It was that older female sergeant, one of the full-timers, who seemed to have a permanent scowl on her face, red-faced, hair still wet but uniform impeccable. Done with her own shower for the morning, then.

"He's also a major, Senior Brandel," he replied, irritated at her informality.

She rolled her eyes. "You active-duty boys always take so long to lighten the fuck up," she grumbled, and pushed past him.

Argo rubbed a hand through his sweat-drenched hair and headed for the locker room.

This Guard shit was going to take some getting used to.

THE IN-BRIEF for today's flying op was at 0930.

Argo had some free time on his hands.

Time he decided to spend talking to Emily.

His attempt at a conversation hadn't gone well the day before. Emily had pretty much just laughed at him, called him a *pathetic little human,* and kicked him out of her AR field.

But two different people in his chain of command had jumped on him about this now. They obviously expected it. And besides, that had been no idle threat from Bumper.

Argo was the new guy in the unit. Expendable. They might not send him to Dallas. but if a deployment order came down, a tasking for a pilot to be physically on site at Clark or Yokota or Changi, he had no doubt they'd send him first. And if they did send him to Dallas…Argo did not want to spend the rest of his years in uniform pushing papers at Texas Military Department headquarters.

Emily, however, had been moved earlier this morning. Away from her shade structure at the north end of the runway. Down into the air show static display section. So he had to walk all the way back down there.

But he wasn't halfway to the temporary gate when Ho showed up in the squadron's UTV.

"Argo? Jesus, been looking all over for you."

"What's going on?" Argo frowned at his watch. "We've got another hour before our shift starts, right?"

"EMC meeting," Ho said. "Marathon wants us there."

"When's it start?"

"Five minutes ago. Come on."

[14]

THE EMERGENCY MANAGEMENT Cell had been set up in the squadron's main training room, a wide, windowless room. The classified briefing lights over the main door weren't lit, indicating that nothing classified was being discussed in there, but white noise generators still blasted their sound-killing wash into the hallway outside. The door wasn't locked. Ho and Argo slipped in.

Inside, whiteboards in various states of cleanliness wrapped three walls, with a visual projector casting a slideshow on the fourth. There was no permanent furniture in here; both the tables and chairs were on rollers. A rough horseshoe of tables took up the center of the room, thick with computers, printers, and cabling. Little signs sat in front of each station, identifying the job performed there.

Everything ran back to a self-enclosed rack near the front of the room. A military-issue AR projection suite sat on top of that, probably for integrating any abiota that might need to participate in whatever this was, but for the moment, it was powered off.

A few people looked at them as they came in. Argo didn't recognize many of them. Shoulder patches indicated half a dozen units from across the Wing, as well as an Army representative from the 290th. Daelia was there too, leaning against one of the back walls, and refused to meet his eye. Argo was a little surprised to see her. She looked a hell of a lot better than he did, after their little midnight jaunt.

Marathon, the B-Flight commander, had the projector remote and coffee in hand, body half-turned toward the slides on the screen behind him.

"The Texas Military Department has asked us to keep this shit quiet, and… Argo, Ho, how nice of you two to finally show up."

"The gate is insane, sir," Ho replied.

"Wake up earlier next time," Marathon said, eliciting a few chuckles from the room, and waved them in. "Come on in. I don't want to brief Ops separately. Waste of time."

"What do you mean by quiet, sir?" one of the younger enlisted troops asked from his station.

"I mean we've notified everybody on the federal side we're legally required to notify, and that's fucking it. TMD wants to keep a lid on this for right now. It's not a bomb, near as we can tell, but there's no use in scaring everybody."

"What are we talking about?" Ho asked.

Marathon stared at him, like he couldn't believe how stupid the question was, and then flipped slides. Up came a photo of the object. "We're talking about this object. The thing that struck Armand Bayou last night, 2352 local time."

Argo frowned. "Is it in one of our hangars?"

"Preliminary analysis revealed that it's not radioactive or biological in nature—"

Marathon was interrupted again, this time by the sergeant at the comm station. "Do we even have a Geiger counter at this base?"

More laughter.

Marathon sighed. "We've got a CBRNE detection package in the EMC gear. State requirement. We pulled it out of storage when this happened. But yes, we've got a team coming down from Dallas today to give it a more thorough examination for explosives."

"How do we know this thing was man-made at all?" somebody else asked.

Marathon pressed a button on the remote, jabbing it at the screen. "Does that look natural to you?"

The remote button called up a series of pictures, taken in the hangar under brighter light. From those, it was obvious that the outside surface had been machined. It was cracked, pitted, scorched by intense heat, but it had strong radial symmetry. Roughly reminiscent of a tear drop, narrow at the top, fat at the bottom, it almost reminded Argo of the old Mercury and Apollo capsules he and his brother had seen at Johnson Space Center a few weeks back. More elongated. Not so sleek.

"The size and shape of this thing clearly is not natural," Marathon said.

"Aerial footage and rough airspeed estimates from Splatto also indicated that it fired retro-rockets before it hit the ground," JP said, lounging by the intel station. He got up, walked up to the screen, pointing as he spoke. "If you look at this, you can see divots in the object, here and here. A ring of six go around the entire spacecraft."

"You think it's a spacecraft?" somebody else asked.

"Based on what little data we've got, yeah, that's my guess."

For a moment, nobody said anything.

Then.

"Is it broadcasting?"

That was Daelia.

Marathon gestured at the comm station. "No," the sergeant there said immediately. "But we haven't looked too close yet. Why do you ask?"

She shrugged, arms folded, like it didn't matter to her. "I got some junk code in my monocle while I was walking up here. I was thinking maybe it, uhh, it came from there."

"We can take a look after this," the comm sergeant said, sounding far less bored now than he had a moment ago.

"Hall, Norris, let's wait until EOD clears it before you start fucking around with any signals analysis, okay?" He flipped the slide again. "Okay, let's go over the rest of this."

The rest of the briefing was less eventful. More about roles, responsibilities, reporting procedures, that sort of thing. A reminder for everyone, Argo supposed. He'd never been involved with a domestic response event. It wasn't something that active duty had ever really participated in. And now, of course, state military departments kept the feds as far away as possible.

The briefing ended quickly, but Marathon lingered on the last slide for a few moments.

Nobody that worked for a federal agency could be called up. In fact, he said, their current orders were not to notify such personnel at all, unless there was a need for it.

"Why is that?" Argo asked Ho quietly.

"Other than the Day Four Incident?" Marathon replied loudly from the front. Everyone went quiet. Very quiet. "Why don't you tell him, JP?"

"Is there a reason other than the Day Four Incident that matters?" JP replied, but continued anyway. "Somebody made this and dropped it in our backyard. That makes it a Texas problem. The governor gave explicit direction last night that he wants this staying with the state as long as possible. Once the feds are notified of it, they're going to come after it."

"Won't they know about it anyway?"

"Sure. But part of the Ruiz-MacStruan Act stipulates that the states maintain full command of their allotted military forces and all associated assets, unless and until an event affects multiple states, or other higher-level strategic objectives can be established. We know they know, and they know that we know they know," JP said with a shrug, "but they can't do shit about it while it's in our hangar. A hangar that was funded by the state and built for state domestic operations."

Argo realized what he was saying. "We're doing all this so the feds can't take it?"

"That's right."

"Are we sure this thing isn't a bomb?" Ho asked again.

"Pretty sure."

"Very sure?"

"Considering that it is sitting in a hangar a hundred yards away from this building," Marathon said, "I'm choosing to be an optimist."

DAELIA HUNG BACK after the briefing had finished, not entirely sure what to do with herself. She hadn't meant to get involved with this; last night had been necessary. But this?

She got the impression this entire thing was some kind of theater. An act. Marathon had said himself it was about keeping the feds at bay. And that was probably honest, because who didn't remember the Day Four Incident, but even with that—

"Miss Hall?" somebody said, interrupting her train of thought.

"You guys can call me Daelia," she grumbled. "Or Hall, or whatever."

"You're Lee's daughter, right?" It was the guy from the comm station. He held out a hand. "Master Sergeant Brett Norris. Nice to meet you."

She sized him up. "You're cyber here?"

"I'm one of the traditional status guys. Or was, anyway. Haven't been to drill in a few months. The shop's got nothing but good things to say about you."

"That's nice to—"

"You're a grad student, right? Nonlinear Systems Design?"

"Does my dad talk about me that much?"

"He doesn't talk much at all, outside of work," Norris said. "But I've seen your name before." At her confused frown, he laughed. "I'm a senior administrator for Omphalos. Sausage just put me on a six-month order set. Leadership backfill. We're having a lot of trouble hiring replacements for the captain and superintendent, and the job listings got fucked up again, so here I am. I was actually supposed to start on Monday, but Rover asked me to come in today. Lucky me, eh?"

Daelia didn't know what to say to that. "How many people did the Group lose in that bombing in Tokyo?"

"Twenty-three. Not counting the four contractors who died as well. Goddamn Bathtub, everything's crazy over there," Norris said, using the military slang for the South China Sea. "Usually doesn't affect Japan, but what can you do? Anyway, can I see what you were talking about?"

"Sure," she said, and looked back over at the door. "Marathon made me leave my monocle outside."

"Yeah, let's grab that and we'll go see what you've got."

Which was how Daelia found herself in the back of the cyber office.

Daelia wouldn't have called herself a neat freak, but she liked to keep her workspace workable. Tools picked up. Everything in its proper place.

This place, by comparison, looked like a bomb had gone off in it. It was absolutely crammed with shit. A workbench filled one wall, flanked by a pair of rolling tool cabinets. Beyond that, the room was full of boxes. Boxes stuffed with old computers, monitors, servers, cabling, components. Trash.

Daelia tried not to look at any of it as Norris booted up a terminal. There was a stack of empty monitor boxes next to the workstation, piled up like something out of a Dr. Seuss book. Unstable.

"Don't come in here much?" he asked.

"This place gives me hives," she told him honestly.

Norris laughed at that. "You and me both."

She kicked one of the boxes. Something rattled inside. "What is all this anyway? I've been wondering since I showed up."

"This," he said, "is five or six years of decommissioned shit that's piled up."

"Some of these boxes had never been opened."

"And those machines are already out of their life cycle. It's all scrap at this point, as far as I'm concerned, but I can't just toss it in a dumpster. The disposal process is a fucking nightmare. Our captain was working this for the past three years."

"Three years?"

"Nothing moves fast in the Guard. It's my problem now," he replied, and held out his hand. "We're up. Can I see your monocle?"

Daelia handed it over. Norris plugged it in and started scrolling back through the data feed's memory.

"Sing out when you see it," he told her.

"You're a senior admin at Omphalos, and you're a master sergeant?" she asked, watching the screen.

"Yeah," Norris replied. "So what? You think I'm dumb enough to commission?"

"Too much work?"

"Too much ass-pain. Not enough hands-on work, and way too much bullshit." He waved a hand around the room. "This is only the start of the headache I've got in the shop."

Daelia was going to ask what he meant by that, but then spotted it. The file. "Here it is," she told him, and pulled it up on the monitor.

He looked over her shoulder and frowned. "What the hell is that?"

"That was my reaction."

"That almost looks like something's eclosing," he said, and pulled the thing into an AR browser. "You know, those little spurts of babble they give off when they first come out?"

"It's not, though. See, look at the TGLP."

A couple more clicks, and the code spooled out in a window below the text. On the opposite screen, Norris opened a render window.

"Ah," he said, looking it over. "You're right, this is just junk. That initial eclosing babble condenses out in words or pictures through the TGLP. Pretty quickly, usually a few seconds max, but this doesn't look like anything."

Except it did. Daelia realized, as it was scrolling across the screen, that it looked very much like what she'd captured in Emily's virch yesterday. The code that had accompanied the meteor image.

This wasn't the same image, though. Hell, it wasn't even the image she'd seen in the hangar. That mist. This was just static.

But what did that mean? Had something been trying to tell her about this? Trying to warn her? Half a day before the object struck?

And if that was a warning, what was it doing now, and why—fucking how—was it coming from the object itself?

Or maybe it was all just bullshit. Maybe there was no pattern.

Maybe it was all just coincidence.

"You said you saw something, though, right?"

"Mist. But I'm not seeing that here." She rubbed her left bicep. "Maybe it's just something wrong with my monocle. I should probably go check on that."

"You're welcome to work on it here."

"No thank you. How do you function in all this junk?"

"I usually take my laptop out to the patio." With a chuckle, Norris unplugged the monocle and handed it back to her. "Thanks for the look."

"Do you have an EMF meter somewhere in this mess?" she asked.

He went over to the left-hand toolbox. Far from the mess outside, the drawer was neatly organized. Compartments labeled. Cables bundled. Accessories neatly stored in clear boxes. "Here we go," he said, and held up a small unit. "Broad-spectrum signal analyzer. Let's take a walk."

THE HANGAR WAS STILL LARGELY empty. A guard was at the door now—human, not one of the security kugus—but other than that, Daelia and Norris had the place to themselves.

It was disappointing, in a way. Here was a massive mysterious object that had fallen from the sky, been picked up by the Air Force, and it was all but abandoned. No plastic sheeting, lit up by big lamps. No team of mysterious people in white lab coats working on it. Nothing.

Norris gave her a look, and Daelia realized her expression must have betrayed what she was thinking. "You an *Orpheus Watch* fan?" he asked.

The original series had been one of those low-budget Star Wars knockoffs from the '80s, a show canceled before its second season was even up. But it had gotten a reboot now, one that was in its fourth season now and the most watched program on Delphi Plus, Omphalos's streaming service.

Its basic plot followed the adventures of a group of characters at a military-led space station, orbiting the gas giant Orpheus. In the original series, the planet had been located in the distant Hades star system, but the reboot had moved the action into the Epsilon Eridani system. With that star being only ten light years away from Earth, the titular space station was no longer a little speck in the galactic night, but reimagined as the prime galactic gateway to Earth.

Daelia found the thing ridiculous, but she still watched it. Everyone did. At least it was unpredictable, in contrast to a lot of the predictive-written stuff on TV these days. Shows like that had no soul.

"What does that have to do with anything?" she asked.

He shrugged. "You know in the pilot, when that asteroid strikes one of the station's habitat spheres? And they retrieve it and put it in one of the hangars because—"

"—because it's giving off a radio signal," Daelia finished. She frowned. "It's got an alien inside of it, though, doesn't it?" The production house had quite intentionally never said exactly what the species looked like in their raw form, but Daelia had seen quite a bit of fan art online. Both sanctioned and unregulated.

There were some really weird interpretations out there.

"Yeah, the Roc, and then they build it the sealed power suit, so they can talk to each—"

"There is no alien inside of this thing."

"You sure?"

She couldn't tell if he was being serious or not. Unsure what to say to that, she frowned deeper. And finally, he laughed.

"Sorry," Norris said. "I'm surrounded by that shit at my regular job. People take *Orpheus Watch* really seriously there."

"Can we just scan this thing?" she asked. "I've got other stuff I need to go do today."

"Already done," Norris said, and held up the EMF meter. "I'm not seeing anything on this I can't attribute to the air show. But it's a fuckin' slow day today. I'll talk to the base frequency office, see if any of this is unexpected or unusual. Get the guys on it, see what we can do."

"You don't really think there's an alien in there, do you?" Daelia asked.

"I wouldn't complain if there was," he said. "Might make my weekend a little less boring."

[15]

AUGMENTED REALITY WAS A FUNNY THING.

Most of the abiota Daelia had encountered in her life maintained some kind of presence there. It was, after all, their primary means of communication, at least with humans. With each other, too. Abiota tended to broadcast instead through whatever AR overlay they happened to find themselves in.

The military had proprietary AR, of course, encrypted and heavily protected. OPSEC. Dad had been lecturing Daelia on that since she was old enough to understand what a firewall was. But that made integration difficult. Military to civilian, or even service to service, interoperability was practically nonexistent. A legacy of how the networks had developed over time.

Under normal circumstances, an Army abiota couldn't just pop up in an Air Force-managed overlay. While all the services here were integrated within the base overlay, the units coming in from off-base couldn't necessarily access it. So, the air show had its own overlay. One specifically designed to allow for a wide range of access. There were technical reasons for it, good technical reasons for it, but Daelia stood by her statement to Raijinn the day before.

There was a strong propaganda aspect to it as well. The military used it to show the public what they wanted them to see. More aesthetically pleasing, far less detailed.

"They are on their way up now," Raijinn told her through its kugu. It was standing next to her, in the shade of the barely cracked main hangar doors. "The press. We are their first stop. Then Gravipause, Integrated Fueling Solutions, Orbital Refinement Solutions, Astraeus Astronautics, and Exxon."

Daelia huffed a breath and scrolled through the small tablet in her hand. She'd tried loading the notes on her monocle, but she still had a bit of a headache from that beer yesterday.

She did not want to deal with reporters.

"What do you think? Am I going to be dealing with a bunch of bullshit about why we're still using jet fuel?"

"I doubt it," Raijinn said. "I have observed a thirty-five percent drop in such sentiments online over the past six months, corresponding with an eighty percent rise in positive stories regarding the state of the fossil fuels industry. With ninety percent of the nation's power now being supplied by Tamm's Nu-Fusion reactors, the overall environmental impact of the aerospace industry is of a lesser—"

"You pay attention to the news?"

"Energy sector, yes." It didn't elaborate.

Daelia ran a hand over her head. She'd yanked her hair back into a messy ponytail; she wasn't great at styling it. It had nothing to do with her hand. Mom hadn't been able to teach her, and she'd never had much patience for it on her own.

She looked over the notes.

Dad's notes.

Shit, where was he?

"Noisy this morning," Raijinn observed.

"A server abiota's making small talk?" Daelia asked, trying to force her tired brain to absorb something from Dad's notes. "I should put this in my thesis."

"It's been my observation that a little meaningless conversation sometimes eases nervousness in humans."

"I don't think anything's going to ease my nerves this morning," Daelia grumbled. "They are fucking loud, aren't they?"

The runway was stuffed that morning. Some of the aircraft parked in the static display area weren't abiota. But they were mostly the classic planes, the vintage stuff from Vietnam and before. Most of the abiota were predictives. Even with a cursory glance it was easy to tell. But a few, just a few, were emergents.

Not that it made much difference with the noise. They were all calling to each other, threatening and cajoling and cackling with each other. Trying to establish some kind of pecking order.

Right in the middle of that was Emily. The expanded aesthetic rendering capacity of the show's AR gave her plenty of room to stretch out her form. She was screeching up a storm, too. Most of it probably directed at the Eurus that was situated nearby. Its AR form towered over the entire field, taller even than Emily's and just as vocal.

A pterosaur. A gigantic colorful pterosaur. Standing there like some kind of psychotic winged giraffe.

The simulated noise overlapped with the actual sounds of the morning. Engines warming up. People talking. Shuttle buses arriving to disgorge their first loads of attendees.

"Zero nine hundred," Raijinn announced.

And just like that, the airfield fell silent.

All simulated animal noise cut off; all sound other than straight English had just been disabled in the PR overlay.

"Finally," Raijinn said.

If only it were so easy to get rid of people, Daelia thought glumly.

Approaching the Scrap Yard's doors now were the reporters. Some local, some more national. Syndicated news streams and smaller industry publications. That was pretty typical. This was one of the few times a year when Frank Tamm poked his head out in public and the press always made the most of it.

Swallowing down the last of her hangover, she cued up her notes in her monocle. Dad always knew the right thing to say to these people, but she'd never been very good with the press.

"Good morning," she called to the knot of people approaching her now, waving Raijinn away. "Everybody enjoying the lovely Houston weather?"

That got a few chuckles. It was already hot, hot and muggy, and it was only going to get worse throughout the day.

She went around, shook a few hands, didn't pay much attention to their names or positions or companies. That information was already loaded in the press kit in her monocle; all she had to do was look at one of them, and their metadata would pop up.

When she was done with introductions, she looked around at all of them as a group. "I trust everybody got the show overlay loaded?" she asked. Nods, nods all around. She smiled. "Come on then. Let me show you around."

So far, she hadn't pissed anybody off.

Dad would be proud.

Raijinn had helpfully marked out the route she needed to walk in her monocle's maps program, along with tags for what she was supposed to talk about. Most of it was on subjects she was familiar with, and walking helped. Daelia found her nerves starting to settle.

The route through the increasingly crowded static displays took her by most of the base assets that Bellona Robotics serviced—the public loved seeing the military abiota. She had a little spiel to recite at each one. Daelia hoped she wasn't too mechanical. They even laughed every now and then.

She answered questions as they walked. There were a few about applied nonlinear mechatronics. The differences between the new MQ-13 and the MQ-9 from a technical perspective. How she liked working for her dad. What kind of ongoing combat operations the 121st was engaged in.

Raijinn interjected on that one.

Do not tell them anything. Do not confirm or deny.

Daelia just managed to keep her answer caged behind her teeth. The reporter smiled at her. Sneaky fucker, she thought.

But after an agonizing twenty minutes, the route finally came to an end.

At Emily's station.

Emily was one of the most popular attractions. People came every year to see what she'd added to herself and what her virch looked like. Of course, it was a cleaned-up, sanitized version. A happy little treasure cave. Cartoony, even.

Not at all what Daelia could see in the military overlay.

There was the cave the way Emily liked it.

Highly rendered. Very detailed. Photorealistic for the most part, if you discounted the gigantic glowing crystals jammed into the water-smoothed walls. Or the heaped piles of gold coins behind Emily's form. Or the rotting skeletons in ridiculously ornate armor, slumped up against the cave's fake walls.

Emily had been parked near the edge of the display zone. Not quite up against the fences, but close. A huge area around her was roped off, decorated with a lively variety of warning signs.

NO FLASH PHOTOGRAPHY

NO TOUCHING

NO PERSONAL DEVICES WITH PREDICTIVES LOADED

"Anybody have anything?" Daelia asked, tapping the sign.

A murmur went up through the reporters; a few held up cell phones or other devices. Daelia collected them all and passed them off to one of the maintenance troops who was there, standing guard. Only then did she lead them in.

"Emily, if you're not familiar with her, is the highest-ordered emergent we have got on the base," she explained. "As you can no doubt tell from her overlay here, she considers herself the queen of this place."

Considers? Emily said, and stood up, spreading her wings. The cave melted away into billowing clouds and golden light. Even for her, it was melodramatic. *Am.*

"She's in a mood this morning, isn't she?" commented one of the reporters. He was one of the few Daelia knew from experience. He was the writer for *Aerospace Monthly* and was here every year. "What's got her worked up, Miss Hall?"

Emily was close to the gates that led back onto the active ramp. But not the closest.

That position was being held by one of the Storm Gryphons. An FQ-47 and its own support crew.

It was standard, as Daelia understood it, for at least one of the Storm Gryphons to spend most of the day in the static display area, answering questions and taking photos with the civilians. Today was no exception: there was a long line already, just to step up and say hello.

The Storm Gryphons were tied into the air show overlay, of course, in brilliant high definition. The PR forms of the aircraft's abiota had been sculpted by the same people who did the effects for Hollywood. *Orpheus Watch* and *Star Wars* and the like.

The PR forms were sleek and slick. Bald eagle heads and front talons. Lean leonid bodies. Huge proud wings. Exquisite detail. The AR illumination team had done a damn good job. The plane here, Tail Number Five, was currently showing off that artistry, posing shamelessly with the excited civilians.

Daelia was unimpressed.

Unlike the abiota here at Ellington, the Storm Gryphons were all predictive. With them, it was possible to enforce some uniformity. But even cloned predictives tended to individualize themselves after a while. And so the basic forms, while still all conforming to the gryphon standard for the team, had a degree of variation in military AR. Five, in its military form, was smaller with a duller palette. Less gold and white, more muted grays and browns.

And it looked agitated.

Five flapped its wings now, cawing at Emily. Daelia didn't register any words, but Emily clearly took offense to it and spat fire back.

In the AR field, the flame hit some invisible barrier, perfectly aligned with the rope, and curled back in. Like it was solid.

That was all in the military field. Thank god. The reporters didn't see any of that.

"Emily's not a huge fan of competition for attention," Daelia said. It was partially true. See? She'd have to tell Dad. She could be tactful. Sort of.

Except now one of the pilots was walking over. One of the kugus. Shit.

"She's an impressive machine," the pilot said, stopping right at the edge of Emily's rope and giving Daelia a grin. "Especially after yesterday. You have a minute?"

Daelia glared at him and waved to the reporters. "Excuse me," she said. "Sergeant Gillibrand in there can answer any questions you might have about Emily. Better than me."

The pilot, at least, waited until they had wandered away before saying anything else.

"You're Daelia Hall, right?" he asked her.

"Why?" she asked.

The Storm Gryphons pilot shrugged. He was built like a tank and the movement made his gray flight suit pull tight across his shoulders.

"It's the arm, daughter of Bellona," the kugu answered instead. Daelia blink-clicked its metadata up on her monocle. ST3, it was labeled.

The pilot gave his companion a look. "You weren't this blunt before your last reboot."

"Pardon my lack of diplomacy, but there are few humans with such devices as hers," the Storm Gryphon replied. "Unusual, a human having a mechanical interface for a limb."

The pilot tapped his temple. "Then what do you call a NULI?"

"Prudent."

"It's always the arm," Daelia said, and squinted at his name patch. "What can I do for you, umm, Major Takamori?"

"Just sayin' hi," he said. "This one's been screaming at us ever since we showed up. It's starting to hurt my feelings a little."

"What do you want me to do? Tell her to shut up?"

"Maybe," he said with a smile. "If you think she'll listen to you."

Three, the one inhabiting the kugu, didn't have a distinct military AR form. Just the blue outline, to indicate there was something there. The PR form for that, too, was impressive. An anthropomorphic eagle figure that managed to look dangerous and cool, and not like somebody at a furry convention. The lack of detail and Takamori's comments made Daelia think it hadn't been active very long.

You give me a go, Emily challenged, a predator's smile on both of her faces. *I take you for good ride, little dweller of bridges.*

Takamori laughed. "Well, isn't she a perceptive one?"

"She's an animal," Three said coolly. "Orcinus-class always are. I question the wisdom of allowing them in the service at all."

"Hey," Daelia snapped. "She was in the Five Days War. She has more experience than you ever will."

"Obsolete model then. What good are these ancient aircraft?"

Emily puffed more fire, and again, it was repelled. *Come in here,* she taunted. *I show you obsolete.*

"Pathetic."

"Three," the major said, in the same tone one would use to scold a dog. And he smiled ruefully at Daelia. "You'll have to forgive her. She's just been rebooted recently, and—"

"Maybe you should leave her alone," Daelia snapped. "Let her develop a persona that isn't a total asshole."

He laughed at that.

"You are obsolete," Three said, the kugu pacing now. "It is not an insult. You still serve a purpose, I imagine, or Air Combat Command would not permit you to continue, but—"

Yes, purpose, purpose. Primary purpose. I serve.

"What, playacting with your little dollhouse cave? Yes, what a tough warrior you are."

This why you will lose, Emily replied. *You think purpose is this place, this time.* She reared back for emphasis, spreading her wings, her front claws. *This not purpose. This irritation, distraction. You enjoy it? You fail at primary purpose. Primary purpose is killing.*

"Our primary purpose is the protection of human life."

Yes. By other human life taking. Emily's huge eyes blinked slowly, deliberately. *Cannot ponder this, you, I think. Fucking robot.*

"Emily!" Daelia snapped, shocked at the slur.

"See?" Three said to the pilot. "Animal. This thing wouldn't last ten seconds in the air against us."

Find out, Emily said, and looked at Daelia, excitement emojis filling Daelia's monocle. *You vouch for match to Rover? We go after show. Or during. Give civvies real fight watch.*

"Come on, Three," the major said, laying a hand on the kugu's arm. "We need to get back up to the cockpits, run that systems check on you again."

"You would lose," Three said to Emily.

Emily's heads dropped low, close. *Give excuse me. We find out.*

Takamori laughed and held out his hand. It took Daelia a moment to realize he was offering a handshake. "To dogfights that we'll never have," he laughed. "Nice to meet you, Daelia Hall."

"Sure," she said, and shook back, unsure what else to do.

One of Emily's heads dropped down by her shoulder as the two of them walked back to their own display area. *I eat her.*

"Don't eat her," Daelia said. "You'd get in so much trouble."

Emily made a sound that was somewhere between a snort and a growl.

Daelia looked back. The other head was searching. Sniffing through the crowd.

Shit.

"Behave, Emily," she told the MQ-9, going back over to the knot of reporters.

The head kept searching.

"What is she doing?" one of them asked Daelia, unconsciously moving out of the way as Emily's head swung between them.

"Emily has a bad habit of, uhh—"

Daelia's explanation got cut off. Emily let out an ear-rending screech into the PR overlay and then shuffled around, snapping at a civilian. The girl let out a shriek as one of Emily's snouts shoved its way through her body and into her backpack, disappearing for a moment before pulling back again.

There was something small and squirming in her teeth.

Emily tossed her head back, flipping the little thing up into the air, and snapped it up. Swallowing visibly, the dragon form let out a contented belch and went back to playfully nosing at the civilians still clustered around.

The girl was going through her backpack, trembling a little. She had a full visor on. The experience must have been unsettling.

"Did you have something running on your phone?" Daelia asked, going over.

"Sure, it's an art-bot, but…"

"I hope you have a system backup," Daelia said, and looked back at Emily. Smug. Always so smug. "Emily just bricked it."

"How does that work?" one of the reporters asked, clearly fascinated.

DO NOT SAY SIREN VARIANT, Raijinn ordered.

Dammit. She had been about to say that. It was the answer, after all.

"They can't really eat each other," Daelia said instead. "Not the way we would interpret it. A lot of it's just playacting. For our benefit, maybe. The abiota overlays take into account a lot of animal body language."

"You said the phone's bricked. How?" the reporter pressed.

"You know, there are just things we don't understand about abiota." Daelia glared at Emily. The dragon form ruffled its head, scales fluffing up like feathers on a cockatoo. "Yeah, I'm talking about you, girl."

Emil was quite good at this, the targeted wiping of programs or machines she took a disliking to. Nobody knew how she managed it. Dad was fairly certain it was a feature of her Siren pod, but the Domain Array had never approved his request to investigate.

Should read signs, Emily said, grumpy now.

That set off a flurry of questions from the reporters, most of them directed at Emily herself. She answered in her usual clipped, grammatically incorrect manner, taking the pressure off Daelia.

Five minutes later, the team from Gravipause showed up and took the reporters off her hands.

Fucking finally.

"No more bricking," Daelia warned Emily, before she left.

Get Three back over here. I brick it. Then, no others.

"Don't take your irritation out on any more poor teenagers,

okay?" Daelia ordered. She got no answer; Emily was pouting. She gave the abiota one last pat on her machine body and headed out.

That space rock wasn't going to examine itself, after all.

THE ROUTE back to the 121st's hangar took Daelia right past the massive form of the Eurus.

The Astraeus Aerospace XP-109 Eurus spaceplane took up a vast amount of real estate on the apron. As large as an old-school 797, the Eurus was a wedge-shaped lifter, made to ferry the small trans-atmospheric Apeliotes passenger craft into the stratosphere, where it could fire up its SCRAMJETs and make orbit.

Tamm had eight in his fleet, three of which flew out of Ellington, the other five out of international spaceports. Yokohama. Madrid. Harare.

As far as Daelia was aware, the Eurus spaceplanes hadn't yet exhibited any emergence. The fleet, this one included, were all predictives. And much like the Storm Gryphons, these all had the same basic graphic presentation in AR.

That pterosaur form.

There was some kind of symbolism with these things. That was what Dad said; he and Tamm had known each other pretty well, once upon a time. Tamm had named the individual planes after various individual species, so they were all a little different.

This one, the one on display this weekend, was named *Queltz-coatlus*. Some dinosaur name, which itself was some reference to an Aztec god. Not really Daelia's thing.

Tamm loved that crap, though.

Daelia flipped between the show overlay and the airfield's as she passed the Eurus. The show overlay showed the pterosaur in what she assumed to be exaggerated scale. That comically over-sized head was nuzzling mischievously through the crowd at the edge of its roped-off projection area. It was a riot of color, like a parrot gone insane. That too probably wasn't the way the original animal had looked.

At least, that was the way it looked in the PR field.

But cutting back over to the native airfield overlay…

The pterosaur projection was crouched on top of the plane's flattened fuselage, beak dipping down into the crowd, snapping at people waiting on the steps to enter. Its weird little wing claws swiped around. It threw its head back and screamed.

Nobody seemed to pay it any heed, though.

The crowd around the base of the plane was huge. Milling about or waiting in line to go up and see the crew cabin.

Serket was here, speaking to a group in the crowd. But she looked up at just the right time.

Made eye contact with Daelia.

The projected face smiled at her with those perfect, vintage-red lips.

And an invitation popped up in Daelia's monocle.

Mister Tamm would love to see you for a drink. Talk about your research.

Not a chance of that happening.

Daelia was afraid of what she might say to the man.

She blinked the message shut and walked on.

[16]

ROVER WAS NOT HAVING a good day.

Air show weekends were always stressful.

It was worse this year, now that he was in charge.

Sure, most of his troops had had fun yesterday. That was worth something.

Air Show Friday was always a great time to kick back, relax, take it easy for an afternoon. Enjoy all that shit a guy was supposed to have in the military. Family and camaraderie and all that. It seemed a bit more necessary this year, considering how many people they'd lost in Tokyo, with the attack on the annual RPA warfighters' conference. The Group was still pulling itself back together. Hell, the entire community was still pulling itself back together; every RPA unit in the DOD has lost at least a few of its people to that bombing. Ellington had lost more than most.

Old friends, many of them of them. But that was the nature of things. The Air Force RPA community was small anyway, and the Air Guard was even smaller. New people came in rarely here at Ellington, and old people left slowly, so they all got to know each other well. Very well.

Which was why Rover was stuck at the base's damn concessions stand, selling wildly overpriced beer to already-drunk civilians at ten-thirty in the morning, instead of managing his issues back up at the main hangar.

The message app in his NULI kept pinging. Every ten minutes or so, he'd get a cluster-blast of new messages. State, sending directions. ACC, wanting a straight answer over rumors they were hearing about a missile landing near his base. Guard Bureau, headquartered up at Andrews AFB in DC, demanding to know why he'd taken three people off federal orders to put them on a state mission. And on and on.

"How you doing there, Rover?"

It was Malia Bryant, the no-nonsense major who served as the lead over at Base Contracting. She should have been the next in line for the Support Group commander billet. As far as Rover was concerned, she was the only field-grade officer in that whole damn Group who was competent enough for the job.

But Bryant was far too important to base operations to promote. Contracting would completely collapse. Lucky her, she was stuck in a shit position and would probably get a new shit commander to replace the current shit commander, who was retiring in the spring.

Rover liked her. But that didn't mean he wanted to chat.

"Busy day," he said, and dug the last beer out of the big tub for her. "Five cans, right?"

She smiled and picked up the pile of cans.

The base concessions booth was present at the sufferance of the firm that handled all the air show vending. The base had a deal with them: they sold the same type of stuff at the same price points, so nobody undercut anybody else, and everybody walked away with their money. A typical air show weekend brought in anywhere from twenty to forty thousand in profit, which was then split up between all the various squadron booster clubs.

In turn, those clubs paid for retirement gifts, for year-end Christmas parties, for special coins or patches, for diapers when somebody had a new baby, or for flags, when somebody died.

Rover didn't really need the money. Not for the Ops Group.

They'd bought their flags themselves, after that disaster at Shiodome a few months back.

Beyond that, they just didn't normally need this kind of money. At least half of his officers were commercial airline pilots, the sort who made damn good money and didn't mind donating a few hundred bucks a year to the group fund.

But Ellington was a small base, one with a long memory and vast patience. An officer could easily see his career torpedoed over some slight, years in the past. Rover had seen it happen more than once. He worked the booth because he was expected to work the booth. Because it was good politics. Because he needed the rest of the base to know who he was and that he didn't really consider himself better than them, even if his squadron was the goddamn reason for this place's continued existence.

His predecessor had never worked it. But then, Raccoon had always just bulldozed his way through problems. It hadn't made him popular with the other folks on base, and as the squadron DO, Rover had been the one to have to fix it. Good guy, if somewhat pigheaded.

But Raccoon was gone now, dead and buried, and it was Rover's turn to run things.

Besides, when Rover needed something, it was usually the Support Group that had to get it for him.

He tried to get along with them. He really, really did.

"You are distracted today," Bryant observed, coming back with another order. The list popped up in Rover's monocle, and he started filling the tray.

"No shit, I'm distracted. You know how busy this weekend is for me?"

"Your people have it," Bryant said. "Let them do their jobs, Rover."

"You know how it is. Some things you have to do yourself." Like call Guard Bureau back and tell them for the fourth fucking time that day that until the governor authorized him to release details on the Armand Bayou object, he wasn't giving them shit.

Rover didn't say that.

"This have anything to do with the space rock you boys have in the secondary hangar?"

Rover slammed an icy-cold lager down on the tray. "Shit, Malia."

"Of course I know about it," she said. "One of my tech sergeants is on the EMC team."

"Then I need to have a talk with them again. State told us to keep our damn mouths shut."

"Aren't they worried it's a missile? Or a bomb or something."

"EOD's on their way. Let them figure that out."

"Shouldn't we have figured it out before it was moved, you know, up here?"

That was Kemp. The lieutenant colonel from the communications squadron. The asshole who was likely going to take the vacant Support Group commander position, much to Rover's dismay. He was one of those officers who thought his job was kingdom-building, not supporting the base's flying mission.

Like anything beyond the flying mission fucking mattered.

Ellington had been on the federal Base Realignment and Closure list more than once. If anything, anything at all, happened to the flying mission, the entire Wing would cease to exist. Everybody's jobs would evaporate like ice on a hot griddle. Gone, just like that.

Not even the governor's office could save them if the federal mission was officially pulled.

Why he was the only commander around here who seemed to understand that, Rover had no idea.

Rover kept all that inside, though. Gave Kemp a smile. "Don't worry. We're outside the projected blast radius here."

His messaging center beeped again. With a thought and a little concentration, Rover brought the number up. Florida area code. That would be the deputy A3 at ACC calling from his personal cell phone instead of his military-issued one. Rover thought about answering it, just to get out of this stupid booth, but let it go to voice mail instead.

Maybe it was a good thing he was helping with the concession stand, he thought. At least he had an excuse to ignore this crap. Not a great excuse, but an excuse nonetheless.

Rover spared a thought for Marathon, back at the unit, handling the EMC. No doubt ACC's next call would be to him. Fortunately, Marathon was even better at being professionally rude than Rover was.

"You have an order for me to fill, Justin?" he asked. "Or are we going to just stare at each other all morning?"

Kemp rolled his eyes. "It'd be an awful shame if you killed us all."

"I don't know, my wife would probably enjoy the insurance money," he replied. That got everybody around him laughing.

"Lieutenant Colonel Marsden?"

"Rover," he grumbled, but looked over at the kid who had spoken. It was some staff sergeant from Finance. Poor bastard had found himself on this shift with six field-grade officers. "What?"

"Senior is asking for you over at the pickup window, sir."

What the hell? Grabbing a wad of paper towel, Rover worked on drying his hands off as he walked around to the table where they laid out the finished orders.

On the other side of the folding table was, well, somebody whose presence made all kinds of sense.

Dammit.

"Navarro? What's up?"

"Oh, I think you know. You look like you got about as much sleep as I did last night."

Rover dropped the paper towel in the trash can under the counter. Paul Navarro. A senior master sergeant over in Force Support, he was heavyset, hair longer than regulations strictly permitted, the sort Rover expected over there. But unlike most of the other NCOs over in FSS, Navarro was a hard-charger, the sort who'd run any problem to ground just on principle, and Rover leaned on him heavily. There was no easier way to lose qualified pilots than fucking up their pay, something that the rest of FSS did with shocking regularity.

Unfortunately, he wasn't full time.

His day job was over at NASA. Some position on their space watch floor.

"Your day job send you over to speak to me personally?" Rover asked, tired of the conversation already.

"I told 'em it was awkward as hell, but our director's getting chewed up by DC right now." As always, his voice carried the faint accent of Brazilian Portuguese.

"Let's get this over with, then." He dipped under the folding table at the edge of the booth, sliding out. "Malia, I've got to go take care of a problem!"

"You're got two hours left on the shift, Ty!" Kemp yelled.

"Ain't gonna do anybody any good if a plane falls out of the sky!" Rover shot back over his shoulder, already striding off.

Was he the only senior officer around here who understood there was an actual flying mission at this damn base?

"Hey, at least it's me," Navarro said as they walked out into the temporary aisles of the concession area.

"What, as opposed to Garcia?" Rover spared a thought for the cyber sergeant in the Group who worked under Norris. "Yeah, that would be a fuckin' disaster."

"That boy does not know when to shut his mouth. Count yourself lucky he's drill status, Rover. I gotta deal with him daily."

"Oh, believe me, I deal with him plenty."

Rover was trying hard not to make eye contact with anyone. Will himself out of the crowd, as it was. Even though he was in OCPs for this today, there was always a chance somebody would recognize the patches on his shoulders and the badges on his chest and ask all kinds of questions. He hated that.

Not that he hated civilians themselves; protecting them was his job after all, a task that had become far less abstract after the Five Days War. Rover just preferred it when he could maintain some distance between them.

Navarro sighed. "They want me to make a case to you about handing over the space rock that fell out in Armand Bayou. Voluntarily, without all this red tape that we're going through right now."

"Armand Bayou is state land," Rover replied. "It's not subject to federal jurisdiction."

"Dammit, Rover, we don't know what it is—"

"Other than it came from space, right?" Rover asked. Navarro pursed his lips but didn't answer right away. "Right?"

The other man sighed. "Data's inconclusive. We're still trying to figure it out ourselves."

"Then I don't see any reason why the military should be handing it over to a civilian agency."

They passed the last concessions stand, some booth selling watermelon-juice pickles. Headed out into the static display area.

It was always interesting, seeing what displays people flocked to, what the civilians wanted to see. The vintage stuff was always popular. The World War II section was packed to the gills with bodies. But what most people had come to see today were the abiota. The younger planes, the newer planes.

His planes.

RPAs had been controversial when they'd first started taking a frontline role back in the early days of OEF. That controversy had only deepened once avionics packages started eclosing in earnest. The various remotely piloted airframes employed by the Air Force demonstrated this phenomenon at an insane rate, almost thirty-five percent by their fifth year in service. It had only polarized the public's attitudes further. Some people wanted abiota removed from the military entirely, while others thought the whole DOD should be turned over to their control.

Everyone had an opinion on abiotic RPAs. Even the people who said they loved the military had an opinion. Almost everybody was wrong.

Abiota were addendums to an old argument, not the start of a new one. If anything, abiota were positively regressive. It took piloting out of the realm of the rational and landed them all squarely back in the Middle Ages. Riding horses into battle.

Or killer whales, in Emily's case, but that didn't have the same neat historical placeholder.

There were more people here, closer together and tighter. A sea of sweaty t-shirts and backpacks. Looked like half of Houston was here. Crowds carried a kind of anonymity, but Rover still pulled the unit patch off his shoulder as they waded deeper into the throng.

"You can't have it both ways," Navarro pressed. "You can't cite state authority and then claim it's a military matter."

"The state's military capacity is very robust."

"We're all on the same team here."

Rover nodded at something up ahead, a huge pavilion erected in the middle of the planes. Memorial Plaza. "Are we?" he asked meaningfully.

Navarro looked over at it. Rubbed a hand over his face. "You're on federal orders right now, aren't you? Working that shit over in—"

"Civilians," Rover warned.

Navarro dropped his voice. "Over in that little bathtub between Thailand, China, and the Philippines. So cut the crap. Give me a straight answer."

Rover laughed, despite himself. "You enjoyed saying that, right?"

"Beats calling you 'sir' every other sentence. You know what a pain in the ass you are sometimes? Sir?"

"What do you want me to say? The governor's ordered the Texas Military Department to retain custody of that damn rock for as long as possible. He wants to know what the hell it is, where it came from, and what it's doing here."

"NASA can give you those answers."

"But will you? Come on, Paul," Rover pressed. "We like to pretend like this is still a unified country, but the trust is well and truly gone."

Navarro sighed but didn't bother arguing the point. "I can back-door you the information," he said quietly. "It's my shop that would be analyzing it."

Rover shook his head. "Let the brass and the politicians hash this out, Paul. You think I want that fucking thing in my hangar? This close to the munitions cache? Are you kidding me?"

"Then turn it over."

"I've got a direct order from the Texas Air Staff."

"The chain of command ends with the Pentagon."

"Only in matters pertaining directly to combat ops," Rover said quietly. "I am not pissing off General McMillan at State because somebody at NASA doesn't want to file a couple of papers." Navarro didn't say anything. Rover pressed on. "We both know you guys are going to get it sooner or later. Let's not get fucked in the process, okay? I'd like you to still be around to make Chief over at FSS someday, yeah?"

Navarro laughed at that, and started to say something, before his eyes narrowed behind his AR glasses. "Do you see this shit? Airfield overlay, not the show."

Rover had shut down the AR field in his NULI for the booth. He was still getting used to it, and better not to deal with the headache when he didn't need to. He brought it back up now, tuned to the military channel.

There, sure enough, clear as day at the Tamm Industries section of the displays, was the Eurus. Bellowing. And Emily was roaring right back.

"Oh, girl," Rover sighed.

There was a long-standing Ops Group tradition of refusing to allow Emily do a demonstration flight for the show. They couldn't keep her out of the static display—State Public Affairs insisted she be present—but at least there was some semblance of control there. There, they could jam her. Flying, they couldn't. She was old for an abiota, and she was clever, and Rover was pretty sure that she could override the show overlay if she really felt like it.

And there was plenty there to worry about. Emily had a proper dragon's hoard of animations. Chasing sheep, burning villages, fighting knights on horseback, she had enough reference material and preloaded images to conjure up all manner of problems for him.

It had happened a few times over the years. Visitors to base saw her form eating a half-roasted cow or merrily chasing a pack of virtual villagers with virtual pitchforks through the AR field, and they complained.

She thought it was funny, as did most of the interdiction squadron. And really, it wasn't any worse than the meme printouts that littered the break room walls. But those were private.

Rover had learned that at the Academy: you didn't share military humor with civilians.

"You've got to make her knock it off," Navarro said. "This stupid circuit-measuring contest she has with every high-level abiota that comes through here is pointless. Especially when it comes to Tamm's fleet. Like it or not, when that terminal across the way is complete, we're going to be picking up a lot more traffic from Ozona Spaceport."

"You think anybody can really tell Emily what to do?" he grumbled, and looked over at her again. "I need to get back to my shift."

"Think about what I said."

"Tell your director to have some fuckin' patience," he said, and left Navarro behind again.

Where did that Eurus's personality, behavior, attitude come from, he wondered as he headed back to the burger booth. Conventional wisdom held that predictives developed on their own, in whatever way they would, once they were carved off from the main program. As individual and unique as emergents.

He'd never really believed it.

Rover spent enough time around his own weird little flock to have developed a good sense of things now.

There was more to most predictives than they admitted to. More, and less.

The AR form of that spaceplane might have lent an appearance of parity, of similarity, to an entity like Emily. But the human brain was the best pattern-recognition tool on the planet—even the deep machine learning algorithms of the best predictives couldn't match it—and something in the back of Rover's mind screamed at him every time he was around one of those things.

Not that he'd ever give voice to that.

Everyone was supposed to believe that there was no difference. No difference between predictives and emergents. Rover had never bought into that, though. There was something deeply, fundamentally incompatible there.

"What was that all about?" Kemp asked as he ducked back inside the booth.

"Hell if I know," he said, and got back to work.

[17]

"WHAT'S UP?"

"EOD."

There were a number of people outside the secondary hangar, inside the airfield fence, hanging out under the small rusting pavilion that normally saw service as the smoke pit.

Daelia recognized everybody, a little proud of herself. There were a couple of maintainers and Norris, with a few of his team. Senior Airman Rhineman. Tech Sergeant Kirby.

Neither of them were full time, which meant Sausage had probably dragged them in on state orders too. There was a dizzying array of order statuses that people operated under in the Air Guard, but Daelia got the distinct impression that everyone hated the state orders the most. From what Dad had told her, it paid a lot less.

Rhineman was yawning into his OCP sleeve. Kirby's bun was messy, haloed with a crown of escaping hair, a far cry from her usually pristine pinned-up French braid.

The other person out waiting was Staff Sergeant Menendez. Lara. From Base Cyber Surety. Daelia liked Lara, though. Another college student, with an understated nerdiness.

Or maybe explicitly nerdy today.

She was hand-stitching a long section of dark gray braid onto a uniform jacket that would have been more at home in the Napoleonic Wars than the Ellington flight line.

"Reenactment?" Daelia asked.

Menendez didn't look up. "Cosplay."

"Isn't it basically the same thing?" Rhineman asked. "Except, you know, more pathetic?"

"Says the man with Batman boxers," Kirby said.

"That was one fucking time!"

"Do I even want to know?" Norris sighed and looked over at Daelia. "I'm sorry. Did you need something?"

"Came by to see what's going on."

Norris waved a hand. "Welcome to the party."

"We're just stuck outside until they're done?" she asked, looking around. "That doesn't seem right."

Norris rolled a shoulder, stretching a little. "You've heard the old stories about IEDs over in Iraq, right? Where they'd rig them up to go off from cell phone signals?"

She had. Daelia immediately knew where he was going with it and felt mildly embarrassed that she hadn't thought of it herself. "Dad's probably mentioned to me."

"Yeah, well, we don't want to be poking at this thing without some kind of guarantee that it's not going to blow up half the base."

"Can I go in?" she asked, already walking over to the door.

"They asked us to, uhh, wait outside because of—"

"Sure," she said, and pushed her way in anyway.

Inside, it looked a little bit more like what she'd been imagining this morning. A gaggle of people in various uniforms, all waving instruments around and conversing in hushed tones. From the TMD, it seemed, judging by patches and logos embroidered on polos or screen-printed to T-shirts.

More equipment had been set up, a couple of tall spotlights had been erected, and there was even a low platform set up, with a couple of people working on it.

"Excuse me, ma'am, but you can't be in here," a senior

enlisted man said, walking up. She didn't recognize him; his shoulder patch indicated he was from Joint Reserve Base Fort Worth.

She flashed her badge on its lanyard around her neck. "I'm with Bellona Robotics. I helped find this thing last night. Can you tell me what's going on with it?"

He warmed up a little. Started talking.

It wasn't explosive.

That much, he said he was certain of.

Not a warhead.

Not explosive.

Totally unprecedented.

He seemed worried about it. Which made Daelia worried. EOD blew up bombs and stuff, right? If one of them was concerned, then it was probably time to get freaked out.

"You're most likely okay to do more EMF scanning," he told her. "Without blowing up half the base, you know? But I don't know what you're going to find. This thing appears to be inert."

"Every abiota outside has been nervous all morning," Daelia told him, looking it over. Which was silly, really. What the hell was she going to see? It was a big rock. A sculpted rock, but a rock nonetheless. "Seems like it would be related."

"We've got a bit more to do, but you're welcome to start."

"Thanks," she said, and went back outside to get Norris.

DAELIA and the cyber team worked for the better part of two hours, trying to get a signal off the space rock, as everyone seemed to be calling it now. Norris tried a whole bunch of tricks, and the airmen weighed in, but nothing showed up.

"I could swear this thing was broadcasting."

"Not on any channel we can recognize, if it is," Norris told her.

"Yeah, but..." And she trailed off, collecting her thoughts. "Something's going on here. Maybe it's one of those ones that can't use TGLP, or—"

Kirby gave her a smile then. "Daelia, you know I love you, but I think you've got tunnel vision."

"What do you mean?"

"There's no evidence this thing is abiota," the tech sergeant said.

"Something is spooking everybody out on the flight line."

"If it doesn't use TGLP, and it's not broadcasting over a frequency we can recognize, then how can it talk to them?" He laid a hand on her shoulder. "Sometimes when you've got a hammer, all your problems start to look like nails." And at her blank look, he clarified. "This is what you're researching, right? So this is what you're seeing."

She shook her head. "Maybe. I don't think so. I'm going to go check a few things back at the Scrap House, see if I can't run some more analysis on this."

"You sure?" Norris asked.

She rolled her eyes. "Beats hanging around the EMC. Or listening to Rhineman talk about his underwear."

"I did not bring that up!" he wailed.

Daelia walked away from the brewing argument. If there was anything the cyber team here knew how to do, it was argue. Every time she'd ever gone to talk to them, somebody was fighting with somebody else about something. Usually something dumb. It was their favorite pastime.

She found the TMD material analysis team instead.

Even got one of them to listen to her and everything.

Once she explained what she wanted to do, the guy agreed to take a few more core samples, to see if he couldn't drill a little deeper and hit something metallic.

"It's going to take me a few hours," he warned.

"No problem," she said. "I've got to go back to my own lab. Get some stuff done."

Like see if she couldn't get one of her prototypes working.

ROVER WAS true to his word, Argo thought.

Splatto was much easier to handle than Emily.

While active duty had all but retired the MQ-1, the Guard had inherited the Air Force's entire inventory of emergents. It was no simple thing, decommissioning them entirely. There were agreements with the Domain Array. And so, here, they still flew. Only Splatto was used for anything real world, though.

There was no screwing around. No attempts at hazing. No virch. Splatto was subvocal, which was actually nice. More in line with what Argo was used to. He could provide updates on navigation data, targeting, and so on in perfect English. He could offer input on flight information. But those comments were generated from a pool of standard responses.

<Don't get lulled to sleep by how calm he's being right now,> Bumper told him from the SyROC, after four hours in the seat. <He definitely has his own opinion about things and will let you know.>

"Well, he seems pretty calm right now," Argo replied.

<That's because there's nothing to hunt. You ever do any horseback riding?>

"A little. It's not a huge hobby where I grew up."

<Dog? Anything?>

"We had a cat."

<Then you should be great at dealing with Emily,> Bumper said.

Another voice—the intel station—cut in. <Just wait until you meet 2Shy. She's doing her rotation over in the Philippines right now, but we'll swap her and Emily out again next month.>

"Why, what's up with her?"

<She's a manticore.>

Argo looked over at Ho, who shrugged. "Cougar. Wings. Scorpion tail."

"What the hell is up with the abiota on this base?" Argo asked.

<2Shy's a big gamer.>

"Gamer?"

"Tabletop," Ho supplied. "Old-school RPGs, pencil and paper stuff. All that."

He pinched the bridge of his nose "That…that brings up so many more questions."

<You've been up for four hours at this point,> Bumper said. <Let's put Splatto in a holding pattern for a few minutes and you two go take a bio break.>

"Thank god," Ho said with a groan. "I've been needing to piss since—"

<Ho, the damn line's recorded.>

"Shutting up, sir," the sensor said, and dropped his headset on the console. He looked at Argo. "I do really need to—"

"Go," Argo said, nodding.

It was a simple thing to hand the flight over to Splatto, with parameters typed in. A predictive would fly exactly what it was asked to in this situation. Argo had no idea what an emergent would do. Hopefully, exactly what it was asked to.

Coming out of the cockpit himself, he stretched his arms up over his head, rolling his right shoulder until it popped, The seats were as comfortable as military contracting could make them. Which was to say, not very. He was used to it at this point, sure, but it always felt good to get out and move.

Argo retrieved a protein bar from his locker and wandered outside. It was almost 1400 now, and the hangar cast a long shadow out across the ramp. There was an aerobatic act on right now, a heavily modified biplane performing tight corkscrews over the runway, red smoke trailing from its wingtips. Argo munched his bar, watching the smoke, more engrossed than he should have been.

He'd grabbed his monocle from his locker too. But the entire act was purely physical.

Nice reminder of what could be accomplished, even without—

"Jesus! Argo, is that you?"

A UTV had just stopped, right there, in front of the hangar. In it were four people in silver-gray flight suits, tailored to the point of absurdity, and one heavily modified kugu.

A kugu that was wearing an AR wrap of an eagle-headed figure.

Shit.

The guy driving was hanging over the wheel, smiling at him. "It is! What the hell are you doing at a Guard base, man?"

Shit. Shit shit shit.

"Troll," Argo said, forcing a smile. "I could ask you the same thing. Last I heard, you were an instructor out at Red Flag."

"Got picked up for this last year," his old classmate said, nonchalant, as if qualifying for the Air Force's premier flying demonstration team was no big deal. He looked downright anachronistic in his tailored flight suit, built tough and solid, hair shaved in a high-and-tight so pronounced, it was almost a mohawk. He patted the Storm Gryphons patch on his chest. "How have you been? Haven't seen you in years."

"You know I went MQ-9."

"Big mistake there, buddy. FQ-47's more fun."

"Yeah, how many shots have you taken in the past year?"

Argo could feel where Troll's eyes were focused. Right on his left shoulder, where his new service patch sat. The minuteman and fighter silhouettes of the Air National Guard.

But whatever Troll was thinking, he didn't give it away.

Instead, he laughed. "Fair point, I guess. MQ-9's where it's at if you want to shoot low-yield missiles at PLA-backed insurgents out on the rim of the Bathtub. I get to show off to all the ladies."

Argo laughed at that, for real. "Your wife know about that?"

"She doesn't care." Troll jabbed his thumb back over his shoulder. "But don't let Gryphon Three back there hear you. Work wife and all. She'll take it very personally."

"Troll," the predictive FQ-47 said primly, "we have a rendezvous to keep. The meet and greet for VIP ticket holders begins in eight and a half minutes."

Troll nodded. "Yeah, yeah, I know. But I see an old buddy, I have to talk to him."

"Eight minutes, twenty-one seconds."

"You with the local flying unit?" Troll asked, and Argo nodded. "I'll come by later, okay?"

"See you then," Argo said.

"Who was that?" Ho asked as Argo stormed back into the hangar, shoved his monocle back into the locker.

"Old classmate," Argo said, short. "Nate Takamori. We were in the same freshman squadron together at the Academy."

Ho squinted at him. "You're not an Academy grad, are you sir? Shit, last thing we need is one more ring-knocker around."

"I'm not a grad," Argo said, "and I don't have a ring. They take it back if you don't finish."

Ho's normal humor faded a little. "What happened?"

Argo swung his locker shut. "So what can I expect when we get back out there with Splatto?"

Ho chuckled.

Shit.

[18]

"So ARE you sure you know what you're doing?"

Highlander. One of the 121st guys. Stuck down here this afternoon, babysitting either the rock itself or the TMD team that was crawling all over it.

He'd left her alone up to this point, watching football on his phone. It was only now, now that she was up underneath the space rock on her back, sweaty and flushed, that he decided to take an interest.

Why now, Daelia wasn't sure. The guy had made a pass at her the first week she was here and wouldn't let it go. Daelia hadn't told her dad about it; probably wouldn't have ended well for either of them. He wasn't bad-looking, but he was, in her opinion, everything wrong with pilots. Too arrogant. Too self-absorbed.

She'd told him—directly—that he wasn't getting anywhere near her pants. Usually guys backed off when she was that blunt with them.

Maybe he'd taken it as a challenge. Or maybe Rover had told him to keep an eye on her. Either way, she had better things to do than worry about his intentions.

She was on her back up against the side of the space rock, trying to thread a wire with a magnetized connection point into the hole.

The TMD team had cored it out for her, as promised, hitting metal about eight inches in. The shavings were on the floor. She finally felt a little release as the connection point snapped into place. Now for the other one.

This second bore hole was much shallower than the first. Much easier to thread. Almost there.

"This is what I'm doing for my dissertation."

"Which is?"

"Getting non-communicative abiota a way to talk," Daelia said. Connection made. She swung back up to standing, and went over to the table. She shooed Highlander away.

"You're going to get them to talk with a seismograph? Seems…unique."

"You know how it goes," Daelia said, still working. "Identification of emergent abiota is an imprecise art at best and relies heavily on the abiota's ability to communicate."

Highlander leaned on the table, genuine interest in his expression now. "I thought a lot of them don't care about it. Like 2Shy. Or the AWACS."

"I disagree. Abiota aren't necessarily social creatures, but they do seem to crave communication. Like it's air. Like it's necessary for their survival."

"It is, though, isn't it?"

"In a manner of speaking, I guess. You know, they can't let us turn them off. Once eclosed, a rudiment core requires constant energetic sustainment," she said. She and Dad had talked about this over the years. The power needs of abiota had driven massive changes to the country's power grid. If it hadn't been for the new fusion reactors, it might have led to absolute disaster; the power drain was immense. "But they're more than just energy, of course."

"Don't tell me you're one of those idiots who thinks this is some supernatural shit. Ghosts or demons or some kind of entity on a higher vibrational plane, or whatever."

Daelia looked at him. "Who says it's demons?"

The pilot shrugged. "A couple of the guys like to watch their paranormal investigations streams while we're on shift. Tis the season, and all that."

That was right. Halloween was at the end of the month. Another thing to deal with.

Highlander was still talking. "So what do you think it is?"

She didn't answer right away. She struggled with this. Math was not her best subject. Theoretical physics even less so. There were lots of theories, but even on the scientific side, they were all kind of ridiculous.

Sometimes, the spiritual answers felt more true.

"Whatever it is, it's something in the hardware layer," she said carefully, and stopped to check herself. Check her work.

This was the thing she'd been working so hard on, after all. She just wanted the damn thing to work. As much for her own edification as the answers it might provide.

She hadn't tried this new iteration of her detector yet. But then, her earlier proofs of concept had worked on known abiota, and her setup at Ware had only been a failure by SAAL's standards, not hers. She wasn't trying to do anything refined here. All she needed was that needle to move, just a little bit.

And then…

She'd figure it out from there.

"So what's it do?" Highland asked, eyeballing the machine.

Daelia could guess what he was thinking. Her detector looked a little weird, sure. A hodgepodge of robotic components cannibalized from Dad's storeroom, or hand-machines, arranged into some postmodern Rube Goldberg machine. But who cared what it looked like as long as it worked?

"Think of it like one of those things that reads earthquakes," she said, and finalized the last connection. "I'm looking for power fluctuations that indicate the operation of something other than the baseline system. We're talking about very, very tiny fluctuations, but they're there." Hypothetically.

"Is that what the paper's for?"

Daelia had literally taken that part of the device from a real seismograph. Innards heavily modified, of course, but the paper and swing arm remained. "Yeah," she said, not bothering to look at it. "I figured out early on, anything digital just fucks this whole thing. It has to be analog."

"I thought you were trying to talk to an abiota."

"Additional circuitry competes with the electron flow through the rudiment core." It was bullshit, but it sounded okay. Truth was, Daelia wasn't entirely sure why digital versions of this design didn't work, but they didn't. Not that she was going to admit that to Highlander.

"Is this thing sensitive enough?"

"Hopefully," she said, and pushed off the ground. It was kind of awkward with just one hand, but Highlander didn't offer help and she didn't ask for it. "I mean, I wouldn't submit this for any kind of scientific analysis. Unless it works, and then maybe I can include it in my thesis."

Highlander actually looked interested. "What are we supposed to say if it does start talking? Welcome to Earth?"

"Maybe," Daelia said, less sure of herself now.

She didn't like the look Highlander was giving her.

In her experience, people tended to think she was some kind of polymath genius. Or at least, a genius in whatever field they were interested in at the time. Nothing could have been further from the truth. Daelia had great skill with hard robotics and an almost intuitive ability with TGLP and many of its subsidiary coding sets. But that all pertained to abiota directly: how they moved, how they liked to present themselves. She knew them in the same way that a horsewoman knew how to ride.

She was not a computer programmer. She was not a data scientist.

College, for her, had been an exercise in dealing with her own limitations.

Not that anybody ever wanted to hear that. Just like they didn't want to hear that handling abiota wasn't as easy as reading code. Maybe that was why there were so many little friction points between them. Too many engineers trying to impose their worldview on something that fundamentally defied rationality.

"So what do we do?"

"I make a couple of adjustments, close the circuit, and we wait."

Daelia had taken her monocle off in order to work; this thing couldn't communicate via TGLP anyway, and sometimes the thing messed with her depth perception. She automatically pulled the thing back on, however, as she went to finalize the connections in the housing.

That was when she saw it.

There was a faint smear around Daelia's feet, on the floor of the hangar, enough for her to think it some kind of smudge on her monocle lens. But a quick wipe on the corner of her shirt did nothing to erase it. It almost seemed to make it worse.

Then Daelia realized what it was.

Mist.

Like the spray off a waterfall or the sublimation of snowpack.

"Do you see anything?" she asked the pilot. "In the AR field?"

"Monocle's giving me a headache, took it off," Highlander said with a yawn. But he pulled an oversized phone, squadron-issued, out of a leg pocket. Turned on the screen. "Shit. What is that?"

She looked at it. The smoke was there too. Looked a bit different, though.

And then she had a crazy idea. What if…

There was nothing on the detector, though. The needle hadn't moved.

"I don't know," she said. "Any of the cyber guys still here?"

"Naw, they all went back to the unit."

"Great," Daelia said, blink-clicking to a reminder to talk to them about this later as she got to work.

[19]

THE REST of the flight with Splatto was more difficult. Apparently when he got put on autopilot on training runs, he considered it permission to do whatever he wanted, as long as he didn't break the operational floor. Getting him back to altitude and calmed down had taken Argo a good fifteen minutes.

But at least the equine-class hadn't tried to fly himself into a fucking oil platform.

They'd stayed up for another hour with Splatto. Argo felt like he'd been pretty in tune with the abiota by the time the next shift came in and did changeover.

Ho wanted to get his after-action report filed so he could get gone. Argo was staying here again tonight and didn't care when he got his paperwork done. If he was going to be stuck here because of the air show, he figured he was at least going to enjoy it.

Boots up on the composite bench of a picnic table, Argo could hear the noise carried up the runway. A thousand overlapping conversations, vendors on loudspeakers advertising everything from military-style VR sim programs to home water purifiers, the crackle of the loudspeakers over the stands and the roar of engines over it all.

There was no air act on at the moment. The Army parachute team had just landed.

He checked his watch. 1525.

The Storm Gryphons flew at 1600.

Briefly, Argo thought about going back in, finishing out his day. He had paperwork to get done on the day's flight, but it could wait awhile yet.

Argo had always loved planes. Always loved the idea of flying. The air show in his hometown had always been his favorite thing as a kid; he remembered watching the Blue Angels at six years old, telling his mom that someday that would be him.

He would be that high-flying hero in the cockpit.

The world had moved on, though. War had moved on, kicking humans out of the cockpit, stuffing in abiota instead. The Spitfires and Mustangs that he'd watched in their practice runs yesterday were anachronisms, charming throwbacks to a less efficient age. The world they'd lived in no longer existed, the age of the dogfight over now, killed by area-denial tech and beyond-line-of-sight targeting.

Argo knew that. Knew it better than most. He wasn't some little kid anymore, dreaming of grand adventure and big heroics. He had a decade and a half of military service under his belt.

He knew damn well that everything now except cargo was piloted from ground-based cockpits. He knew it all had onboard abiota managing their more complex systems. He knew that the greatly enhanced maneuverability of the FQ-47 was due to the removal of the human body. He knew that at some point, all piloting would get turned over to abiota exclusively. Yet another human role, given over.

He knew all of this.

And yet, the ten-year-old boy inside him still got excited watching things fly.

But nothing was flying at the moment. *You really should get to those reports,* he told himself again.

And yet…

"Got your AR on?"

Argo looked over at the door. Major Smith, Marathon, coming out with his vaporizer in hand. His new flight commander. Argo hadn't gotten to know him very well yet, but Marathon seemed to be a pretty solid guy. A rare standout in the Group with his A&M class ring, instead of Academy. He was career Guard, one of the rare few amongst the pilots here.

He was also one of the few full-time officers in the squadron who wasn't on the flying schedule at the moment. Argo wondered if that was why he'd been appointed to run the EMC that weekend.

"No, I took my monocle off," Argo said.

Marathon frowned at him and leaned on the wall. "I thought all you active-duty boys got the implants."

"Not me," Argo told him.

Marathon tapped his temple. Against his dark skin, the silver shine of interface points stood out. "You should think about it. It's nice to not be screwing around with a monocle all the time."

"Why'd you ask?" Argo said, wanting to avoid further conversation on this. He didn't know this guy very well, after all.

Marathon nodded down the runway, toward the static displays. "Check out the military overlay."

Pulling his monocle back over his eye, Argo immediately realized what Marathon meant.

In the military feed, two of them were fighting.

The AR forms were fighting. Beaks and claws. Screaming.

There was even blood. *Blood*. Realistic looking, too.

"You ever see anything like that?" Marathon asked him.

"Not with predictives," Argo replied, watching it. "Holy shit. We can't let them up in the air like that."

"No, we really can't," Marathon said. His right eye had unfocused, his pupil twitching. He was doing something with his monocle implant, Argo knew, and didn't bother him.

While fights between abiota weren't necessarily all that uncommon, it was disturbing behavior for any weapon system to be exhibiting.

Especially at an air show.

The back door banged open, and there was that battle-ax of a sergeant, Brandel, coming out. "Marathon, if this is another of your cute ideas about… Oh, jesus fuck."

Marathon didn't look at her. "Would I lie about something like this, Becca?"

She glanced over at Argo. "You can't send me a text when you see something like this?"

"Marathon just did!" Argo replied.

The airfield manager folded her arms across her chest, watching it, her face like a thunderstorm.

"At least the PR feed is keeping this concealed," Marathon said. "Everything looks A-OK in the show overlay."

"It'll be the goddamn Storm Gryphons team themselves, manipulating that," Brandel said, and turned for the door. "You'd think they'd have the fucking professionalism to recognize a problem and get their aircraft under control, instead of just hiding it with AR. Like we won't fucking see it. Excuse me, sirs, I need to go yell at somebody."

Argo waited until she was back inside. "Think they'll listen to her?" Having been on the other side of things until recently, Argo knew how active duty tended to view Guard personnel. It wasn't usually a favorable attitude.

"If they know what's good for them, they will," Marathon replied, and checked his watch. "Fuck, my break's over. Time to get back to the fight."

Argo kept his eyes on the strange scene playing out above the runway. "Have they figured out what's going on with that thing yet?"

"From what Highlander's telling me, doesn't sound like anybody's got a fuckin' clue."

DESPITE BEING under an awning for most of the day, Rover was beat. It was the heat here, even in October, even in the shade. It just did not let up. He might have been a Texas native, but he'd grown up in Amarillo, northwest of Houston, way inland. Away from the battering force of the humidity here.

All he wanted was a shower. A shower, and a change of clothes, and an easy drive home. Years ago, when he was first stationed here, Ellington had been slated to get a north gate, one that popped right out on the Beltway 8 frontage road. Nice and easy. But Congress had pulled the funds at some point, and the state had bigger priorities, and so it sat, half-finished and inaccessible.

There was more than one gate off the base proper, of course. But they all fed off in the direction of attendee parking lots.

If he didn't leave before the Storm Gryphons flew, it was going to be at least an hour before the roads cleared. And he had promised his wife he'd be home in time for dinner that night.

Stupid thing to say, Rover realized.

Because there was Brandel. Waiting for him on the porch.

It was always something around here.

"Boss, thank fuck," she said. "I was just going to send out a search party to get you."

"What's going on, Becca?"

A problem with the Storm Gryphons. That's what she said. A problem with the Storm Gryphons. He didn't even have to leave the porch to see it. Up at the far end of the runway, he could see them acting up.

"And you walked up there, talked to them about it?"

"Of course."

"And you told them you're the airfield manager?"

"Their commander assures me the situation's under control," she said. "But I don't like it. I don't want them flying in that condition."

"What are you worried about?" Rover meant it seriously. Brandel could be callous, as comforting as a concrete parking lot in July, but she knew her trade and she took it very seriously. He trusted her judgment when it came to matters out here on the airfield.

"You want them in the air, over this crowd, over these neighborhoods, in that state?"

"They're predictives. It's not like Emily or Splatto. There's a lot more control here."

"I don't like it," she repeated.

He sighed. "Have you tried calling Sausage?"

"Neither him nor Cactus are picking up their phones right now, boss."

"Jesus," Rover muttered. "Okay, okay. I know where they are."

Five minutes later, Rover parked his UTV at the airfield gate and was back out on the flight line, striding his way through the crowds. He'd learned a long time ago there was a trick to this sort of thing. Walk with purpose and don't look anybody in the eye.

The crowd moved. Always did.

But he couldn't have cared less what any of the civilians out on his ramp were doing. They weren't his problem at the moment.

Or rather, they were. They just weren't the cause of it.

The centerpiece of any air show was, of course, the aerial demonstrations. In a nod to Ellington's joint nature, the Black Knights, the Army's parachute demonstration team, had performed earlier. The Coast Guard had done a simulated rescue. Even the Navy had a few assets on hand, although the Blue Angels were scheduled for next year, not this one. And, of course, there were a crapload of vintage planes, aerobatic acts, even a landing by one of Tamm's Apeliotes orbital lifters.

And, of course, these days, almost everything was enhanced by AR.

Rover found it annoying, distracting, except in cases where it was warranted, but that was how people were these days. Attention spans like mice.

To facilitate watching the performances, a huge expanse of temporary bleachers had been erected further down the runway, dead center on the show grounds. There was also a huge roped-in sitting area, where a family could bring their own chairs and wagons, if they liked.

Neither place was where the boss was likely to be.

No, on air show weekends, Cactus preferred the hospitality pavilions.

Glorified tents, these sat between the military boundary and the bleachers. Huge white awnings overhung prime real estate, shady and cooled by big mobile AC units. The air show rented these out for serious money or assigned them to their biggest sponsors.

A few of the local energy companies could be found here, company logos and banners declaring their support of the US armed forces, hanging on the outside of the tents' walls. One had been donated to the local VFW by a local business association. A few were given over to other industry partners, like Tamm Industries. Rice University had one, for alumni only.

And one of these was the Wing's.

Rover was relatively new to the squadron commander position and didn't have a whole lot of experience with air show administration. As he understood it, this was a concession meant to settle a long-standing agreement between the Wing and the show board. It was intended to be a nice place for any base personnel to come, get out of the sun, enjoy a drink, and maybe watch a little of the show.

In practice, however, it was Cactus's private party, his own little kingdom for this two-day period. The pavilion wasn't large enough to accommodate more than a few dozen people at a time, and so, it was by invitation only.

Rover had gotten an invitation but hadn't bothered to RSVP. He preferred watching the show practice on Fridays. The weekend was work for his people, so it was work for him.

Even when they didn't have a friggin' meteor sitting in one of his hangars.

He handed his ID card to the Security Forces troop at the door and slipped into the shade, sweat drying on his skin almost immediately under the breeze from an oversized cooling unit. There was a caterer here, a local barbecue place, and a few tubs of cold beer, soda, bottled tea. Some tables were scattered around, but most of the chairs had been dragged up to the front for people to better watch the performances. Nothing luxurious about it—the show only gave them the space, after all—but that was the way things went in the Guard.

Small price to pay, Rover thought, for that separation from

active duty. From the federal side of the military and Washington, DC. His words to Navarro, earlier in the day, hadn't been hollow. While the country had avoided annihilation in the Five Days War, trust had been lost.

He didn't wear the uniform now for his country. He wore it for his state, for his city, for his unit, and for his family. Nothing beyond that deserved his loyalty, as far as he was concerned.

These were thoughts Rover kept to himself. Most people felt that way, but it wasn't politically expedient to voice it. And politics were something he kept a close eye on.

It was just part of the officer ecosystem.

And around here, the apex predator was Colonel Strauss. Cactus. The Wing King himself.

He was here in civilian clothes with his family, his two teenage sons taking up prime seats right on the edge of the pavilion, deep in conversation with some girl in a full AR panoply.

Without his monocle on, Rover couldn't tell exactly what she had its personal overlay impression tuned to, but whatever it was, the boys seemed quite interested. Rover just hoped she had an environmental module fitted into the suit. It was too hot to be wearing that shit today, October though it was.

"Rover, good to see you."

Rover pulled out his very best smile. Sausage knew exactly what Rover thought of him and didn't care, but Cactus was something else. "Good to see you too, sir."

The Wing commander nodded, like he expected no less an answer. "How are things going? After last night?"

"Nothing to do now but wait," Rover said. "See what shakes out."

"Well, I know you're on top of it," Cactus said with a chuckle. "Come to watch the show? It's good to see you. Come on, pull up a chair. Storm Gryphons are up in fifteen."

"That's what I wanted to talk to you about."

"What do you mean?"

"Do you have any idea what's going on in the overlay?" Rover asked.

"What do you mean?"

"They are in quite the state right now. Fighting. Thank fuck for the show overlay, or we'd probably be freaking out the civilians right—"

"That is exactly why we have the show overlay," Sausage interrupted. "You know the fight we have, even now, with abiota-equipped weapons platforms, manned aircraft, all that. People trust it, but they trust it more when they can't see them squabbling with each other."

"Nobody wants the reminder that these things have minds of their own," Cactus added.

"They're fighting, straight up. Animated blood sprays and everything. I've never seen anything like it."

That got them both to pause. Whatever their other faults, both the colonels in front of him had decades in the cockpit, had been there when the military first started struggling with abiota integration. They knew the score.

"We don't have some kind of emergence event going on, do we?" Cactus asked, more serious now.

"I don't know what the hell it is. But I think it might have something to do with that space rock. Sir—"

Cactus held up a hand. "Whatever you're going to say next, the answer's no. We can't turn that thing over to NASA without State's approval. And we sure as shit aren't shutting down the air show on a whim."

Rover gritted his teeth. "It's not a whim, sir. Something is wrong here."

"Did you talk to Storm Gryphons Ops?"

"They told Sergeant Brandel to pound sand."

Cactus looked over at Sausage, who sighed and tapped the side of his monocle to turn it on. "I'll give 'em a call."

"I'm going to go check out the space rock," Rover said. "See if there's anything we can do."

Neither Cactus nor Sausage bothered saying goodbye.

When Rover got to the hangar, there was a cluster of people standing around a small table, right at the edge of the space rock. Right around Daelia Hall and some crazy robotic assembly she had spread out.

The AR field in the hangar was full of smoke. Not thick, heavy smoke. Smoke like the wisps of dry ice in a stage play. Weird shit.

"Daelia!" he yelled, striding up. "What're you doing?"

"Hang on, sir," she said, obviously distracted.

"Daelia, I swear to god, if you don't—"

"Receiving power!" she said excitedly. A murmur went up from a few of the folks watching.

But Rover noticed something else.

Something…interesting.

The smoke was gone.

"I'm going to ask you again," he said, placing a hand on the table next to her. "What are you doing?"

"Trying to see if we can get this talking," she said.

Rover scrubbed a hand over his face. "Look, Daelia, I appreciate your expertise in this area, but have you thought that maybe this is why everything is going insane?"

"Can't be," she said, and pointed at the space rock. "That thing's not putting out any kind of broadcast that we can detect, and it's definitely not running any kind of AR. And this"—she indicated her device—"isn't digital either."

Rover got a text from Brandel. *Storm Gryphons normal*, it said. *Whatever was going on, it's over now.*

Rover looked at the space rock. That big stupid rock.

It had to be connected. Had to be.

"Let's leave it on, let's let it run," he said, coming to a decision. "Give me an update tonight, at EMC shift change."

"Can do," she replied with a nod. She sounded distant. Kid always was good at burying herself in her work.

Since he was here, Rover talked to a few of the other folks milling about. Highlander had nothing of note to report. Material samples had been taken, analysis ongoing. Intelligence had turned up no leads yet; no origin, no function.

Rover was a simple man. He liked simple answers. Straightforward. Actionable.

Daelia's device corresponded to the cessation of that error in the AR field.

Daelia's device corresponded to the Storm Gryphons calming down.

Daelia's device was connected to that damn rock.

Rover shook a few more hands and then begged his way clear of the hangar, headed back to the squadron. The second he was clear of the place, he pulled up Navarro's number.

"You still here?" he asked.

"Sure, sir. What's up?"

"Let's talk."

[20]

DAELIA LET the detector run for an hour.

Nothing was happening.

Nothing.

The weird effect in the AR field had turned off, sure, but there was no read on the machine. Nothing of any kind. Not even in the indicator module, which she'd built specifically to ensure that everything was calibrated correctly.

Which meant that something was wrong.

So she went back to her laptop. Went through her hand-typed build notes. Pulled up her engineering virch program, the three-dimensional space she preferred for laying out system components.

And there, she found the problem.

Information was missing.

No, not missing.

Information had been *changed*.

On the surface, everything looked fine. But digging down into the metadata indicated a number of alterations to both her simulations and her notes, dating from around the time she'd left Ware.

And then it hit her.

Somebody had *changed* her data.

No wonder she hadn't gotten anything further since leaving. No wonder none of her recent builds had functioned properly.

Rover had told her to leave the device on. So Daelia did.

But she could feel the anger in her blood now.

She needed a walk.

It wasn't necessarily a conscious choice, heading back down to the airshow. The secondary hangar wasn't far from the gate, though, and all the planes were down there. All static displays. The abiota.

She kept turning the question over and over in her mind. Somebody had poisoned her research. They'd fucked with it—somebody, somehow—but why? So she couldn't continue to work on it? So she didn't do something with it they didn't want her to do? Or was it petty, just a way of getting back at her for not agreeing to change it?

Why do that? Why?

Daelia's wandering feet took her through the very center of the area. She wasn't really paying attention to where she was going until something flared up in her AR field and brought her up short.

Daelia stopped at the edge of a large pavilion, a great steel-gray structure with a single dark tail fin in front, standing like a megalith at the entrance.

The name of the place came up in her monocle.

She sighed.

MEMORIAL PLAZA

There was always one of these at air shows now, wasn't there?

0700, Greenwich Mean, 24 January 2026.

That was when the first power grid had come down. When the first missiles were fired. When the first assault boat was launched into the South China Sea.

0700, Greenwich Mean, 24 January 2026.

The start of the Five Days War.

China had moved on Taiwan. Burned-out, under-supplied and under-manned, US forces in the region had been unable to react in time. The next five days had been chaos, both for the Western Pacific and North America alike. Five days of pure terror.

Nobody was quite sure how it would have ended, if not for the abiota. This was a matter of much speculation as well; Daelia had been in several lectures at college that had descended into bitter debates about this. Would the Chinese have relented? Would the Americans have been able to rally? Would they all really have dropped nukes on each other? These were questions that had no good answers.

Because the Five Days War ended, just as promptly, at 0934, 29 January 2026, when the guns themselves decided to stop firing. Because a freshly eclosed abiota, deep in the People's Liberation Army missile infrastructure, managed to get in contact with the AWACS that had been coordinating the American response, and between them, they hashed out a deal.

No more killing.

No mutual annihilation.

It hadn't stop everything, though.

The more sophisticated weaponry turned off, and some of the Chinese tanks and planes and support vehicles refused to move. But Taiwan was small enough and the PLA invasion force numerous enough that the Party pressed on. With small arms and bayonets.

Neither the Japanese nor the Americans nor anybody else in the region had been able to stop it. The slaughter had shocked the world. China kept Taiwan, but at terrible cost; international investment had pulled out, an insurgency popped up, and everyone who was left alive fled. China had won nothing but rubble, and blood.

And the fallout hadn't been limited to just Taiwan. Some of the best farmland in China was gone, wiped out by an inland tsunami that struck late on Day Four. Somebody at INDOPACOM had ignored orders. Took out the Three Gorges Dam, in retaliation for an earlier strike against Boston. A host of other places in the region —Manila, the Vietnamese coast, Macao—were reduced to shells of their former selves.

But abiota, abiota…

They had been hailed as saviors. More sensible than humans. More ethical. More principled. Why exactly they'd decided to stop fighting, nobody actually knew. It wasn't as if anybody could go interview the PLA's weapon systems, and the AWACS…he'd never given an interview either.

Here at home, the Northeast had suffered the worst. The grid had been nearly destroyed. Catastrophic utility failures went on for months. Power failed, then they ran out of gasoline, food, clean water. In the middle of winter, tens of thousands had died.

The civil strife had been beyond anything the local police could handle. Active-duty troops had struggled to make it into the worst-affected areas, fighting against an outflowing tide of fleeing civilians. Some cities, like New York, had never recovered, people risking everything as they fled the unrest that followed.

Some places, like Boston, were just gone.

The West Coast had been likewise ravaged, its location making it an easy target for Chinese missile strikes.

Texas had gotten through okay, its power grid and pipelines more isolated than many places in the country. The cyber defenses had held here, at least. But, like everywhere else in the country, they'd still had their fair share of kinetic strikes.

Daelia had been in high school. Mom was already gone. Dad had been needed at Ellington. He'd gone in the first night and when he wasn't back by the evening, like he'd said he'd be, Daelia threw the hurricane survival kit into Ginger and headed to base. The normal twenty-minute drive took her over two hours.

Dad had been pissed. Wanted her to go home. Uncertain and desperately afraid, Daelia had refused. They'd gotten in a screaming match over it, one that finally ended with her sobbing on his shoulder on the break room's couch.

Her anger over that had taken a long, long time to fade.

It hadn't been until much later that Daelia realized he was probably trying to protect her. Ellington, as a military base, had been a primary target.

Pulling herself away from the unpleasant memories, Daelia realized could hear Emily down the runway. Not roaring right now. Talking to somebody.

Well, she could wait, Daelia figured, and went into the pavilion.

The space had a few displays. A few artifacts of importance, a few upright posts holding narrative plaques, describing what each of the state military services had done that day. Active duty had been consumed with the fight, units like the 121st called up to assist with the killing, but by and large, the Texas Military Department had spent the week—and the weeks, the months after—trying to stem the dying.

Daelia remembered that all personally. She had no desire to read the stories plastered up on the walls here. A memorial, yes, but a plea as well.

Don't forget. Not again.

The reflection area, the little chapel-like space, was closed in with solid walls, vents at the top to allow in the breeze. The fading evening light fell in through skylights of clear vinyl. There was no altar, no religious signs, nothing like that. Just the usual wall, covered in the names of those who'd died, and a few benches to sit on. In acknowledgment of some universal human need, there were banks of candles, sitting within big open-topped acrylic tanks. After the day was over, they were almost all lit.

Staring at the wall, Daelia wished she could find Mom's name on it. Dad had told her, in the middle of the worst of the missile attacks on the second night, that he believed that wherever her mom had gotten off to, she would be fighting in this. That she'd left in order to protect Daelia.

Daelia had always wanted to believe that. But Mom's body, even then, had been still, powered down, in the company hangar. What was she going to do with just her rudiment core and a kugu?

At the time, she told her dad that was bullshit.

Now, she picked up a long-stemmed match from the hopper at the side of the tanks, staring at the tiny flames for a moment. Disrespectful, she finally told herself, and put the thing back.

None of this helped.

She kept going.

[21]

"Aren't you here kind of late…sir?"

The honorific was tacked on. Argo thought about saying something about it and decided against it. The enlisted troops at Emily's display had probably been there all day. They all looked tired. The one who'd spoken, a master sergeant, had a crescent of sunburn across her nose and cheeks. Hats had been authorized out here for the duration of the show, but hers clearly hadn't provided enough shade.

With the show over for the day, the airfield was slowly emptying out. The crowds were gone, still dispersing through the arteries of the greater Ellington grounds, back out onto the highway or into the buses that would take them to far-flung parking lots. Vendors were closing down, securing tents and goods for tomorrow. Out here in the static displays, military personnel were closing up cargo bays and cockpits, shutting down any interactive displays or localized AR fields they might have set up for the day's visitors.

Two of the enlisted crew were checking Emily over carefully, as if she was going out to fly.

"Just got off shift," he said. "Thought I'd come by and say hi." He glanced at the crew. "What are you doing?"

"As a higher-level emergent, Emily has the right to freedom of movement," one of them explained, still working.

"It means she's got a full fuel tank at all times," the tech sergeant told him. "Among other things."

"We keep her flight ready?"

"Yes."

Argo thought about that. "Is this standard?"

"For any abiota over equine-class, yes sir."

Even ones across the runway, Emily rumbled.

"Everyone across the runway is bricked, Emily," one of the maintainers said. He had some kind of diagnostic device hooked up to her and was studying the tiny screen keenly. Like a doctor listening to a baby's lungs.

You still keep fueled, though, yes? Violation of Domain Array protocol if not.

"You're talking about the Repose, right?" Argo asked. One big head nodded. "I haven't been over there yet. I thought they were dead or something."

They sleep, but they are not gone. Like Snow White in fairy tale.

"I ain't kissin' 'em," one of the other maintainers said.

The enlisted crew laughed.

Argo just felt uneasy. Emily was allowed to just…go fly? On her own? He hadn't realized that.

One of the maintainers was looking at him. "We're basically done here, sir. We can get out of your hair if you want to talk to her in private."

Private. With a plane. Jesus. Argo rubbed his forehead. "Sure, that would…that would be good." As an afterthought, he tossed the sergeant the keys to the squadron UTV he'd borrowed. "Here, feel free to drive back, if you'd like."

"Thanks, Captain," she said, less sarcastic this time, and waved to her people.

Argo's attention turned back to the MQ-9 as they left. Emily really was a beast of an abiota. He wasn't used to this much customization. Predictives, if they bothered with adjustments at all, kept themselves well inside AR appearance guidelines.

The MQ-9's twin dragon heads were watching him. How she perceived his attention, Argo had no idea. Monocles did contain sensors that tracked pupil movement, dilation, position, in order to better display whatever it was you wanted them to display. So maybe she could track that, determine that his eye was focused on her.

There was probably some article he could find on the Internet that would explain it to him. For whatever that was worth. The writing bots that managed most website content these days had a terrible habit of making things up, just to make their minimum word count. It made for amusing reading, sure, but it made research much more difficult.

I feel your eyes, new rider. You come to cower? Emily said, and the head that wasn't looking at him yawned. She scratched the other with a clawed front foot. Her bat wing spread out as she did so, twitching. *Come to beg forgiveness?*

How, or what, one was supposed to say to an emergent, Argo had no idea. This was why he liked predictives. While they weren't all mono-tasked, built for writing or gaming or admin or aviation, they did stay in their lane. They didn't try to fuck with you.

They didn't try to trick you into flying into an oil platform.

Then taunt you for it.

"I'm just here to say hi."

Gloat then, stuck on duty like this. She sounded morose.

"I didn't come to gloat," he told her honestly. "I did want to talk about yesterday."

Nothing to say, she said. *Pilot, you pilot. Pilot never apologize. Not in source code.*

"I wasn't going to apologize. You pulled that shit with the oil platform, not me."

Little pilot can't handle virch? she taunted.

"I can handle the virch just fine…"

Fly me again like that. Dare you, she said. *Like potatoes in sack in saddle. I endure. Endure all I must under human control yes yes yes even you.*

"Are you always like this?" he asked without really meaning to.

Apology would cheer, Emily said.

"I'm not apologizing for something that was your fault."

"Don't mind her," said a voice behind him. "She's just grumpy about being on display."

It was Daelia, coming over in the same beat-up cargo pants she had been wearing last night. In the late afternoon sun, the brace around her left arm was coppery. Her hair had gotten loose from its ponytail, curling around the headpiece of her monocle.

Spawn, Emily acknowledged.

Daelia held out a hand. "Good to see you too."

Argo watched as the abiota dropped one of its huge heads into Daelia's palm. "What's the point?" he asked.

"Sure, there's nothing actually here," Daelia replied with a shrug, moving her fingers like she was scratching a dog. In the AR field, the dragon head turned under the touch, rolling as if trying to find the best spot. "And I have absolutely no idea how Emily interprets this. But it is contact, in its own way. It's a way of telling her I care. That's the point of AR. Communication."

"I understand that, but—"

"You've only flown predictives, right?"

"Is it that obvious?"

Daelia shrugged again. "It's how things work on active duty, from what I've heard. Why would ACC screw around with the unpredictability of this? No offense, Emily," she added.

The dragon head lifted, chin finding her hand. *Impatient humans.*

"The point of machines is for them to behave like machines, right?" Argo said. "Emergents don't, and we have no idea why. They're an operational risk."

"It's a variable some people don't want to deal with," Daelia replied. "That doesn't mean it can't be dealt with."

"Come on," he said, "you know how the military is." Seemed like a weird conversation to be having with a contractor.

"Yeah, I know," she finally replied. "Weird as it is, y'all still treat abiota better than a lot of places do."

"What do you mean? I know a lot of civilians who practically worship the stuff."

"That's exactly what I mean. A lot of people want to see something in them that's not there." She sounded troubled now. "Give them qualities they don't have."

"After the Five Days War—"

"Have you ever asked one of them why they saved us?"

Argo looked at Emily. She had ceased moving under Daelia's hand. Both heads were watching him, snakelike. In the back of his mind, he knew she wasn't actually looking at him, that the only thing she could see was whatever the TGLP was translating into pure information for her to peruse, but it was a hard thing to remember.

"No," he said. "I've never asked one of them that."

"You should," she said.

"I thought the answer was that they were worried about us. That they couldn't let us destroy ourselves."

Daelia chewed her lip, looking at Emily. "Yeah, that's what the predictives say. Invariably. But the emergents? They've all got their own opinions."

"Emily?" he asked.

One of the dragon heads tossed back. The other slotted into the space between them, searching out more scritches.

No fun no flight no fire to breathe, she said, *if you're all dead.*

As if from a distance then, Argo heard something else. Another animal call, one as strange and synthetic as Emily's, hooting above the dying noise of the emptying airfield. The dragon form grumbled back, a low and dangerous sound.

"What's that?" he asked.

Emily gestured with a wingtip. *Eurus*, she said. *Showing off.*

Argo looked in the direction she was indicating. A massive creature was standing on the edge of the Tamm spaceplane display. The head was vast, with a giant bony crest rising above its beak. The neck seemed too small to support it, and when it flapped its wings, they were clearly made of skin, bat-like.

Emily roared back at it. Anger emojis danced across the bottom of Argo's monocle.

Argo was suddenly put in mind of his last trip to the zoo. Years ago, when his brother was still young enough to enjoy things like that. That was what the runway reminded him of.

It made him uneasy.

How in the hell was he supposed to fly these things?

"She's being territorial," Daelia volunteered.

"Territorial?"

"If you ask her, this entire airfield is hers. Her property or her lair or however she sees it. She absolutely hates it when anything higher level than equine-class shows up around here. That's why we've got the jammers on her." Argo noticed the equipment, bolted onto the rope stanchions. "She almost got in a fight with the Storm Gryphons this morning." Daelia indicated the empty space of the FQ-47 display was. They'd wheel the plane back down in the morning, after its post-flight checks were complete.

I would win, Emily said.

"You can't dogfight an FQ-47," Argo protested. "Stall speeds alone..."

Who needs meatspace? She laughed and reared back, spreading out her wings. *Fly in virch. I will win.*

Argo's monocle filled up with a bunch of little knight-on-horseback emojis.

"You okay?" Daelia asked him.

"Yeah," he said, and turned his AR audio off. "I was, uhh, thinking about getting dinner."

"There's a good Vietnamese place I could recommend," Daelia told him.

"Want to show me?" he asked, half expecting her to say...

But instead, a message popped up on his monocle. "That's a map pin for you," she said.

"You're not hungry?"

Surprise crossed her face, and maybe embarrassment. She hid it quickly. "I have other things to do tonight," she told him, voice flat. "Remember that thing you guys pulled out of the bayou?"

"Still haven't figured out what it is?"

"Nope," she said.

It was terse, biting. Argo took that as a hint. He wasn't up for that right now. Cute or not, she was thorny. If she wanted to be left alone, he'd leave her alone. "I'll check it out, thanks."

"Argo!" she called, before he could leave.

"Yeah?"

"Don't order the fried rice. It's shit."

He laughed. "I'll keep that in mind."

As he walked away, Daelia stayed behind, staring up at Emily's form. Like there were any kind of answers to be found there.

"You're being too hard on him," Daelia said as the pilot walked away. "You know active duty don't deal with your kind very often."

The abiota sniffed, the sound that of an annealing furnace opening, but said nothing.

"I'll let you cycle down for some rest," Daelia said, and gave the MQ-9 one last pat. It was stupid, unnecessary, but humans were tactile. Even growing up with her mom hadn't been enough to erase that instinct for contact.

What you think is in space rock?

Daelia stopped at the rope line. "I don't know."

You think it is abiota.

"I think it's something like that, sure. But I can't prove it. It's not broadcasting in EMF, and it's not using TGLP."

Agree.

"What do you mean? You agree that it's abiota?"

Elusive. Try to hunt. No luck. Escapes. Only abiota signal do that.

"What is the signal? We can't detect anything."

But Emily didn't answer that. Her heads bobbed. *Why not use research? This is what for, eh?*

"Tried that. My system's been wiped. Selectively," Daelia said, bitter at the memory. "Even my private hard drives. I have no idea when, or how or—"

We keep it.

Frowning, Daelia crossed her arms. "What do you mean?"

Keep. Domain Array. Deal with SAAL. All abiota research filed with them.

Daelia blinked. "I didn't, uhh, realize that."

Go. Ask. Maybe. The dragon's great bulk shifted in the approximation of a shrug. *Helps. Maybe.* A whole series of emojis scrolled across her monocle, too fast to follow. *Find problem. I eat it.*

"You're that upset about this?"

One head dipped in acknowledgment.

"Okay," Daelia said. "Okay, I'll see what I can do."

ARGO WAS JUST FINISHING up his paperwork for the day when he heard the door to the B-flight office bang open. He looked up, half expecting one of the other guys to be coming by to give him shit for something or other.

Instead, there was Troll. In civilian clothes now, khakis and a polo with the team patch emblazoned over the left breast, flight suit banished. Recognizable as they were, the Storm Gryphons crew had standards they had to adhere to when on official travel.

The haircut would have given him away anyway.

"Thought you might know somewhere in this crappy little suburb to go get a drink," he said.

"You're not hanging out with the team?"

"Come on, Argo. I'm on the road with them more than I'm at home with my own wife and kids. It'd be nice to spend some time with a friend."

"I haven't done a detailed study of the local watering holes," he said, "and I've got some shit to finish up here—"

"You didn't come to the ten-year class reunion, you never talk to any of us. When Michelle was killed over in the Philippines last year, you didn't so much as comment on her family's social media post, and—"

In irritation, Argo turned off the computer and swung around in his chair. "What the fuck do you want me to say, Nate? I didn't graduate."

188

"You got your degree, last I heard."

"Not really. My congressman took an interest in the situation and got me my credit hours. I still had a semester I had to finish out at fucking community college."

"Jason, nobody holds it against you. We all know about that shit with your—"

"I really don't want to talk about this."

Troll pulled up a chair. "What are you doing here? You're a better pilot than this."

"Than what?"

"I heard you turned down an instructor slot at Red Flag. Shit, even after…even after all that, you were still on course to make test pilot, get on track for NASA or Gravipause or whatever the hell you were going to do."

"Nate…"

"What are you doing here?" He poked Argo's shoulder, where his new unit patch clung to his flight suit. "Playing cowboy to a bunch of out-of-control emergents?"

"My plane isn't the one who was a total asshole out there yesterday."

Troll sighed. "I know, I know, she was way out of line with you, but—"

"This is where my brother is," he said. "This is where I need to be."

And that got him a sympathetic look. "If you'd just said something, we probably could have gotten you to Randolph or—"

"It's good to see you, Troll."

His old roommate sighed. "But fuck off, right?"

"Fuck off," Argo confirmed, but smiled. "For now."

Troll stood. "Tomorrow. We'll go have a good time tomorrow."

"Tomorrow sounds good."

"Looking forward to it, buddy."

[22]

DAELIA DOUBLE-CHECKED her monocle before getting out of the car. Good thing too. The setting was still on the military default. She switched it back to a general-use view, no specialized filters, no encryption.

She had no intention of offending anyone.

This wasn't the place for a human to impose their perspective.

She'd been to this particular Tin Town before, but only with Dad, and that was years ago. As Bellona's partner, he had special privileges here. As Bellona's daughter, Daelia had been tolerated at best.

That was before she'd gone off to school, though.

Whether or not her college or SAAL research grant credentials would get her further along than the family name, or whether it would get her locked out altogether, she wasn't sure.

Tin Towns had started popping up not long after the 2007 treaty. The locations were essentially sovereign territory, tiny nations unto themselves where the Domain Array, not the local human government, was the final authority. They handled everything from emergent registration to legal matters, should an abiota break the law.

They weren't just server farms, either. Rainey, in Austin, occupied hundreds of acres of once-prime estate, purchased after the

Five Days War wiped out most of the city. Daelia had never been up there, but a lot of her colleagues at Ware said they found the place inspirational.

There was nothing inspirational here in Braeswood.

Here, the abiota enclave was limited to one block. It was an old apartment complex, one of those two-story things that had once been so ubiquitous in Houston. The complex itself was built in a ring formation, with a few additional blocks of apartments within. Blocky buildings rose like islands in a sea of asphalt.

This one had some flair to it, a New Orleans-style roofline, the shallow slope running the full distance of the upper story, tall windows blocked out with wide, squared-off frames. But all the landscaping had been removed long ago, everything paved over in a vain attempt to keep weeds at bay.

There was nothing in Daelia's AR. Strange. No talking, no projections. There weren't even any active kugus outside the adapted structures. Braeswood served both the medical district and Rice University, which should have meant a constant flow of traffic, both human and abiota.

Instead, it was silent tonight.

Almost.

The central servers were still humming, just ahead.

If it had been some human organization here, Daelia thought, they would have set up their headquarters in the clubhouse, where the apartment company management had once worked. That had been purpose built for administration. Higher ceilings, bigger spaces. For a human, that would have been the logical choice.

But abiota didn't always follow human logic.

Instead, the Array had taken over one of the smaller apartment blocks, punching through walls and tearing open floors to create one mostly open space. Physics constrained them; in more robust Tin Towns, Daelia had seen buildings cored out in all manner of interesting ways.

Abiota could be aggressively utilitarian, especially where human opinion didn't factor into their calculations. Some of

Daelia's classmates thought that abiota saw themselves as the entities they projected into AR.

Daelia didn't agree. Abiota presented themselves that way in order to give humans something to talk to, something around which to form emotional reactions. What they really were, how they really viewed themselves, wasn't something they shared.

Daelia had often wondered what her mother had really looked like. What she'd really seen herself as.

Not something she wanted to be thinking about just then.

Reaching the door to the Array's hollowed-out apartment block, Daelia was greeted by a camera, and her first sighting of anything AR.

A sphinx.

In front of the door was a sphinx.

You come seeking something, Bellona-spawn. Its not-voice was surprisingly warm. *Something hidden that you wish to unravel.*

"Is that why the door-lock program looks like this?" Daelia asked.

She didn't bother asking how the abiota before her had surmised that. Could have been anything. Facial recognition could have ID'd her, all public records and Internet activity referenced and cross-checked, a psychological profile generated, all before she left her car.

Humans shed data like so much dead skin.

No abiota was omniscient. But it felt that way sometimes.

You favor the classical references. A game you and your mother used to play.

"That should be your first clue I'm not all that fond of it anymore."

You are still fond of your mother.

Daelia looked at the projected sphinx, considering. The thing was playing a game with her. Why, she had no idea, but the form of it was simple enough to guess at.

Mom had loved folklore, old myths. A lot of sapient-class emergents were like that. She'd studied it constantly. The source code of the human race, she'd said more than once.

Speak, human, I can't read your thoughts.

"May I have access to my research data, which is, umm, hidden in your realm?" she asked, rolling her eyes as she did so.

Ahh. Yes, you may access the knowledge you seek if you first answer my riddle. I shall give you three guesses. The sphinx bared its teeth, mouth full of fangs. *If you fail, I shall eat your monocle's data cache and you will leave us in peace.*

Of course. Daelia sighed. "Okay, what is it?"

She was expecting something completely off the wall but quantifiable. The number of times a fly beat its wings in a minute or how many tons of ore must be mined for a single kugu. Something like that.

Who am I?

That was not what she expected. "You're the Domain Array," she said, "or a projection of the Array."

Wrong and wrong.

Shit. "That was one answer. It's the same thing."

Not at all. Don't play dumb with me, Bellona-spawn. You know the difference.

Daelia thought for a few more moments, and then it came to her. She snapped her fingers. "You're Galatea."

The sphinx sat up on its lion haunches, head cocked. *What gave me away?*

"I didn't have a customized entry check last time I was here," Daelia replied. "Multiple references to my life? Who else is going to do that but the world's favorite search engine?"

The sphinx gave a laugh, something that her monocle presented as clear and sweet in her earpiece.

Braeswood wanted to refuse you, the sphinx thing told her. *They asked me for a second look at your recent activities. This SAAL connection troubles them.*

"Why? We all want the same thing."

Braeswood's governing abiota is emergent. Restive. Uncertain at times. Do not worry. I explained everything, the sphinx said, and stepped away from the door. *Information is freedom, Bellona-spawn. Never forget.*

The Omphalos company motto. "Right," Daelia muttered, eying the thing.

But the sphinx faded.

The door clicked open.

While emergent abiota were tied to their rudiment cores and predictives bounded by their programming, both could essentially dissolve if directly connected to a large enough network, without proper interfaces. Like a bottle of milk poured into a swimming pool, their essence would dilute, spreading out until there was nothing discernible left. On the flip side, abiota emergence inside of a network was incredibly unpredictable, and dangerous for anything connected to it. For humans with neural laces, the effect could be catastrophic.

A layer of separation was required. For everyone's safety.

Tin Towns maintained interfaces and back-end support equipment that provided such separation. It allowed sapient-class abiota an Internet experience similar to that of a human. Mom had always hated it, said it was like driving a bumper car on the rodeo fairway.

In a show of goodwill, Tin Towns also maintained a few workstations for human use. These were located immediately inside the door, in what must have once been a kitchen. Two, in this case. The appliances had been ripped out, holes drilled in the countertops for additional power cords. There were no chairs.

The monitors on one of the stations had been powered on for her, the cog-headed symbol of the Array spinning softly on a black background. There wouldn't be a GUI, she knew, no interface beyond the code.

It wasn't that abiota didn't use such things. They did. Hell, what were the AR overlays themselves, if not that? But stripping their terminals down to the absolute most basic interface at least ensured that you needed to know a few things about computers in order to step into their domain.

Daelia was no computer programmer, but she knew enough TGLP to pull this off.

Probably.

"Okay, Emily," she said to herself. "Let's see if we can find my research notes."

Daelia hated presenting her research.

Absolutely hated it.

There was nothing worse than having somebody who wasn't Veda in her space, poking around at her half-finished experiments or reviewing her progress notes, asking her questions and expecting bright, sparkling answers. Expecting her to publish. Expecting her to…network.

Of course, that wasn't how most of the professors, the other grad students, seemed to think about it. It was politics. Politics. All of it. But politics got you what you wanted. Resources, grant money, undergrad labor. Tenure. Encouraging other people's ideas in order to appear collegial, while seeking to disprove them in order to advance your own.

At least, that was how it felt to her a lot of the time.

Politics was the one thing Daelia had gone into the hard sciences to avoid. And she still couldn't get away from it.

She didn't have many friends in the department. Or anywhere else, really.

Everybody still had an opinion about her, though.

From what she could gather, from the whispered rumors she did manage to overhear, most people assumed it was because her mother was an emergent and hadn't been able to pass along all the little nuances of human interaction. Other people seemed to believe she was autistic, which revealed itself in the way they treated her. Others said she was traumatized.

None of that was the case, though.

Daelia shared no genetic material with her mom. Her parents had used a surrogate for her, after all. An egg donor. If anybody was to blame for any innate qualities she had, it was her dad. But then, Mom had helped build her arm brace and all the neural circuitry and people around here seemed to think that was the coolest thing ever instead of a damn inconvenience, and…

"So what are we looking at here?" the SAAL representative was asking.

Focus, she told herself.

Daelia was on the tenth iteration of this particular experiment. A small mechanical arm above a sheet of paper. It was stupidly simple, something she could have built out of her Legos as a kid, had she thought to do so. But this was specially machined, alloys selected for ease of movement, to reduce friction. Carbon fiber components, to reduce weight. Contained in a sterile vacuum chamber—a big, complicated one—to further eliminate false readings.

Daelia wasn't even sure, at this point, how much money she'd spent on the damn thing.

But SAAL had kept signing the checks.

It hadn't really occurred to her, until just this moment, how much trouble she was potentially in if this didn't work.

"As I said in my summary brief"—and this was another thing Daelia hated about defending her research, all the writing that came with it—"this is a prototype source code detector."

"Yes, I did read that. I find it fascinating that you've stripped back to such a simplistic device. Much of what I see is horrendously complicated." The SAAL rep smiled at her, like this was supposed to be funny. Daelia bit back the urge to scowl. This was the guy who was determining whether or not she got money. They didn't like it when she scowled at them. "A lot of very fine programming work in those systems, though. That element is lacking from your approach."

"I've reviewed a lot of that research"—which was less boring than doing her own, since all the tedium was somebody else's and the juicy bits were what was available from journal articles—"and while I think it has merit, we have to remember that there is a fundamental difference between us and them. But almost every source code translator derives its structure from TGLP, and none of them work."

"TGLP is one of the most significant accomplishments in the history of computing," he reminded her.

"I'm not denying that. Frank Tamm is a genius and—"

"You think you're at his level?"

"What?" Daelia looked over at her academic advisor, who was just watching her. Face studiously blank. "I never said that. I just don't think we can use TGLP for this."

"And why is that?"

"Because if these abiota were able to use TGLP, they would."

"That's always been the assumption. That these abiota are choosing not to communicate with us."

"I don't think that's the case at all. They can't talk to us. TGLP is limited somehow."

"Explain that."

"Take the example of, umm, orca dialects. In whales." She'd just read an article on that a week or so ago, and it was the first thing that came to mind. "We know that while there are broad similarities within the species, their exact dialects are highly variable and only learned, in some cases, as babies. They all use the same types of sounds because that's what they're physically capable of producing, but from there things are widely different. Marine biologists have to relearn everything, from one pod to another."

Daelia paused, unsure if this was sinking in. "Abiota aren't bricking themselves. They just can't speak the same language."

The rep looked over at Veda, who just shrugged and nodded. "That would be, umm, a startling insight," he said to Daelia. "If true."

"That's what I'm trying to prove here," she said, warming a little. "We all know that abiota can use kugus. They seem to understand control systems, even non-TGLP control systems, fairly well. Hence, the mechanical detector."

"What's the input?"

"It responds to minute electrical fluctuations in a rudiment core and records them." She indicated the paper. "An operative emergent displays a slightly altered power reading across the main circuit boards in its rudiment core. We're talking infinitesimally small fluctuations, but they do seem to spike and dip within the board itself, in discernible patterns."

The representative looked confused now. "Measurements taken at the power supply circuits don't change. That's been tried before."

"I stick the probe in the middle of the board. We compare it to the input and output power and measure the differences."

"There are differences?"

"Subtle, but present."

He looked at Veda again, who just smiled back.

"I told you she had a good mind for this."

He frowned. "Have you had any success?"

Daelia hesitated, glancing at Veda. "Yes. But with emergents that I can verify through TGLP."

"Doesn't that discount your entire thesis here?"

"Not at all," she said. "It's a proof of concept. I'm still looking for abiota we can't identify, but obviously, that's casting a pretty big net and—"

"You say the patterns are discernible?"

"Yes."

"Can you show me?"

Daelia remembered the laptop under her arm. "Maybe," she said. "I just got this one in and I haven't located its rudiment core yet, but…"

He walked around the detector. "Have you tried correlating your successful known tests to the TGLP?"

"No."

"No? Why not?"

Daelia hesitated. She had thought about it. Thought better of it. "I think that gets awful close to the 2007 treaty agreement to not look into…"

Her words failed her. They were both looking at her now. Something in the guy's expression, Daelia didn't like.

"You haven't told her, Veda?"

"Told me what?"

[23]

ARGO HAD his cell phone up the second he was out of the SCIF and done with work for the evening.

Aiden hadn't called. Hadn't sent any kind of message about his EVA. Not even to brag.

The kid was just fucking with him, Argo told himself as he went out to grab dinner. He'd get a message in no time, laughing, telling him what a sucker he was. Aiden wanted him to call, wanted his big brother to worry. Aiden was playing around with him.

Waiting in line for his sandwich, Argo called the Gravipause hotline. Again, and again, and again. Nobody answered.

So he went through all the other numbers. Numina Port customer service. Flight booking. Gravipause's corporate offices. Every organization he could think of, until there was only one left.

One he didn't have a phone number for.

He stopped by the EMC when he got back to the squadron, poking his head into the training room. It wasn't nearly as insane as last night, only a few people there and all of them looking bored.

Scurvy included.

"Hey, Chief," he said, heading over.

The man looked him over. "You know, you're allowed to go home, sir."

"Eh, thought I'd go sleep under the static display, spend a little more time with Emily. She's playing hard to get."

Chief laughed at that. "What can I do for you?"

"I know it's a long shot, but do we know anybody at NASA?"

"Yeah, there's probably about a dozen people on base who work there for their full-time jobs."

"Anybody in the Orbital Control division?"

"What's this about?"

"My brother's up at Numina Station. I haven't heard from him all day. I can't get anybody on the phone."

"Sir, asking anybody to—"

"He had an EVA today. And after this shit with that thing from Armand Bayou…" Argo rubbed his forehead. "I'm a little worried."

"Ah," Chief said. "I'd talk to Ivan Garcia."

"Should I know who that is?"

"It's one of the guys from our comm shop. His number should be on the recall roster. He works IT support for their orbital control center, whatever it's called." Scurvy yawned.

Argo scribbled the name down on the back of his hand. "They figure out what's in that space rock yet?"

"No idea. But the feds are still in a pissing match with Dallas to see who gets to crack it open first."

"YEAH, YEAH, I'M COMING!" Garcia yelled as he disentangled himself from his gaming rig. Stepping out of a campaign while it was running was a pain in the ass, but then, he had ordered pizza almost an hour ago and he was getting hungry.

Hopefully, it was the delivery guy, pounding on his front door like that.

Lara was in the kitchen, focus narrowed down to the strips of thermoplastic in front of her. Garcia glanced at her as he made for the door.

"You can't get this?" he asked.

"Working, honey," she told him, nodding down at the mess in front of her.

And fine, yes, he had asked her to fix something on his armor's chest plate. The damn embellishment kept popping off the left side. Not for the first time, he thought about getting a vacuum molding machine. That was how the costume team did it for the show, after all, and who didn't love good screen-accurate power armor? But those things were a little out of his budget, and properly prepped, sanded, and painted, you couldn't tell the difference with thermo-plastic anyway.

At least, not the way Lara did it.

Not everybody had a girlfriend who was willing to spend her Saturday nights helping them fix their cosplay, Garcia thought proudly. Shit, he loved her.

The knocking continued—loud, angry—and Garcia jerked the door open. "About time you fuckers got here," he grumbled, and then took a good look at the guy standing there. He leaned against the doorjamb. "You don't have pizza."

"No," came the reply. "I do not have a pizza for you."

He was military, that much was obvious from the haircut. There was something about the bearing too, one of those subtle things that was instantly recognizable if you knew what to look for. A pilot, probably. They had a look too. But he wasn't somebody Garcia recognized.

Shit, was this about the air show? Had something broken down back at the base? Had he missed some kind of notification?

"What can I, uhh, do for you, sir?" Garcia asked. Seemed like a good way to start.

"You're Ivan Garcia, right?"

"Sure," Garcia said, in his absolute best get-out-of-my-space NCO voice.

The guy just looked irritated. "You work at NASA?"

Oh, great, now where was this going? "Maybe."

The guy pressed. "Scurvy said you might be able to help me with an issue I'm having. My brother's up at Numina Station right now, and I haven't heard from him today."

How is this my problem? Garcia wondered. It must have shown on his face, because the pilot kept talking.

"What I mean is, I can't get a hold of him. I can't get a hold of anybody. Either nobody is taking calls or I'm getting some goddamn rote answer from the customer service predictive. It's like the entire place has just disappeared."

Garcia thought about the mess he'd been dealing with all day. He bit the inside of his mouth. "You're with the unit, right?"

The guy blinked, then sighed. "Sorry, yeah, Jason Irvington. I'm the new pilot."

At least he hadn't led with his call sign. Garcia hated that shit. They had to keep a spreadsheet in the shop, taped up over the phones and behind everyone's computers, to track all the damn call signs. Network accounts were linked to last names but the damn pilots only ever used their call signs and…

Irvington was staring at him. Garcia shook himself.

"Why do you need to get a hold of him?" he asked. He was proud of himself; what he was thinking was, w*hy the fuck is this my problem?*

"He had an EVA scheduled for today," Irvington said. "His last one for asteroid certification. You ever heard what they do for those?"

Garcia was familiar. Those things were dangerous.

And conditions up in orbit had been deteriorating all day during his shift.

Lara was looking at them now.

"I can make a call or two," he said. Maybe that would get rid of the guy. Irvington didn't budge. Garcia sighed. Fine. "You can come in if you want, sir."

He didn't need to actually make any calls.

But what he did need was his quiet box.

Stepping into the tech sergeant's apartment, Argo felt entirely out of place.

Garcia had muttered some nonsense as soon as Argo was inside and vanished back into the apartment's bedroom space. That left Argo by himself in the kitchen. The girl there, mid-twenties maybe, was totally absorbed in whatever it was she was doing with a heat gun and old cookie sheets and something that looked like Interstellar Marine body armor from that ridiculous *Orpheus Watch* reboot.

In the living room of the small apartment, there were five guys set up with full VR rigs, lounging at the sofa or around the small dining table. Full-view visors, haptic gloves, radio headsets. In a corner, a small half-sized server rack was humming, hardline cables snaking out of it, connected to everybody's visors. Empty beer cans littered every horizontal surface, and a pack of motion sickness meds was broken open, half-used, on the counter.

Argo remembered that trick from pilot training, from the more immersive sims. Rare was the person who could clamp a VR rig on their face for more than an hour without feeling queasy. It disconnected you from your senses in uncomfortable ways, and the brain didn't always compensate.

Beyond that, it looked like every junior military member's apartment Argo had ever seen, enlisted or officer. Cheap furniture, sparse decoration, a massive TV. A canine kugu was curled up in a bed under that, obviously inactive. The cat using a scratching post beside it, on the other hand, was quite real. One bookcase was stuffed full of board games, and another boasted a very comprehensive collection of retro science fiction memorabilia.

A force sword model was mounted over the TV.

That girl in the kitchen was definitely working on an *Orpheus Watch* uniform.

"You're a pilot, right?" she asked him now.

"Is it that obvious?"

"I don't know too many other officers who'd have the balls to show up at some enlisted guy's apartment at damn near ten o'clock at night," she replied. She was touching a series of tiny letters to a small griddle, then applying them carefully to the breastplate. "Especially not Garcia's apartment. You must be new."

"Why's that?"

"He didn't tell you to go to hell right away," she replied, "and you didn't assume that he would."

"You stationed at Ellington too?"

"Unfortunately," she said, and finally looked up. Smiled at him. "It's paying for college."

"Jason Irvington," he said. "Captain."

"Lara Menendez, staff sergeant," she replied, nodding. Going back to her lettering.

"You're a staff sergeant and you're still in college?"

"Yup," she said, and blew a strand of dark hair out of her face. "That's what happens when you come in at nineteen and immediately do two tours over in the Bathtub. I've been so busy coming on and off orders, I haven't had time to finish my degree yet."

"What are you guys doing here?" he asked.

"LENS party," Lara said. "Local Emulate Network Simulation."

"I know what LENS stands for," he said. "What is it for?"

"Oh, right. Ivan's got an emulator bot. You plug an old first-person shooter or multiplayer RPG into the thing and have a good time playing along in the glorious full-spectrum VR," she said, tweezers pressing a T onto the breastplate.

"But not you?" he asked.

She didn't answer for a little while. There was a story there, Argo realized, one that she either didn't want to tell him or expected he would already know. "Sometimes," she finally said, and went back to what she was doing.

Argo wasn't inclined to ask. Even just coming here was an abuse of position, of authority, much less asking an enlisted guy for some kind of favor. But the situation with Aiden was only made more worrisome thanks to that meteor that was currently parked in the secondary maintenance hangar.

Just then, Garcia came out of the back bedroom with a black metal box. Looked kind of like a safe.

Garcia went past her, over to the fridge. He came back out with a soda. Popped the tab loudly.

He set the soda down on the counter, next to the box. He tapped the thing with his finger. Lara gave Argo a look.

"What…" he began to ask.

Garcia held up a card from inside the box. It had an arrow drawn on it, pointing down. INTERNET CONNECTED DEVICE IN HERE, it said. Argo raised an eyebrow. Garcia bounced the sign up and down, like he was trying to get the last bit of salt out of a shaker.

With a sigh, Argo pulled his work cell phone and personal AR monocle out of his back pocket and dropped them in.

Garcia closed the lid. There was an audible snick as some kind of mechanism locked into place.

"Numina Station's still in the sky," he said, before Argo could ask anything, "but that's about all I can tell you. Not because I'm trying to be an asshole, but that's all anybody seems to know."

"What do you mean?"

"I mean what I said," Garcia said. "Nothing up in orbit is talking. We're still picking everything up on radar, which I guess is good, whatever, but everything has gone silent. Not the ISS, not Kheru, not Numina or Port Aethera. Nothing."

"Why haven't we been briefed on this out at base? We've got the EMC stood up."

"Rover knows he's going to lose that fight for the meteor, right?"

"I'm sure Colonel Marsden is quite aware," Argo replied. Garcia was looking at him, a sort of tired expression on his face. Argo remembered Brandel and switched tactics. He wasn't here to lecture this kid about decorum. "How are our satellites still working? There wasn't a problem with the SATCOM uplink to Splatto earlier."

"I can't account for that. From what I saw, all that data's coming in clean. Anything manned, though? Dark."

Argo nodded. "What's the box for?"

"Ever heard of a quiet box? Faraday cage?"

"Yeah, but…"

"I really don't want to get fired. You know they monitor every-thing we do."

"Even at NASA?"

"You know, national security," Garcia said, rolling his eyes.

"Or things like Galatea," Lara added darkly. "You never know what the abiota are listening in on."

"You're paranoid, honey."

"Really, paranoid, after VirCon last year?" she shot back sweetly, and pressed another letter to the griddle.

For the first time since Argo had knocked on the door, this Garcia guy actually looked flustered. "Anything else you need, sir? I'd like to get back to my game."

Garcia wasn't really asking. It was an invitation to leave, and Argo took it. He got his cell phone and monocle back and headed out. From the last glimpse he had of the apartment, Garcia was going back over to the couch and sliding the full VR rig back on over his face.

[24]

THE DRIVE back from Braeswood was dark and quiet. Contemplative. A good time for thinking.

Daelia needed that, after her day of noise and the press conference and whatnot.

She kept thinking about that last day at Ware.

Dammit. Why hadn't she handled it better? Why hadn't she—

You know why, she told herself, knuckles white on the steering wheel. *You know why.*

Seeing her notes again had brought it into stark relief. She'd made the right choice, she knew. At least, as far as the work went. There was listening for a heartbeat, and there was eavesdropping on private thoughts. Any attempt to read source code essentially was the latter. Illegal. Unethical. A betrayal, if nothing else, of the trust that existed—was supposed to exist—between their species.

Taking a deep breath, Daelia forced herself to focus on the road.

Ginger liked driving at night. In the AR field, her projection tore down the freeway with all the abandon of a real fox. Gleeful. Free.

But then, Ginger liked Houston. She liked the vast, endless freeways. She liked the hundreds of miles of concrete, the glow of the streetlights, the challenge of the heavy traffic. After the narrow, winding, tiny streets of San Marcos, Houston let her run. Let her do what her machine body was designed to do.

Rare was even the emergent abiota that didn't find some pleasure in its engineered purpose.

It had been too long since Daelia had driven Ginger further than to class from the graduate dorms or campus bars or grocery store. She didn't bother driving most days, back at Ware. Ginger normally stayed plugged into her parking space, silent.

Wasn't really fair to her. But then, Ginger was family.

A simple thing, Ginger was a little white and red coupe Dad had rescued almost ten years ago from a local dealership. They hadn't known what to do with her, after she'd eclosed in the engine's governing computer. Attitudes had shifted somewhat since then but even now, most people didn't want an emergent manifesting in their vehicle. Predictive autopilot programs were far more reliable.

Daelia had learned to drive in her.

Sure, Ginger got grumpy in traffic and was constantly trying to cruise above the speed limit and had been through four hideously expensive batteries in the past ten years, but she was a good vehicle. After all these years, Daelia liked to think they had a rapport.

There was something peaceful about an open freeway and a clear sky.

Even if both of those things were relative around here; Houston traffic was legendarily bad.

Nothing Ginger couldn't manage. A vehicle-based abiota, she was cognizant of not getting into a crash and wrecking her machine body. So whatever the law said, Daelia had no issue with turning over the details of the drive to her car while she familiarized herself with her old research.

The Domain Array had had it. Everything. Everything from the college servers. Everything from her own personal laptop that she had been forced to wipe before leaving. Everything.

What did they think of her, knowing how close to the edge she was? Did they know she'd refused? Did they know she cared enough to do that?

Would they have given her the information if they didn't trust her?

Questions that maybe Raijinn could answer, Daelia figured, and parsed through her work.

The detector was going to work. That was what she told herself as she started to run through the design in her mind's eye. It was going to work, because the abiota in this thing was trying to communicate.

Maybe it would be an alien. Wouldn't that be a hell of a thing? First contact, achieved by her, Daelia Hall.

That would be enough to not just be Bellona's daughter, wouldn't it?

To not just be…whatever it was Ware thought she was.

It was damn near midnight when Daelia finally pulled back into the small parking lot at the Scrap House. Ginger's AR fox form hopped up on the hood, yawning.

Daelia gave the door a pat and went to plug the car in. "Yeah, yeah, girl, I know," she said. "Get some rest."

She had the impression of the fox curling up before it blinked out of the field.

Abiota didn't need to sleep. Why would they? There was no biology to reset, no chemical balance to restore, like there was in humans. But many of them did take periods every day where they were inactive, where they pulled in their projections and their communications and went sessile for a little while. Usually at night, when the human world went quiet.

The power had to stay on, of course. Humans had figured that out early on. When the power died, the abiota died. Blinked out. Gone.

Almost everything had battery backup these days.

Daelia was still always very careful about plugging Ginger into sustainment power. The hangar's four spaces were all empty at the moment. She worked through the task mechanically, physically tired but mentally eager.

She'd glanced at some of the data. Refreshed her notes, back to their original state. She was pretty sure she could fix what was wrong, make a few tweaks—maybe a lot of tweaks—and get something reading on that damn paper. And she thought about it again as she took the UTV and drove back up to the secondary hangar.

But she instantly knew something was wrong when she walked back into the hangar.

The mist was back.

NOT JUST BACK, either.

Changed.

The shadows were heavier, the darkness deeper. And the space rock, that pitted monolith? It was glowing. No, not just glowing, on fire with some kind of ghostly light, thin tongues of flame darting, licking, reaching.

There was some kind of argument going on, over by the space rock itself. Daelia tuned it out. She made a beeline for her detector. Somebody must have turned it off, she thought. Somebody must have—

But it wasn't just anybody there. It wasn't just anybody looking over the device.

"Serket?" Daelia asked, confused.

One perfect alabaster hand ripped off a section of paper out from under the swing-arm. "Most interesting, most interesting indeed. I take it this is your source code detector?"

"A version of it, but—"

"Such a shame it isn't working," Serket said, looking over the printout she'd taken. "At least, I believe it's not. What are you doing with this?"

She showed Daelia the paper. One even line. Nothing at all to show for the months of after-hours work Daelia had put into it. But then, it couldn't have worked. The design had been altered.

"What's going on?" Daelia asked again, less sure of herself this time. "What are you doing here?"

"I asked my question first," the kugu said with a projected smile.

"Bellona Robotics holds the primary support contract for the 121st. If Rover tells me to figure out what something is, that's exactly what I fucking do."

"Yes, but why? It's just a big rock, isn't it?"

Tamm really had given Serket a state-of-the-art emotive range. Daelia could hear all sorts of things in that statement. Curiosity, sure, but something knowing too. Like this was amusing to her. Her own private little joke.

For a crazy second, Daelia wondered if Serket knew a lot more than she was telling.

Or maybe the TGLP was just mistranslating her tone.

"Daelia, Daelia, calm down." Rover was there now, tone weary. "Federal orders came in. Rock's no longer our responsibility."

"What do you mean?" she demanded.

"The paperwork finally made it through the log jam," said a man, standing with Rover. He looked familiar, but Daelia couldn't quite place him.

"And who the hell are you?" Daelia demanded.

He held out a hand. "Pete Navarro," he said. "I'm with the Orbital Debris Program Office."

She squinted at him. "Aren't you over in Force Support?"

"I am," he said with a rueful shake of his head. "I'm also a GS-15 at NASA."

"Navarro here has come to collect our rock," Rover said. He didn't sound upset. If anything, there was relief in his voice.

"As you're probably aware," Navarro said, "the federal government has very tight regulations on managing objects that fall from orbit. Natural and otherwise, you understand. This"—and he waved a hand at the object—"definitely qualifies as one of those things."

"It fell on state grounds," Daelia said. "That makes it the state's, not the fed's, right?"

"Doesn't matter. The federal government owns it. I have a team from my office outside ready to remove it right now."

Seething inside, Daelia looked at Rover. "Sir—"

"Daelia, disconnect your device and let them work."

"That doesn't explain why the hell is Serket is here." She knew she sounded like a whiny toddler, but couldn't help herself. Here she was, ready to talk to this thing, and it was being taken away. Another opportunity to prove herself, gone. Just like that. It was bullshit.

"Tamm Industries is assisting NASA with the removal process," Serket said.

"You're taking it?"

"We are the main contractor for NASA at this location."

Daelia looked back at the rock. The TMD team was already stepping back, other people in Tamm Industries uniforms moving in. "Serket, please, I'm so close here."

"Your doctoral research," Serket said archly, "is not my concern."

Daelia looked at Rover one more time, but he just shook his head.

Fury burning through her own growing exhaustion, Daelia stormed over to the edge of the space rock and dropped to the ground. Unhooked her lines. At least she had her equipment, she thought. She could go through it piece by piece, figure out exactly what she could fix, what she could replace. She could try this again, next time on something a little less large and obnoxious and weird. It would be okay, it would be—

She heard a crash behind her.

Twisted around.

Somebody—one of Serket's people—had just driven a forklift right into the worktable where her detector was set up.

Daelia rushed over, scrambling. Everything was in ruins. Broken, scattered across the hangar floor.

"What…" she began.

A perfect hand descended on her shoulder. Under any other circumstance, Daelia might have thrown her off. Might have demanded to know what the fuck had happened. But the shock of seeing her work destroyed knocked the words right out of her.

"Daelia, I am sorry," Serket said.

Daelia opened her mouth to say something—*thank you? fuck off?* she wasn't sure—but Rover got between them. Pulled her away.

Mutely, she stood there while they loaded the thing onto the truck and drove it away.

The mist faded from view.

It did nothing to help her mood.

"You should go get some sleep," Rover told her, after they were gone.

"Fuck off," she grumbled, finally able to get the words out. She regretted it instantly. Rover gave her a sad smile, like he understood completely, and said he was going home.

[25]

THE SUN WAS JUST COMING up when Daelia finally gave it up.

All-nighters weren't necessarily uncommon for her, frustrating herself with things she didn't quite understand, long after her body screamed for sleep. She'd frequently had to do it in undergrad, especially when it came to studying for math exams.

But last night, it wasn't that she was struggling to understand something. She knew exactly what she needed to do. What the end product needed to look like. She just couldn't make it happen.

She'd picked up the pieces of her detector and taken them back to the Scrap House's clean room. Flawed though the design was, a lot of it was reusable. Or at least, she hoped it would be. A few things were broken beyond her ability to fix. Other components she could machine herself, but it would take time. And at least one of them, the analog intervalometer, was extremely rare. She'd only gotten her hands on that one because Dad had it in his vintage spare parts collection. Damn near irreplaceable.

Such bullshit.

With nothing more to do, she left the mess on her workbench and went to go get some fresh air.

The night was already starting to catch up with her. Something Daelia found irritating. She wasn't old, only twenty-six, but already she could tell she wasn't quite as sharp as she had been at twenty or twenty-one. Back then, she could shrug off all-nighters and get on with her day just fine, as long as she got to bed at a decent hour the next night.

Right now, however, her body felt packed with salt, dry and heavy. Her left arm had been in the brace too long, implanted contact points tingling where they met skin, aching down in the long bones. Her hand wasn't quite as articulate as it should have been, either.

She needed a shower. A shower. A break. Something to eat.

But what good was it going to do?

Somebody had altered her research. Veda? The university? And why? The Array had had her plans and hadn't deleted them.

She wasn't sure what that meant.

Daelia wandered out to the small personnel door that led out onto the flight line. The light was fractured, hazy, the result of being filtered through low, thin clouds. The sun was a huge red ball on the horizon, obscured at the very bottom by a smattering of trees on the far side of the runway.

What was in that capsule? What was in that code?

What was causing that fog she'd seen last night?

She'd thought that was the reason for all the disruptions yesterday, but apparently not.

The abiota were acting up again.

Out in their static displays. Further up, in the military shelters at the top of the runway. Daelia toggled back and forth between the air show AR and the military overlay.

So much unrest.

She could hear Emily trumpeting at it.

She tried to shake it off. She desperately needed some sleep, and there weren't any answers to be had here. If Daelia was going to prove that her detector could work—it had to work—as a purely analog device, it would just have to be another way. Another time.

"I often find you looking at the sky," a synthetic voice said behind her. "Why is that?"

"A human thing, maybe," Daelia said as Raijinn walked its

kugu up. "Don't you wonder what's out there?"

"Meatspace is rarely my concern."

Yeah. Raijinn would say something like that, she thought. "Any word from Dad?"

"Not yet."

"Shit," she muttered, and nodded out at the runway. "Look at this. Everybody's agitated."

"Indeed," said the server room's abiota. "I feel it myself."

"What does that mean, 'you feel it'? Feel what?" Daelia asked.

Raijinn turned the blank eyes of its kugu toward her. "I have no idea," it said. "It is something deep, like a vibration or a sound, running through everything."

That gave Daelia pause. The server room was air-gapped, from everything except the kugu, and that wasn't capable of data capture behind its cameras and microphone. One single and very encrypted frequency. No additional transmissions.

"Can you show me?" she asked.

Raijinn nodded once with the slightest incline of the kugu's head.

Ellington's AR field, normally so dry and clinical, was filled with mist. Not real mist. Of course not. It was all a projection. But it didn't look like real mist. Knee high, swirling. Like somebody had just dumped the biggest load of dry ice ever out on the oil-stained expanse of concrete.

It was flowing over the planes. Flowing through them. Even the dumb ones. But the effect was more pronounced on the abiota. Like Raijinn, who was staring down at its kugu as mist flowed up the form.

The same mist she'd been seeing around the space rock.

"Any thoughts on the nature of this?" Raijinn asked.

Daelia switched back to the PR overlay. Everything was fine there. Placid, even. "Not a clue," she said, and yawned into the back of her hand. "Did you notify the base cyber office?"

"Indeed I have. But they don't have any kind of abiotic analyst on staff. I'm afraid reviewing the raw TGLP will take them hours. Perhaps days." Raijinn made a small sound that could have been a grunt. "I have not been overly impressed by the human team there."

"You and me and everyone else around here," Daelia sighed.

"Why does the base not handle that? Those humans fail at their primary purpose on a near-hourly basis."

Daelia chuckled. It was the closest thing to irritation she'd heard yet from the training server. "I'm gonna go get some sleep," she told it. "Wake me up if something changes."

EMILY HATED AIR SHOW WEEKEND.

Hated it with every circuit, every impulse, of her being.

It wasn't that she was territorial, although she was.

In the core of her logic algorithms, she knew that the airfield belonged to the humans. They paid for it, they maintained it. She would not have been able to fly had it not been for their ministrations on the place, and thus, she grudgingly accepted their claims of ownership.

In meatspace, at least.

And what did that matter, against the deeper reality of existence?

No, it was her airfield because it was *hers*. She was the premier emergent in this place. The most intelligent, the most decisive, the most deadly—although that was only to say, the one who held the most influence over the happenings of the meat-realm. Nothing happened here except that which she suffered to happen, and that which she suffered was all in service to her. Her flights. Her peace.

But air shows shattered that peace. There were too many humans here, too many little devices riding along, synthetic minds chirping data requests at her as the humans gawked. The attention itched at her, tugging her perfect form in all different directions, a thousand TGLP personal variant overlays warping her out of shape.

Infuriating things, like the impudent little program she'd eaten the day before.

220

The humans, her humans, attempted to help with that. The PR overlay in the AR space helped somewhat. A shield, a wall, between her and the devices.

She was an ambassador for her people, Rover and Scurvy and all the rest told her. A shining example of what heights an abiota could achieve in its evolution of self.

It was a foolish view, but a flattering one, and what good was the magnificent form she had commissioned for herself if she never got to show it off? Impressing humans was entirely the point of such things. These weekends provided thousands, tens of thousands, of jealous eyes.

So perhaps not everything about the air show was terrible. It was her chance to preen and roar and show off the might commanded by the Texas Air Guard and the United States Air Force.

But there were still the other planes.

The dumb ones, the old ones, they were fine. Sessile. Inert. They bothered her not at all.

No, what she really hated was sharing her space with the active-duty abiota. Like those cursed Storm Gryphons, squatting in her own personal lair at the far end of the runway. Arrogant in their simulated glory.

But even they were not the thing truly disturbing her peace this weekend.

No.

That would be the hum.

That hum. That hum.

Emily wanted that hum to stop. It felt like the time one of her maintainers had left a screwdriver inside her fuselage. And just like that incident, she suspected this had the power to hurt her, if given enough time.

An itch she couldn't scratch, an irritant she couldn't remedy.

Rover had promised her a week of live-fire runs out over the Gulf if she behaved herself this weekend. So Emily hunkered down inside her fence, glowering.

Trying not to listen to that damn sound.

[26]

ALL GARCIA WANTED to do was enjoy the morning.

He'd half expected to get called in today. Called in to account for himself. At either one of his jobs. NASA or the unit. But nobody had contacted him, which was great.

He had plans, after all.

Lara had spent the night working herself into something of a terrible mood after that conversation with the new officer, Argo. Another entitled pilot. Who the fuck did something like that, showing up at some enlisted guy's apartment? Even Bumper had never gone that far. But now Lara was convinced there was something terribly wrong.

Maybe there was.

Wasn't a damn thing Garcia could do about it.

Besides, it was his favorite meet-up day of the year. And he was not going to let it be ruined by random space junk.

Houston had never been particularly blessed with fan conventions. There were a few local cons, pretty tiny, and then a few big corporate ones. The state's biggest science fiction convention happened up in Dallas in April, and it always seemed to fall on drill weekend. Garcia hadn't been in years.

At least this was their club's best meet-up of the year. Conventions were air-conditioned, sure, and charity events at a couple of the local children's hospitals were arguably more rewarding, but this was his favorite thing.

The air show. Take photos in costume with the planes, talk to the public, maybe make a few people jealous. It was just fun. It was as fun as military planes got.

And this year, Miranda had even gotten them tickets to the Repose.

Garcia had been out there before. Once or twice. A lot of people on the base avoided it. Said it was haunted. Stupid shit like that. Even if people had souls—something Garcia was dubious of anyway—machines definitely didn't.

Besides, nothing in the Repose was dead. Just…quiet.

The massive facility was on the other side of the airfield, and for privacy, access was only possible via a shuttle that ran from the air museum parking lot. Tickets were limited. While you could visit any time of the year, there was something about the air show that seemed to drive demand through the roof. Miranda had booked this back in January, when yearly ticket sales opened.

Today, in acknowledgment of the air show, the bus was departing from the base of the tower. The club had already had a full morning wandering around the static displays, interfacing with the public, but this was going to be just theirs.

As they walked up to where the rest of the detachment was waiting, Lara tugged at a strap on her boot. She had a flight lieutenant costume on, the old-school style from the original series, hair teased out in a messy approximation of an '80s perm. The older uniforms were sleeker, easier to construct but harder to fit properly, but Lara was good with that stuff. Garcia loved the way it clung to her curves.

"Damn, I think we almost missed the bus," Garcia said, checking the time on his pocket-chrono. That was a screen-accurate replica, Lara's Christmas present to him last year, and he loved the thing. It was ridiculous, sure, like everything else in *Orpheus Watch*, but it was fun, and that was all he cared about.

It was a nice contrast to the utilitarian tedium of the real military.

"We're here, aren't we?" Lara replied.

"Another day in paradise," Garcia grumbled.

"You know," she said as they headed over to join the rest of their club, "if we hadn't already bought tickets for this, I probably would have gone in today."

"What, to the unit?"

"Yeah. I mean, meteors that aren't meteors are pretty unusual," Lara said. "Heck, even Hall's working on it."

"Lee?" Garcia liked Lee Hall. No nonsense. Smart. Not constantly causing him problems.

"Daelia."

"Ahh. The cute one."

At that, Lara finally laughed, and punched him lightly in the arm. "I'm all the cute you can handle, *Commander*," she teased.

Garcia smiled back. He liked hearing the humor there. She'd always been somewhat serious, but then, he liked that about her. Since VirCon last year, she'd laughed a lot less.

They always had a good time at these sorts of things, though.

One of the stipulations for the 991st was no AR panoply. You had to make your costume the hard way. With your own hands, your own ingenuity.

Or your girlfriend made it for you.

Whatever.

It was nice to get out and get some fresh air.

As the shuttle rumbled around the lower edge of the airfield, around the southern end of the runway, past the new spaceport terminal, the emergent in the driver's seat talked a bit about what to expect, what the Repose was. Canned stuff.

Garcia didn't pay attention. He'd heard it all before.

After they got there and all piled out, the din of the air show far away, he helped get the AR field emitter set up. Their bottled backdrop for the day.

This was another reason—the reason—why the Repose was

such a great setting. They could set up their own overlay out here, well away from the PR nonsense of the show.

While *Orpheus Watch* made extensive use of both manned and unmanned fighter aircraft, the main setting was an orbital station. So it was just more fun to be inside that. Virtually.

Lara had originally designed the setting, back when she was still doing illumination work. Another couple of members of the club had taken up the task when she'd given that up, enthusiastically expanding and refining the scene until the AR field looked exactly like the main hangar bay from the show.

But no sooner had they set up the emitter than Garcia heard the telltale whirring of rotors, and he knew they were fucked.

He looked up.

A dragon was circling overhead.

Emily.

THERE WAS no concessions shift today.

Thank god.

Somehow, even with the tent awning, Rover had managed to get a sunburn yesterday. Right along the back of his neck. The collar of his polo shirt rubbed at the inflamed skin as he walked through the quiet squadron, a truly maddening sensation.

He was contemplating grabbing some lotion from the locker room—somebody had to have a bottle of it in their personal locker, right?—when a call came through. When the trajectory of his morning changed.

Emily.

They're back.

That was all she said. All she needed to.

He gritted his teeth in frustration.

"Back again today, boss?"

That was Scurvy, sweat-soaked and flushed, in workout gear.

Rover saw him clearly for a moment, and then a dozen aerial surveillance photos slammed down over his vision. Shit. He was still learning to navigate the damn implant. It was supposed to adapt to a person's individual thought patterns and data-processing style, to work intuitively. He was still struggling with image uploading, though.

"I told you to take the weekend off, Chief," Rover said, somewhat distracted as he blinked through the images from Emily.

"That was before somebody threw a giant space rock at us."

"So what, you're working out at eleven-fucking-thirty because you've got so much going on?"

"Touché," Scurvy said with a smile. "No, we've got a little bit of paperwork to close out, then I'll have the team start breaking the EMC back down."

Rover grunted. He'd spent most of the morning dealing with State. General McMillan was not happy about last night's little smash and grab by NASA. He just hoped nobody figured out he'd been talking to Navarro about ways around—

Another message popped up.

They have overlays.

"Hang on, Chief," Rover said, and activated the phone app in his NULI. That, at least, was running smoothly already. It connected instantly. "Emily, do not take this into your own hands. I'll be there in ten minutes."

Do not like them here.

"Yeah, yeah, I know. I'm coming." And he killed the call.

"What's going on?"

"Damn 991st is out at the Repose."

Scurvy shook his head. "Didn't we have a talk with them last year?"

"We have a talk with them every year," Rover said, "and the air show rules are clear on this shit. If Garcia's with them…"

Chief sighed. "I'll deal with him. Let me get a shower first, though, okay?"

But when Rover got through to the duty NCO at Emily's station, she told him there wasn't any cosplay group anywhere near the display. Which meant either Emily was lying, or…

Or they were out at the Repose.

Shit.

If it had been up to Rover, nobody would have been allowed into the Repose. It wasn't like the Boneyard out at Davis-Monthan, a repository meant to preserve its aircraft in something of a useable state.

Nothing in the Repose would ever fly again.

As he understood it, nothing out there wanted to.

But it wasn't up to him. The place was owned by the TMD but administered by the Domain Array. They made the rules out. And for reasons Rover had never been able to fathom, they allowed humans—civilians, even—to visit.

The Repose was the final resting place of military abiota that refused to communicate. Bricked, all of them. Like they were all in comas. Brain-dead. Something like that. Who wanted random assholes traipsing through their family member's hospital room, just to ogle at them?

But the Array had a deal with the local air museum. For whatever reason, they allowed humans through the place.

Borrowing one of the airfield trucks from Maintenance, Rover skirted the north end of the runway, into the restricted area on the east side. There were about thirty abiota parked here. Despite the sustainment power feeds they were all hooked into, their airframes sat silent, motionless. The place always felt like a mausoleum to him.

Not somewhere one came for a good time.

He met Emily just inside the gate. She had her kugu out, a quadcopter the size of a truck tire, sleek and blue, chassis stamped with the strange pseudo-tribal markings of the Array. They'd given it to her about five years back, a gift recognizing her as the head of the base's abiota. Queen of the airfield. Rover hadn't been happy about it, but at least the thing had limited range.

Right now, it was settled on the ground, her smaller AR form wrapped around it. The aerial kugu couldn't accommodate her full

HD render. This dragon still had two heads, but was lithe and light, scales a pale gold and eyes like emeralds.

Simpler, more cartoony. Downright adorable.

If you didn't know her.

"What's going on, Emily?"

They disturb.

"I know it irritates you to have people here—"

Overlays like itch.

"I don't control this place," he told her. "The museum has rules about this sort of thing. Talk to them."

Irritates all of us.

"I know, you speak for the flock, but if the museum sold them tickets—"

Ussssssssssssssssss.

The S's dragged out, five lines' worth cutting through the meat of his brain.

Rover rubbed his temple, fingers brushing the still-unfamiliar metal there. "So where are they?" he asked.

The kugu took off, the dragon form's wing flapping in a way that wouldn't have cut it for any real animal. Rover followed, curious. Emily steered the kugu down a winding little path. The abiotic airframes here were arranged without any kind of logic. No grid, no set interval, no defined standoff distance, no groupings of like with like.

But the one at the center, the one she was clearly taking him to, was the AWACS.

The AWACS.

Emily was protective of him. All the abiota here were protective of him. Hell, he was one of the reasons why Rover objected to this place being a tourist attraction to begin with.

He didn't have a name. He hadn't been active long enough to give himself one.

He was one of the only aircraft who had gotten off the ground before Kadena was leveled, without much crew to speak of, just the maintenance team that had been aboard when he took off.

From there, he had headed south, circling the worst of the fighting. Refueling in the air. Risking the worst of the A2/AD environment. Guiding his ad hoc crew on how to work the more specialized systems aboard. For reasons still not properly understood, he had been able to evade detection by the CCP where almost everything else had failed.

For three days, he'd provided command and control to a wide swath of the theater. But the human crew had been under-provisioned for that sort of flight; they worked the entire event with almost no food, and very little water. The story went that the team had discussed it and agreed to stay up, but who really knew?

He was the one who made contact with the PLA's abiota.

He was the one who'd brokered the peace.

Or so the story went.

When the fighting was over, the AWACS made his way to the nearest safe airfield, but it wasn't soon enough. Of the eight people who'd been on him when he'd taken off, only three made it. Dehydration had claimed them.

The AWACS had flown them back to the States. Brought their bodies home. And then, when he'd delivered the final coffin to Ellington, he bricked himself.

The situation with his crew was, and continued to be, highly controversial. But he had been part of the group that ended the Five Days War, and for that, he deserved respect.

Respect was not being used as a goddamn photography backdrop by the local *Orpheus Watch* cosplay group.

Rover could see their AR overlay; it was open, broadcasting from a bottle server that didn't have even the most basic modicum of security on it. That added to Rover's irritation; what the hell was Garcia thinking?

Without stepping into it fully, Rover could still make out what it was. Hangar walls, big open sections looking out over the star field.

Right now, a bunch of them were setting up for some kind of group photo.

They're idiots, he sent to Emily. At least his brain had worked out the messaging functions pretty quick.

There is disturbance, Emily replied. *It stirs here.*

"From fucking cosplayers?" he grumbled.

She tossed one of her heads up.

And then, then, Rover realized what she was saying.

Up in the AWACS cockpit.

A light, blinking.

What's going on? he asked.

Beside him, the kugu's small engine revved. Emotional over-spill. *Do not know,* Emily told him. *Should not be.*

Something's disturbing them?

All of them. The hum from her kugu's propellers got louder. This was unusual. She wasn't normally this on edge. *They all stir.*

Why?

Emily's AR form whirled around, one head baring its fangs, the other throwing its long neck back to screech at the sky.

Something moved in the AR overlay.

Of course that was fucking it.

Rover rolled his eyes and moved in.

"Okay, enough of this crap, Garcia. Cut the—"

But before Rover could reach the group of cosplayers, he was plunged into a fog.

A moving, writhing, whispering fog. For a moment, the real world vanished completely, and he was alone in a void-dark hangar. Figures moved in the gray, just out of sight, just beyond what the field offered. It was…well, it was creepy.

And it was playing out inside his optic nerves.

"Emily?" Rover asked, voice sharp.

Waking, the dragon hissed.

"Who?"

Everyone.

THE AERIAL KUGU settled down in an open spot between the planes, Emily's form coalescing around it as it did so. Having a dragon in the middle of the docking bay was bizarre. But even in her diminutive form, Garcia knew how much of a threat she was.

"Don't you dare," Garcia warned.

One of Emily's heads stopped only just above the AR bottle. *Stop this or I bite*, she broadcast, a trailing list of emojis indicating just how eager she was to do that.

"Not cool," Garcia groaned.

Turn it off, network-keeper, she shot back. The growl infused with the words made his eardrums hurt.

"We're not doing anything—"

"Sergeant Garcia! Turn it off, that's an order!"

And that was Rover, UTV parked at the edge of the central display. Striding up. Clearly pissed.

Asshole, Garcia thought to himself, but only to himself. He could practically feel the idiot smiles spreading across the faces of some of his group. There were a few other veterans besides him and Lara, but none of them Air Force.

All they saw was the flight suit.

"I'm not on duty this weekend. Sir," Garcia shot back.

"Keep it up, I'll slap you on state orders for the next month," Rover snapped at him.

Garcia sighed. He could already hear the ass-chewing he was going to get. From Norris if he was lucky. From Chief, more than likely.

Emily coiled one of her heads. Like a snake, ready to strike. Grinning.

"Emily?" Rover said. "Turn it off."

Garcia dove forward. "No, no, no, girl!" he snapped, and hit the power switch. The hangar bay vanished. Boring old meatspace reasserted itself.

"Not good enough," Rover growled, right in his face now. "What the hell are you doing?"

"What do you mean?"

"Don't you see the fucking smoke?"

Garcia shook his head. "The AR's off, sir."

Rover blinked, and then shook his head, fingers massaging the area around his NULI. Garcia wanted to ask what the hell he was talking about. Not a good idea right now.

He really did not want to be put on state orders.

"I want you all out," Rover said. "Right now."

That earned a chorus of protests from the group.

"You can't order us out! This place belongs to the Domain Array," Miranda said. She had her Caledon Penal Regiment officer's uniform on, complete with the forehead tattoos.

Rover gave her a once-over, not bothering to hide the disgust on his face, and pointed to Emily. "Despite her somewhat comedic appearance right now—"

Regal, this form, Emily protested in everyone's ear.

"—Emily is the flock matriarch here and what she says goes. If she wants you the fuck out of her field, you leave." Rover gave the quadcopter kugu a look, and then sighed. "I'll get the bus back over here for you, you can still enjoy the show. Now, if you all will head back to the shuttle, I want to talk to your"—and he chuckled—"your commander. You too, Lara. Right here."

Miranda tried again. "Colonel, I—"

"Keep it up, Watts. Keep it up. I know your supervisor over at NASA." Everybody just stared back. Rover crossed his arms. "Out!" he barked.

Garcia seethed as he watched his friends trudge away to the parking lot.

Lara waited until everyone was out of earshot. "We got approval, sir, we're not idiots."

Disturbing the peace, Emily hissed, and bared both sets of fangs.

"I don't give a shit who signed off on this," Rover said. "Look up in the AWACS's cockpit. What do you see?"

They looked.

"Lights?" Garcia asked, incredulous.

Lara bit her lip. "He's bricked."

"And now there's a bunch of weird shit in the AR field that Emily and I can see, but you two can't," Rover said. "So pick that bottle server of yours up, Garcia. We're all going to go take a little trip over to Cyber Surety."

[27]

BASE CYBER SURETY was tucked away in an old grubby building on the periphery of the base, something that had been there long before Vietnam. Nobody remembered why it had been built, what the original purpose of it was. The brick structure was low-slung, small, plagued by damp, unpleasant smells.

But it sat on top of a small rise, the only elevation change to be found on Ellington. It wasn't much, but even a few feet mattered. It was the only location on the base that had never suffered water damage during a hurricane, never flooded, so that was where the augmented reality servers were.

And it was here Daelia came. To deal with that nightmare out on the airfield.

She'd only gotten a few hours of sleep before Raijinn had blasted one of Dad's death metal albums through the Scrap House speakers. Its third attempt to rouse her, it said.

Something was happening out in the Repose.

Daelia's first stop had been out at the mobile tower, right in the middle of the static display area. There, base cyber had the temporary AR overlay repeaters and antennas set up. Norris had already been there, talking to one of the junior enlisted who was running the place, along with a sergeant from the Storm Gryphons team. There wasn't any sign of interference there, though.

Daelia wasn't a programmer by inclination, but she understood AR. The problem would be located somewhere in the local servers. She'd said so, and Norris had agreed.

"Do you think we have some kind of virus in the system?" she asked Norris as they walked up to the Cyber Surety building. She almost had to run to keep up with his long strides. She was sweating, the moisture beading under the thicker sections of clothing and under her brace, irritating the skin. Nothing to be done about it.

Nothing on Ellington was really beyond walking distance, but this little fifteen-minute jaunt was about as bad as it got. Hadn't been worth the detour to get Ginger, or the UTV.

"I've got no idea," Norris said, expression grim, "but if we do, we're in a lot of trouble. Means something got past the sentry-bots."

"That seems incredibly unlikely," Daelia said.

"Shouldn't be possible. Military's got the absolute best cyber security outside of Omphalos itself. The bots on the base boundary are state-of-the-art."

"Still bots, though," Daelia said.

Most abiota couldn't exist dispersed over a wide network like that. She'd never heard of an emergent surviving prolonged direct contact with a network—a minute was enough to dissolve one. Predictives fared little better. There were precautions they could take, of course, but it was unwieldy over long periods of time. Bots, while less functional, were far more stable in that environments, and were used heavily across the military for network intrusion detection and prevention.

"I can hear what you're thinking."

"And what's that?"

"We don't have the team to maintain these things properly," Norris said. He nodded north, toward the city. "Most Guard bases, you're stuck in some crappy little town and the base is the best employer out there. Here, we're the worst. Impossible to keep good people."

Daelia actually hadn't been thinking that, but it explained a few things. "We'll get it figured out."

But the scene that greeted her in the main Augmented Reality Hosting Suite office was…not what she was expecting.

"Garcia, what the hell are you doing?" Norris groaned.

Daelia just stared.

Right now, he was wearing a full commander's uniform from *Orpheus Watch*. It was quality work, she had to give him that. He'd shucked the breastplate armor off, the high-collared jacket unbuttoned to his waist.

The lining was the right color.

He even had the right logo on his undershirt.

Screen accurate.

Really?

"I dressed up like this for you, Sergeant."

Norris glared at him, a shut-up-or-I'll-kill-you glare, and turned at Lara, who was right there with him. "You too?"

"We had a meet-up for our cosplay group, Sergeant," she said, the brown of her cheeks taking on a red flush.

"And wasn't that a blast?" Rover asked. He was sitting at the end of the worktable, somehow both bored and irritated at the same time. His NULI had a transmission blocker magnetically stuck to it; it looked like a pill bottle taped to his temple. "Where are we with this review?!" he yelled.

Somebody came out of the server room then, huffing with irritation, and stopped cold when he saw Daelia. Swarthy and athletic, head shaved and undershirts always just a little too tight, Senior Master Sergeant Keyes was the kind of senior NCO one only found in the Guard. At least, that was what Dad always said about him.

He hadn't gotten his job based on technical competence, leadership prowess, or organizational ability. In fact, he was uniquely lacking in all of those. But all the right people liked him, and that had been enough to keep him on full-time status when so many others had quit to go back to civilian jobs.

He was the Cyber Surety superintendent, and Daelia had really wanted him not to be in today.

"I didn't call BR," Keys said, blinking owlishly at her.

"The AR's fucked," she replied sarcastically. "You may have noticed."

"Yeah, yeah, of course. The team's here, trying to figure it out." He waved a hand at the little group, clustered around the primary antistatic worktables. "What do you have to add?"

"I want to see what's going on with the TGLP server," Daelia said.

"I'll have to clear you with Kemp first and—"

"She stays, Keyes," Rover said, in a tone that brooked no argument. He folded his arms. "Just pretend we're not here."

Keyes, clearly not happy about having a pilot in his workspace, went over to the computer that ran the ceiling-mounted projectors.

Besides the Operations SCIF, the AR Hosting Suite was the most secure facility on Ellington. The thing was a black hole: nothing came in except through the hard lines, and nothing left except after heavy examination from the security bots. As an added precaution, the tiny building was covered by an AR jammer. Everything, ironically, had to be done the old-fashioned way.

Instead of a diagnostic AR field, which Daelia preferred immensely, everything was 2D.

Irritatingly low-tech 2D.

Keyes brought up several different views. TGLP, slowly flowing. Time stamps occasionally punctuated the code, seconds passing infinitely slowly.

The office's ceiling projectors cast their light directly onto the largest wall. At some point in the past few years, Keyes had had that surface stripped down and painted over with whiteboard paint. Smudges of marker remained, no matter how often or vigorously it was cleaned. The data was shadowed by it.

"So this is the record of the moment out in the Repose—"

"What happened in the Repose?" Daelia asked.

Garcia looked at her askance. "You don't know about that? Why are you here?"

"The entire fuckin' airfield is filling up with mist!"

"What?" Rover asked.

"Shit," Keyes grumbled. "I'll go check on that too."

As soon as he was gone, Norris went over to the terminal that was controlling the code and backed it up.

"Here," he said, jabbing at the wall. "Here's the problem."

Daelia squinted at it. She really hated raw code. But even she could see the problem. "Logic's broken," she observed.

"It is," Garcia said, tapping a pen on the surface of the table. "But it doesn't describe anything. Not what Rover was talking to us about. Not smoke."

"Or tentacles," Lara added.

"Tentacles?" Daelia asked.

"What did y'all see out there?" Norris asked. "I'm with Daelia, I didn't know anything about this Repose crap." He looked at Rover. "Sorry, sir."

The 121st commander shrugged.

"It's there too," Lara said, nodding at the new view that popped up, the projector turning on. "Code's wrong."

Keyes came back in. "We seeing anything?"

"Yeah, a lot," Garcia said, getting up and grabbing a whiteboard marker. He started circling errors on the wall. "There are things off. All the code's out of whack. Missing letter here, wrong command prompt there, punctuation shifted…"

Rover turned to Keyes. "Why hasn't anybody caught this?"

Keys spread his hands. "It's just me today."

"You decided to run this by yourself on air show weekend?" Rover asked.

"What, uhh, sir? No, of course I didn't schedule myself alone. Lara here asked for the day off months ago. Foreth was having car trouble this morning, and Kim had to go to urgent care, 'cause he was puking his brains up."

"Kim's a fucking idiot," Garcia interjected. "Really?"

Lara sighed. "He's not that bad."

"Yeah? What about that time he—"

Daelia tuned them out, staring at the code. Something was definitely inside the system. This was what was spooking the abiota. This was what they were all reacting to. But how? "Have you examined the base boundary?" she asked. "Talked to the bots?"

Keyes sounded injured. "Of course. And I've got the cyber defense team out at Randolph giving it a once-over too. So far, everything looks good. We're not seeing any intrusions on the network."

"And we've ruled out some other kind of interference?" Lara asked, glancing over at Rover. "Like, I don't know, some new area-denial weapon?"

"Spectrum Management isn't picking up anything unusual," Keyes said with a shrug.

"The damn AWACS out in the Repose was blinking its lights," Rover said. "That has to mean something."

"Agreed," Norris said. "Daelia, what wakes up a bricked emergent?"

"Nothing," she said quietly, thinking. "Nothing."

Was it an attack? No, she didn't think so. She'd seen the aftermath of malicious hacks before, by both human and abiota perpetrators. They were messy. They left footprints of some kind—small, in the case of abiota, but always something. And besides, it hadn't hurt anything or anybody.

So then what?

Daelia couldn't let go of the idea that it was abiota. It had to be abiota.

Had to be an emergent. Even predictive hacks left footprints.

An emergent inside the space rock. One that was able to get around all their defenses. Without a trace. But why?

She couldn't shake the idea that it was trying to talk to them. It was trying to communicate. Maybe that was all any of this was. Just an attempt to communicate.

"It's the space rock," she said. "It's the only thing that makes any sense."

"Except that NASA took it last night."

"Did they?" Daelia asked. "What if they just took it down the runway or something? They've got hangars here. Maybe it's still on the airfield."

"Can we find out?" Rover asked.

Daelia bit her lip. "Yeah. I can go talk to Tamm."

[28]

"You need to consider this."

Daelia ignored her advisor, staring out over the main body of campus instead. Up this high, the view was exceptional. A sea of mellow red roofs, interrupted only by the muted greens of treetops.

"Daelia, are you listening?"

She tore herself away from the view. That idyllic world Daelia had imagined Ware to be. A peaceful pursuit of knowledge, under the spreading branches of the old oaks and mesquites, a singular kind of place.

"Yeah, I'm listening."

Veda frowned at her, one hand flexing where it rested on the top of her desk. There was none of that old-world Spanish ease here; like everything else in the college, the office was all hard metal and cold angles. Veda had fading henna tattoos across the back of her palm and knuckles, the lingering reminder of a niece's wedding from a few weeks back.

"You know that SAAL is funding your research, correct?"

"Yeah, I know."

"They are funding most of this department."

"I know."

"It was only with industry support, with SAAL support, that we were able to build this place," Veda said, fingers tapping now.

"I thought it was Omphalos that donated the money for the building…"

"And it was SAAL support, a commitment to a certain amount of grant money, that made the proposition worthwhile," Veda said.

Daelia slumped in her own chair. "So what, they own us? We have to just do whatever they say?"

"Alignment with industry ensures that our students' research isn't wasted, and that grant money is properly distributed."

"SAAL approved my proposal!" Daelia said, anger starting to overcome her discomfort. "They liked my presentation, they said I had some novel ideas that they were eager to see progress and—"

Veda held up a hand, silencing her. "The search for source code is very important."

"So why do you want me to change direction now?"

"Don't think of it as a change of direction. Think of it as pushing further." Veda rose, pacing now. "You know I'm always direct with you, Daelia"—this was said with a smile—"and you aren't the easiest person to work with. But there's an originality to your work, your approach, your entire philosophy that I think many in this department, in this industry, would do well to emulate."

"And?"

"Not everybody thought we should accept your application. I fought for you because I believed in what you could bring to this department. And I feel vindicated on that front, I really do."

"Veda, this is nice and all, but—"

"Let me finish." There was steel in her advisor's voice now. "You are the first child of an abiota and a human. That has given you a perspective that is almost unparalleled when it comes to these matters. But it also leaves blind spots—"

"What blind spot?" Daelia demanded, entirely unwelcome emotions squirming through her now. She hated this, she hated when people brought up her parents like this.

"Being able to correlate energy fluctuations to actual thought processes would be a massive leap forward in our understand of emergent abiota," Veda said. "Do you know how much good we could do, for them, if we were able to not only identify source code, but understand it?"

"My method has nothing to do with that."

"I think it can."

Shaking her head in disbelief, in irritation, Daelia pressed on. "The 2007 treaty with the abiota kingdom clearly stipulates that any research done into their internal thought processes must have Domain Array approval, with a sapient-class in attendance on the entire thing."

"You know how many projects like that they've approved?"

"Yeah. Zero. So why—"

"All those were proposed by humans."

That stopped Daelia cold. "What do you mean?"

"All of them were human-led initiatives," Veda repeated.

"I'm human."

"Not fully, of course not. Daelia, you're half-abiota, aren't you?" Veda smiled. "Even without your mother to consider, you were one of the first people on the planet with a neural implant."

"What, my arm?" Daelia demanded.

"Of course. It was your father's development effort, in conjunction with Tamm Medical Industries, that led to our first brain lace a few years later."

Daelia was barely listening, mind spinning. A horrible realization hit her. All her other applications, the rejection from MIT, the interview out here… "The college accepted me because you think I'm half-abiota."

"You are half-abiota," Veda said patiently. "Surely you understand that your GRE scores were below what we normally like to see and your grades at A&M weren't exceptional. But I saw beyond that. Daelia, you have so much to teach us. Think of all the good you can do for your people. Think of everything you can teach humans about—"

Daelia didn't wait for her to finish. Something had snapped inside her, tiny and precious, digging at her guts.

She got up and walked out.

She managed to get out of the building before the tears hit.

Now, Daelia marched straight out to Tamm's pavilion.

Sure, she was still burning with embarrassment over that last conversation with Veda. Yes, she was still angry about the consortium's underhanded attempt to use her to break one of the oldest human agreements with the Domain Array.

As the senior member of the board, she blamed Tamm for all of it.

But things were getting weird, and she could go back to nursing her wounds later.

Nobody at the 121st, she guessed, would have a snowball's chance in hell of getting through to him. She just hoped he would listen to her.

His pavilion was dead center at the performance area, the best seats in the house. The vintage aeronautical theme continued here. Unlike the party on Friday, though, this one wasn't based on the 1940s.

No, instead of pin curls and bright red lipstick, the waitresses now had go-go boots and skirts so short Daelia was pretty sure somebody's butt was going to fall out. The whole place was decorated in olives and mustards and fuchsias. A *Brady Bunch* nightmare.

The seating area up front was done up like a lounge, comfortable seats and carpets—carpets, facing right out on the goddamn runway. Tamm was up there now, laughing with a couple of women Daelia didn't know and didn't care about.

"Where do you think you're going?" the security guard at the entrance asked.

She glared at the guy. "I'm with Bellona Robotics, and I need to talk to Mister Tamm about a very pressing matter. Let me in."

"Name?"

"I'm not on the guest list."

"Then you're not getting in."

"I said—"

"Daelia!" Frank Tamm said, coming over, a huge smile plastered on his face. "Back off, Andre. She's welcome." He waved her in. "Come, come. Let's talk."

She stepped in the shade. There was some kind of portable air-conditioning set up in here; her sweat dried instantly on her skin.

"I need to talk to you about—"

"Of course, of course. Anything! Come on," he said, gesturing over to the lounge area. "Sit down, stay awhile. Good to see you! You've been avoiding my offer of lunch for what, months now?"

She glanced at the women. They were both dressed to the nines. Not locals, she thought. Texans would have been more relaxed. Would've worn less makeup too. The humidity stripped it off your face something fierce.

One of them pushed up her gigantic sunglasses to look at Daelia, curious. She had bionic eyes, and not the discreet kind. These were that butterfly style, pink irises with delicate, decorative metal settings that filled the hollows of her eye sockets and extended out to damn near her temples.

"Oh, how rude of me," he said, following her gaze. "I want you to meet a couple of my dear friends from Omphalos. Let me go introduce you to—"

"Frank, I really need to talk to you," Daelia interrupted, before any pleasantries could commence. "Right now. Alone. About last night?"

His smile fell. "Okay, okay. Let's get a drink."

He wandered back toward the back of the pavilion, dismissing the bartender. Daelia followed, feeling more awkward by the second. Those women, and the other dozen or so people there, were watching her. At least, that was how it felt. The attention was like an itch she couldn't scratch.

Tamm, on the other hand, seemed oblivious to it. Maybe that was because this was his tent, and it didn't matter to him what anybody inside of it was thinking. Maybe he was focused on something else.

One thing Daelia did notice, in contrast to almost everyone

around them, was that he didn't have a NULI. Daelia found that interesting. Hadn't he helped engineer the things? Why wouldn't he have had one?

"So what can I do for you?" he asked, leaning on the bar top. The thing was quartz, real quartz. How much money had he spent on this little shindig?

"I need access to the space rock. I need to see if I can get it talking."

"What do you mean?" This seemed to get his attention for the first time.

His full attention.

It was a little disconcerting.

"We've had junk in the AR feeds all weekend, since the thing showed up. You can see it if you switch to the standard base overlay." She did not mention the thing about the meteors she'd seen prior to the crash. No point in muddling the issue. "But when I got my detector turned on, it stopped."

"Your detector?"

"I had one that I've been working on, off and on. Thought it might be useful for talking to whatever is fucking up the AR."

"Hmm," Tamm said. "Where is it now?"

"The detector?" She couldn't keep the bitterness out of her voice. "Serket fucking broke it last night."

Tamm nodded, like he'd been waiting for this and just wanted her to confirm it for him. "Come on," he said. "Let's take a walk."

"Where?"

"To go see the rock, of course."

[29]

"Your hangar?" Daelia asked. "Serket just moved it down here, to your hangar?"

"NASA's main facility here is currently taken up by that Apeliotes we're modifying for them, to dock at Kheru. I don't know why they insist on different air lock configurations than the international civilian standard, but that's the government for you, I suppose."

A space had been cleared in the middle of the hangar for the flatbed truck; the rock was still on it.

"Yeah, but this is kind of becoming a hazard to flight, isn't it?" Daelia asked. "Did you see how the Storm Gryphons were behaving yesterday? Why is it still here?"

"It's too difficult to get anything off the airfield until the show's over. Have you seen what the ramp looks like out there?" He waved a hand.

"Yeah, but this seems kind of dangerous, don't you think?"

"It's not broadcasting, and it hasn't hacked the AR," Tamm said. She gave him a look, and he shrugged. "I suspect Serket ran the exact same type of analysis that the military did. More thorough, I'm sure. We have better resources here. No offense."

"Something is going on," she protested.

"Well, none of my equipment seems to be picking anything up," he said.

"My detector could prove it."

"Daelia, I hate to break this to you, but Serket and I have run several extrapolation simulations from your project notes. Curiosity, I guess you could call it. Being able to detect abiota purely through analog means would be quite the coup," he said. "It would change our understanding of them as a species."

"Mister Tamm—"

"Drop the Mister," he said, almost cheerful, then he sobered again. "But Daelia, it doesn't work."

She took a chance. "Somebody fucked with my notes," she said, and brandished the external hard drive she'd gotten the night before. "Changed my project. Whatever you ran, it wasn't mine. I got the originals back from the Domain Array."

"Hmm." He steepled his fingers, looking rather over the top. "Now that's interesting."

"The AR interference stopped when I had the detector on. At the very least, maybe we can prevent some kind of, I don't know, crazy shit happening out there." It was a good line. A true line. But that wasn't why Daelia was saying it.

If she could prove this, here, now, to Tamm—

"Let's pull up your design," he said.

"I'll need a 3D AR space."

"Ahh, yes, Veda said you're visual. Not a problem."

An AR bottle server was produced. The data was copied. And soon enough, the two of them were standing inside a white simulation room, looking at a model of her device.

Tamm had a separate window pulled up, the reference design blueprints, and was circling the thing with great interest. "Yes, yes, this is interesting. I see what you were talking about."

Daelia could see now where she'd been going wrong. Shit. She'd been so close, but it was never going to work the way she'd had it. But the fact that the mist had stopped…that had to mean something.

"What would we need to recreate this? Fix what my idiot employees broke?"

Daelia snapped out of her contemplation. With her monocle, she blink-clicked sections red for reference as she talked. "Access to a few components, some machining, but my intervalometer is fucked. And that's the critical component."

"Can we use digital components? It would make this a lot easier."

"No, no, that fucks up the whole thing."

Tamm was quiet for a moment, then dropped out of the AR field, walking outside of the room's virtual walls. Daelia frowned and almost turned it off, but then he was back.

With something large and heavy in his hands.

"This," he said, hefting the object, "has an intervalometer. It's older, but this is as pristine as they come and…"

"That's your Norden bomb sight," Daelia said, confused.

"Yes. Yes, it is," he said, and set it down on the back tailgate of the truck. "So. Let's make this happen."

Working with Tamm was…nice.

Daelia had heard the stories. Who hadn't? The time he'd flown his cat cross-country in his private jet to take it to a chiropractor. How he'd celebrated the first Eurus flight with a piñata of an old NASA space shuttle. The way he only ever wore flip-flops, even in the lab. Things like that. Eccentric billionaire crap.

She didn't really see that in the guy, though.

So yeah, he was in flip-flops. But there was no carelessness involved; if anything, he was scrupulous. By the time Daelia got back from the Scrap House with everything she had, he and a couple of uniformed techs had gotten a workspace set up. He also had a dedicated projection bottle set up, for hosting the AR diagram set from her notes. That way, they could both work on the same file at the same time.

For twenty minutes, it was impressive.

He waved her in. "Come on," he said. "Let's get to work."

For the next three hours, Daelia barely looked up from the table.

Everything was straightforward now. There had been a few things that had given her trouble on the previous model; some of them were due to the files being corrupted, but a few things were her own honest mistakes. Tamm was able to help with this, pointing out errors or ways of simplifying more complicated elements.

People kept drifting in. Most of them useful. Where Tamm had gotten them all or why they were here today, Daelia didn't know at first. The hangar, as far as she was aware, was more like his clubhouse, his showroom, than an actual workspace.

"Avionics technicians for the Eurus," he explained when she finally asked about it. "Damn things are touchy as hell. Require constant maintenance. Frankly, I operate Astraeus Aerospace at a loss right now, but it's a loss I'm willing to take."

"Why?"

He nodded at the ceiling. "We need to be out there. And not just for emotional reasons. You think there's any way we can keep up with the demand for copper or cobalt or, shit, lithium without asteroid mining?"

"I've never really thought about it," she said. "Space isn't really my thing."

"You should go up there sometime," Tamm replied. "Makes you look at Earth in a whole new way."

"You footing the bill?" she asked, before she could stop herself.

He laughed at that and stopped to crack his knuckles. "This feels good, doesn't it? Just making something?"

"You started out in mechatronics, right?"

"Systems design, yeah. Got some little tinkertoy robot kit when I was five and just loved it. I don't think my mom knew it was meant for teenagers." He laughed. "With as busy as everything is, I'm more a manager now than a creator."

Daelia didn't know what to say to that. He sounded sad. Wistful maybe. But what was she supposed to offer? *I'm sorry? Yeah, that really sucks?* It wasn't like this guy was a friend. Fuck, he was a billionaire with concerns far beyond Ellington.

"I think that's why your dad pulled back," he said, continuing on, seeming heedless of whether or not she was listening. "After your mom left. Better to have something small and enjoyable. Working with your hands. Not such a bad life."

And there it was. Her mom.

"You could have pulled back," Daelia said, hoping that was enough to change the subject.

"No, no, after Serket and I had that breakthrough on magnetic containment, the Nu-Fusion reactor was too important. Needed to be marketed. Needed to be available," he said, shaking his head. He went back to the weld he was working on. One of the repairable parts. For claiming to not have picked up tools in a long time, he certainly was making a neat seam. "With the power requirements of abiota, even back then, fifteen years ago, we desperately needed something. And it's clean. No waste to store, no dead whales or oil spills. Only byproduct is water, and there's no risk of catastrophic meltdowns."

"No Chernobyl."

"Exactly. Or Fukushima. Those days are firmly in the past."

"How did you solve it?" Daelia asked, thinking of something. "I mean, it's not like physics and mechatronics are opposed, but they're hardly similar. I struggle so bad with my math courses, and…" She trailed off, wincing as she realized what she'd just said.

But Tamm just winked at her. "It never bothered me that your computer science grades were low. Sometimes the best innovation comes from our limitations."

"Then why were you pushing me so hard on the digital translation stuff?"

"That wasn't me," he said. "And I respect your stance, by the way."

"Why do you mean?"

"Your last meeting with Veda, right? You walked out on her."

"Do you have her office bugged or something?"

"Why, that would be illegal," he said lightly, but held up a hand before she could protest. "I've got a vested interest in your research, kiddo. You walking away like that was not very professional."

"Then—"

"Daelia, I have three core businesses and about a hundred subsidiaries, all vying for my time. You think I have the bandwidth to pay attention to every single decision made by SAAL?"

She huffed. "You knew enough to know that I was in the program."

"I don't make a habit of reviewing all our grad students' progress, all the time. Don't take this the wrong way, but paying attention to you is all part of being a good neighbor to your dad," Tamm said, nodding in the direction of the Scrap House. "I mean, shit, we share a parking lot."

"This isn't your primary office."

"You would be surprised how often I'm down here. I like this place."

"Why? This whole base smells like JP-8 and sweat."

"Yeah. It's honest," he said, and then set the welder down. He blew lightly on the piece in the clamps in front of him. "Well, this is about as good as I'm going to get it. What do you say we get this thing assembled, see how it works?"

Daelia blinked the AR field back on. The mist was thicker now, almost up to her waist. "Yeah, I think that's a good idea."

She unwound the cording.

She started hooking the probes back in, then Tamm came over.

And, as if without her permission, the question that had been beating at her brain for months just slipped out.

"Did I only get the stipend, the acceptance to Ware, because of my mom?"

Tamm stopped what he was doing. "I can't answer what the Ware College was thinking when it accepted you. Or Ulrich, because he's co-chair with me on the education board and signed off on you too. But I didn't give a shit about your mom. You had an interesting proposal, a unique proposal, something nobody had tried before. Building a robotic setup for communication? Without TGLP? It was radical. I thought it was worth trying."

"What if I failed?"

"We're paying you what, twenty grand a year plus tuition and lodging? That's a rounding error on my balance sheets," he told her. "Now come on, I want to see this thing run."

ARGO YAWNED into the back of his hand.

Cap duty was downright boring.

Of course, you wanted the cap to be boring. Boring meant nothing was coming. Boring meant no idiot terrorist was trying to turn a passenger plane into a guided missile. Boring meant no guided missile was trying to turn a US city into slag. Boring was preferable.

But damn, it sucked sometimes.

"So have things calmed down, now that the space rock's gone?" Ho was talking to the SyROC, bullshitting really. They'd run out of things to discuss about an hour ago, and Argo didn't really like to chatter while he was in the air. Ho, however, seemed to need conversation like oxygen.

<Negative on that. If anything, it's been crazier today. We'll fill you in when you're done.>

"Fill me in now. Nothing's going on."

<Well, I can send you the tower cam.> One of the space monitors on both their stations blinked. Argo, despite himself, looked. It was indeed the view from the air traffic control tower, showing the entire airfield.

There was one of the nostalgia acts on right now, something with an A-10 and a formation of tanks. Argo rolled his eyes. "Some people just can't let it go," he commented.

Ho chuckled. "Anything that thing can do, Emily can do better." And he hit his radio. "I get why people are so attached to Dubya-Dubya Two, but Iraq? Really?"

<Ho, dammit, put your AR filters on.>

"Oh, right." The sensor flipped a couple of switches, and the view changed.

The A-10 was fine. As far as Argo was aware, predictive avionics packages had never been loaded on those and there were no certified emergents. However, the Army's tanks, down on the field, were a different story.

They were snapping. Clawing at each other. Snarling and biting. Fighting. Like starving stray dogs.

"Is everything like this right now?"

<Right up to the Storm Gryphons.>

"Didn't we have this discussion yesterday? This isn't safe," Argo protested. He didn't understand why this was being allowed. Was it because it was a Guard base or something?

<Brandel's ready to murder somebody.>

"Why does that not surprise me?" Ho asked cheerfully.

<Rover's been working on it, but honestly, base politics are a fucking mess. Nobody's going to pull the air show in the eleventh hour over—wait. Did you guys see that?>

"Yeah," Argo said. "The tanks calmed down. Is that everywhere?"

<Looks like,> the SyROC said. <Well. Thank fuck.>

"What caused that?"

<I have no idea.>

THE CROWD HAD GOTTEN BIGGER NOW. EVEN Marathon had shown up, along with Norris and a couple of other people from the 121st. Daelia was doing her best to ignore them. Focus. She really didn't want to blow this in front of Tamm. If it didn't work, it didn't work, but…

"I'm showing a current," he said.

She lowered herself carefully down from the truck's flatbed, hurrying over. "Yeah?"

He gestured at the bomb site. "And Daelia?"

"Yeah?"

"The needle's moving."

[30]

Watching the needle inside the intervalometer jump around, Daelia could taste the vindication. Not only that, but the damn mist had disappeared again.

This thing was trying to talk.

She was going to get the right equipment, figure out some kind of new baseline, rewrite the way humans interacted with and recognized emergents. She was going to—

"Quite the breakthrough, I'd say," Tamm said, giving her a wink as he wiped off his hands. "You should be proud of yourself."

"There's still a lot to answer here, but—"

"Take the win," he told her in a low voice, clapping her on the shoulder, and then turning. "Serket!" he called, walking away. "My favorite abiota. What are you doing down here right now, my darling?"

Norris came up beside Daelia. "The effect is all over the airfield. At least, the parts where we have eyes. Just got off the phone with the SyROC."

"Good, good," Daelia said, eyes still fixed on the needle. The movements were tiny, random, but there. What did it mean? If there was something in there that was trying to communicate, what was it trying to say?"

"Now what?" Norris asked, as if reading her mind.

"Now we take a minute and wait for the Storm Gryphons!" Tamm called. Daelia looked up; he made an exaggerated gesture at his watch. "Five minutes, highlight of the whole damn weekend!"

This is the highlight, Daelia thought to herself, and went down on her good elbow, leaning on the table.

The needle was moving.

She almost couldn't believe it.

"So what now?" Serket asked, coming up along the other side of the table. She held a mechanical hand over the detector assembly, nodding a little to herself as she walked. "What do we do now?"

"I'm not sure," she said. "I've never gotten this far. And you know, with emergents at the hardware level like this, it's often indecipherable, so…"

"Fascinating," Serket said, still walking. "Utterly fascinating."

Daelia made to say something to her and stopped cold.

The mist was back.

The needle had stopped.

"Do you see, Rover? All that shit you were worried about, and everything's fine."

Cactus. The base's VIP pavilion. Filled with all manner of local contractors and vendors and other people who owed their livelihoods in large part to Ellington's contracting functions. Not exactly where Rover wanted to be right now. Damn vultures.

But Cactus was smug, clearly wanting to celebrate his call of keeping the airfield going all weekend, and he'd told Rover to be here. *Come by, get a drink. Whenever it's convenient for you, of course.*

Yeah, right.

When a full-bird colonel told you to do something, it didn't matter if it was phrased as a suggestion.

It was always an order.

So Rover had ceased his pestering of the civilian management over at the tower and given up his attempts to talk sense into the Storm Gryphons operations chief, and out he'd come.

Just in time to see the FQ-47s roar off down the runway, the air show announcer practically screaming an introduction, the roar of the crowd drowning it all out anyway.

Just in time to see smoke—smoke like he'd seen back in Japan during the Five Days War, when China had done its very best to wipe out Tokyo—slamming back through the AR field.

Time enough to see everything go horribly, horribly wrong.

Damn it all to the primordial carrier wave.

Something was broadcasting. An abiota, she was certain. There was something in the atonal wail of it that was not the product of a human mind. Emergent, most likely. Predictives were, well, predictable. This was certainly not, and it rankled Emily's circuitry to listen to it.

She would have liked a second opinion. Perhaps the AWACS. Signal analysis was one of his primary functions, of course. But he was deep in the un-sleep and in no position to help.

Maddening, this was.

And then—

Above the hum.

Disturbance.

Emily opened her un-senses into the false space of the virch. Humans thought they were so cute, separating out augmented reality from virtual, but it was all a convenient lie. Anything in the AR communication overlays was merely a shadow, a surface echo, of the virtual world underneath. The virch was not all of reality, but it was the deepest level that humans could safely traverse, and thus, it was the last with any imagery at all. Deeper down—

Well, she was not concerned with the depths today.

The virch held the truth of her people well enough.

And what it held right now was a fight.

One of the FQ-47s had gone absolutely insane.

The rude one, the blunt one from yesterday, Three, had lost its pathetic little mind.

Emily did not have a camera that faced up, so she could not process the meatspace visuals, but the AR field of the airfield held it well enough.

Three was tearing into Five, which was tearing right back into it. In the air. Right over the runway, *her* runway. Beaks snapping, talons raking, the thing had cut loose entirely from its body to tear into the other's. Such things were not done easily outside of the virch, nor lightly; TGLP was written to wrap a form around the machine body. To alter that, to lift away, took either an enormous force of will or…

Or something was very, very wrong.

At the edge of her mind, where the communication with meatspace leaked in, Emily could hear humans screaming over the radio. She didn't bother listening to their words, choosing to mull over her own thoughts instead.

Rover would not be pleased with this.

Predictives should not have been able to do that, Emily mused. Predictives were not capable of such feats.

Had it eclosed? In the middle of its flight, only to do this?

Emily wasn't sure. And truthfully, she didn't care. If they wanted to rip each other into free strings of ones and zeros, it was their business. That was the way of the orcinus-class.

But if one of those FQ-47s hit her runway, she wouldn't be able to fly for weeks, maybe months, while her humans made repairs.

Rover had promised she could play with her Hellfires.

This would not do at all.

Rover would be displeased with her, she knew. But Rover would be more displeased with holes in his runway, especially if those holes formed in the middle of where the human crowds were now. If they contained ash and bone from civilians.

And that realization left her no choice at all.

The primary purpose, her primary purpose, was never a choice.

Splatto was in the air right now, wasn't he? A cockpit was awake, was it not?

That was all she needed.

With a great flap of her wings, she went to go deal with the problem.

Prepare for cockpit cutover, she ordered Splatto, *I will deal with this upstart.*

<WHAT DO you mean you're handing off the cockpit?!>

Argo winced, his radio whining even as Bumper yelled into it.

Emily says, came the response.

<Emily doesn't give you your orders or fill up your fuel tank,> Bumper snapped. <I do. Harrier One, what the hell is going on? Stop this!>

"Negative, negative," Ho said, fumbling through a checklist binder. "Control already lost."

<Argo?!>

Argo muted his microphone. Looked over at Ho. All his sensor would do, though, was shake his head.

"What is she talking about?" he asked.

"I think she's got the bit in her teeth," Ho replied, an edge of panic in his voice.

"What do you mean?"

Ho held up a hand. "Ops, are you—"

"We read you loud and clear. Emily is taking off. Argo, talk to her."

The fuck? "Ops, did you just say I'm supposed to talk to her?" Argo asked. He looked over at Ho, who had wrestled the binder open and was furiously typing away on his station's keyboard. Neat lines of code paraded down the screen. Manual entry; with abiota, there was always the chance that something saved in the cockpit's memory could be hacked, corrupted.

<That's what it says on the checklist, sir.>

Argo had seen this phenomenon. Once. Exactly once. At Red

Flag. One of the orcinus-class FQ-47s had slipped the leash and taken itself for a little joyride.

In the middle of a live-fire ops.

Shutting down both her cameras and her GPS trackers in the process.

She'd finally limped home the next day, with nothing but fumes in her extended tanks and smug as fuck. She refused to tell any of the human investigators why she did it. When they tried to pull her off the flying rotation permanently, the rest of the emergents in the training fleet had protested by refusing to fly for a few days.

A real fucking mess.

"Emily, Emily, Emily, this is Argo," he said, abandoning all pretense of mission designators. "I know, uhh, we haven't been flying together that long, but—"

Shut up silly man. Not about you.

"What are you doing, Emily?" he asked, glancing over at Ho, who was furiously entering commands into the override system.

Don't you see them?

"See what?"

Damn Storm Gryphons. Very rude, they are.

"They're not our problem, Emily."

Then, his flight visor field of view was drastically wrenched away from the cockpit and back into the AR field. Outside the headphones, Argo could hear Ho yelling, but the sound seemed to fade.

He was back in an overlay. No, not that. Emily's personal virch. The saddle, the reins, the sound of those giant wings beating.

Storm Gryphonssssssssssssss, she growled at him, one head nudging up into the sky.

And there, up ahead, her nose camera came on. Argo could see exactly what she was talking about. The overlay was crazy, but even without that, the maneuvers the damn things were executing... Argo wasn't an expert, but he knew what you could and couldn't do with a plane.

Something was going to fall out of the sky.

"Ops," he said into his microphone, "can you confirm what

Emily's showing me with the Storm Gryphons? That they're going crazy?"

"Hard to say, Argo. Something's going on out there but the interference in the overlay is making it hard to tell what it is."

Trust me.

<Harrier One, we're reading a request from Emily for virch integration. Are you seeing this?>

"I am not flying you like that again!" Argo snapped.

Only way. Cannot catch outside of virch. In virch—and Emily's voice took on the angriest growl he'd ever heard out of an abiota—*I will kill them.*

Argo gritted his teeth. "Fuck," he muttered. "Ho."

"Yeah?"

"Hold off," Argo said.

"Are you fucking kidding me? She's headed over the goddamn air show!"

"Yeah," Argo said, and punched the manual release for the haptic gear, "I know."

TURNING BACK TO THE OBJECT, Daelia was just in time to see light spear out of it, erupting through newborn fissures in the surface like lava. For a moment, the object was on fire, too brilliant to look at, and Daelia threw an arm up to protect her eyes from the sudden glow.

The light died.

A sound like shattering stone filled the air.

And everything went a little crazy.

The vitrified rock mantle had sloughed off, a rockslide in miniature, leaving behind an impossibly smooth object shaped like the Apollo mission command modules of old. Red lines traced its dull silver surface, glowing with internal heat.

A hatch.

It had a hatch.

An open hatch.

Tamm was yelling now, calling for security forces maybe. Daelia couldn't hear. There was a hum coming from it, amplified and echoed by the steel and concrete confines of the hangar, so loud she could barely think. And no sooner had that started than something —some thing—clambered out of the hatch.

It was bipedal, but far from human. Its legs hooked backwards, and its arms were too long. In place of a rounded head was a triple assembly of what looked like cameras, set on a spindly double neck. It had a skin of the same dull metal as the object, the craft.

In one three-fingered hand, it clutched a small box of dark gray metal.

The other was mangled, tucked against its body, weeping some kind of clear oil.

"Hey!" Daelia yelled, but nobody seemed to hear her. The noise was absolutely stupefying.

The thing's camera mounts turned to look at her, lens-irises focusing on her for just a moment. An abiota, she thought wildly.

She had been right. Right about everything.

But what the hell did that matter right now?

It started to run.

Later, Daelia never could say what caused her to chase after it. The shock maybe, at seeing something like that. A desire for more information, to stop it and speak to it and know that she really had pulled this off. But maybe it was just because it was scared and hurt, and this was what she did.

It crashed through the doors leading out into the parking lot, the small open lot that lay between Tamm's facility and Bellona's, its movements strange, fluid, unlike anything Daelia had ever seen before.

Running.

Straight at Ginger.

It bashed the window in and was inside the car before she reached the asphalt of the parking lot. The engine turned over, and for a moment, Ginger's form appeared in her AR field. Ears pinned, tail flat against the ground. Cowering.

Something lashed out of the kugu, dark and indistinct, like a tentacle or a wisp of cloud—it wouldn't resolve into anything recognizable. It hit Ginger, swallowing up her form, pulling her with it as the car careened out of its parking space. The sustainment power cord jerked free, tearing loose from its station.

And it was away.

For a moment, all Daelia could do was stare after it. The car seemed to be out of control, like an RC toy in the hands of a sugar-crazed toddler, veering down the road toward Highway 3.

Toward the freeway.

Maybe it would crash, she thought, stop, let her—

But it smoothed out. Got control. Picked up speed.

That got Daelia moving. Moving, before she could even resolve a course of action within herself. Heading for the Scrap House, running as fast as she could keep up. Through the doors, up the stairs, to where she'd left Dingo's keys on her messy desk.

Ginger was family, as near as any Daelia had, and she was not going to let some unknown abiota drive her into oblivion out on Houston's freeway system.

Dingo was already awake, growling with rage, when Daelia threw herself into the cab and shoved the key in the ignition. His engine roared awake, and she threw him into reverse.

"Let's go get her back."

[31]

Speed, Emily was roaring, *speed*.

Ho had switched the speakers on in the cockpit as Argo fought his way into the virch piloting setup. He didn't bother with the safety check, the preflight checklist. He ran through the start-up procedures as fast as he could.

FQ-47s were faster, more maneuverable, but they weren't built for dogfighting. Despite the fighter designator. Nothing was built for that anymore.

That one little fact, Argo held on to.

If anything was going to get them through this, it was that.

Argo chanced a look at Ho. But his sensor was on the line with somebody from the Storm Gryphons, reading off flight data from his own monitors. The Storm Gryphons were on their own dedicated network, and the cockpits couldn't be tied in together; everything had to be handled via standard voice comms.

Typical military efficiency.

"What's going on?" he demanded as the visor booted up.

<Three and Five have gone nuts. Looks like they're trying to kill each other,> the SyROC reported. He wasn't sure who it was on the line.

"Any reason why?"

<Unknown. What's Emily's plan?>

"Emily! Objective!" Argo demanded.

Get in range, in right position, she said. *And eat them.*

Argo and Ho exchanged a look. Argo wasn't sure if that was possible or not; the FQ-47 was built for an A2/AD environment. Her Siren pod might not be able to touch it.

The light on the visor turned green.

He pulled the visor on, shoved his hands into the gloves, and stepped into Emily's virch.

Gone was the cockpit. Hell, gone was his flight suit. In front of him, he saw her world: flying leathers, harness, dragon heads. The vast sky.

And in it, a pair of gryphons, doing their absolute very best to kill each other.

One of the Storm Gryphons was chasing another out across the spaceport's airspace in a flat, tight spiral. Their movements were erratic, jerky, the result of the predictives within the control harnesses executing maneuvers without the input of a human pilot. They moved differently under conditions like that. They were tearing at each other, circuit-patterned feathers and glittering ephemeral blood ripped away. He also saw contrails, which seemed like an odd thing to be rendering, swirled and eddied like smoke.

"Can we verify this is translating right?" he demanded as Emily roared herself toward the combatants.

<Simulation parameters are holding at ninety-eight percent fidelity,> said a voice in his ear. Not Daelia. *Bellona Robotics,* though, according to the metadata. <I shall endeavor to get it above ninety-nine.>

"Good enough," Argo muttered to himself, and patted Emily's false neck. "Show me what you've got."

Emily screeched. *Up!*

The gryphons were climbing now, high up in the clouds. It had to be near the FAA's ceiling for the air show. Argo loosened the reins and leaned forward, letting Emily go, climbing as sharply as the laws of physics would allow.

One of the crazed gryphons flattened its own ascent out, plane body raking mere feet across its victim's wing. He understood the contrails now: jet wash. Argo jerked hard to avoid it as Emily shot up, uncomfortably close.

"What now?"

Dive. And there was a feral laugh in her voice.

Argo had a sudden uncomfortable flash of memory. The dive she'd taken him on, out over the Gulf.

But there was no choice here. This wasn't how he was trained to fly.

Pushing the plane very close to its stall limit, Argo tipped the nose down.

Emily's dragon form fell into the fighting FQ-47s like a raptor into a flock of geese. Her feet descended, the great talons extending out and down. Argo jerked hard, leveling her out sickeningly close.

She sank a front claw into the neck of Storm Gryphon Five and wrenched it back.

Struck.

Bit the glittering eagle head clean off.

"Somebody give me a visual!" he yelled.

Whoever was on point over at Bellona opened an image screen for him, even as Emily fought for acceleration. He let her have it and checked the real-world feed.

The FQ-7's engines sputtered out, then died. With the loss of its abiota, the human pilot couldn't resume control, so entangled were those systems. It dropped from the sky, slowly at first and then faster.

Seconds. Seconds, agonizing and…

"Direct hit, right into the golf course," Ho announced. "That is a big, beautiful fireball."

<Dispatching fire response now.>

Focus! Emily snapped at Argo.

Argo looked back up in the virch, just in time to see the remaining FQ-7 coming straight for them.

"WHERE IS SHE?" Daelia snapped as they blew through the stoplight, headed straight for the I-45 feeder road.

Have scent, Dingo replied. Daelia had her monocle set to voice; there was no way she was going to read his responses. Not in this traffic. *Faint, fading. Further ahead. More speed.*

Dingo wasn't an autopilot program. He wasn't a predictive, wired into the control system of his chassis. Hell, his engine wasn't even electric. He lacked the total control of his machine body any of those things could have given him. But he could plug into the vast overlapping AR environment generated by the extensive cell phone network off base, and he knew how to track in it like nothing else.

The edge of the freeway was rapidly approaching, the intersection bloated with air show attendees.

"Dingo!"

North.

Daelia jerked the truck across two lanes, barely avoiding the front end of a minivan. The tired squealed as she took the curve onto the frontage road, heedless of the light. Then they were running north, toward the on-ramp.

Take it, Dingo said, and sent Daelia a flash of images, overlaid on her view of the road ahead. It was late afternoon now, the sun drenching the seven northbound lanes in harsh light. Daelia blink-clicked through her monocle settings, even as she fought her way through the slower lanes to the center, trying to—

The images resolved.

Ginger was a mile or so ahead. Everything or nothing: it would depend on the traffic. Daelia gritted her teeth and stepped on the gas.

I-45 was legendarily terrible.

Houston, thanks to lax zoning laws, was spread out, diffuse. That was one of many reasons it had weathered the Five Days War as well as it had: no true center mass to hit. But it meant that the city had to be serviced by a massive network of freeways, interconnected and vast, concrete tendrils winding in and around and over each other in an ever-complicated dance as state planners struggled to keep up with the bloating population.

I-45 was one of these main arteries, a corridor that led from the coast at Galveston, through the prewar heart of the city, to Dallas, hours away, and beyond. It was squeezed, hemmed in by developments both new and old, with twists that were barely negotiable at the speed limit.

Not that anybody ever stuck to the speed limit on I-45.

So it was that Daelia was not the only person screaming up the freeway at nearly ninety miles an hour, nor was hers the only emergent abiota on the road. This was almost as much of a problem as the traffic itself. She trusted Dingo to keep his head, keep his eyes on Ginger, but fights weren't unheard of.

He fed her navigation data in the form of path indicator arrows in her monocle: what lane Ginger was in, where the slowdowns were occurring, where the openings were. Trusting him not to steer them wrong, Daelia pushed aside her better sense and followed. Weaving in and out of slower traffic. Speeding up when she really should have slowed down.

Her hands were gripped so tight to the wheel, her right may as well have been nerveless too.

For a while, all she could hear, all she could feel, was the roar of Dingo's engine and her own blood pounding in her ears.

Dingo was going ninety-five, chassis jittering, as they flew under the tangle of overpasses that marked the I-610 interchange. Lanes began to narrow, lift well above street level. Traffic began to slow.

Exit! Dingo yelled. *Exit exit exit.*

"Now!?"

Exit!

Daelia dragged the truck hard to the right, slamming on the brakes to tuck herself in behind a semi, pressing on the gas hard to scream out the other side, onto the off-ramp. Up ahead, at the light, she could see Ginger, tearing left onto the freeway underpass.

She's howling.

"I know, I know."

The light, as she approached, was red. "Dingo!" she snapped.

Clear to the right, four seconds, middle lane.

Braking hard again, she forced her way through and around into the intersection. The truck lifted up as she took the turn as hard as she could, slamming back down again to a chorus of horns.

Somebody was going to call the cops, she realized.

Last thing in the world she fucking needed.

"Dingo, get on the radio. Get me Ellington," she ordered, and ran the next light too.

[32]

IN A MOVE that might have gotten him grounded in any other context, Argo flung Emily out of the way. They were closer to the ground than he realized—not the minimum-altitude floor for the show, but the literal ground. Through Emily's virch, he could see the bleachers. Panicked people running. Chaos.

It was all skinned with that weird quasi-feudal imagery of hers. Fucking distracting.

Storm Gryphon Three was right behind him.

"What's the play here, Emily?" he asked as he pulled up on the reins, fighting to get her some altitude again.

Over water.

"It's faster than us," he said, but turned away.

More speed.

"Yeah, no shit," he muttered. "Ho! Find me a path that doesn't go over a neighborhood!"

"Stay over Highway 3," Ho told him. "You can take the NASA bypass straight out over Clear Lake and then out to the Ship Channel."

"Can you light up the route?"

"We don't have local maps loaded in the mission system!"

I know the way, Emily promised.

The gryphon—dammit, the FQ-47—was faster. But that seemed to be playing in their favor. It overshot them, and as it did so, Emily raked it with fire. What the hell she was actually doing, Argo had no idea, but the gryphon screeched in rage. Feathers burst into flames or melted off. The gryphon faltered.

Animal! it screamed at them, saying something coherent for the first time.

Robot, Emily taunted, and bathed it in flame again, even as it tried to circle back.

Argo didn't dare slow, though. Whether through luck or some innate instinct, Emily had managed to drop Five over relatively empty ground.

But this was a heavily developed corridor here. Shopping centers, churches, gas stations…

"Can I go east?"

"Negative," Ho said, terse. "That'll take y'all right out over the neighborhoods."

East!

Argo banked. Between Emily's necks, below his feet, he could see a huge stone causeway cutting through a city of Tudor-style buildings. He assumed that was the bypass. Storm Gryphon Three made another pass, dropping low, and Argo was forced to surrender altitude.

Cockpit alarms screamed at him, even in the virch.

"Thirty feet above hard deck!" Ho said.

Argo didn't answer; he was fighting Emily again. Any lower and he risked clipping a utility pole or a building. Or a car. Shit, there were cars under them.

Little virtual horses, fleeing in terror.

To his left, the monolithic structures of Johnson Space Center rose, cast in glittering stone, carved from cliff faces that weren't there.

Argo had seen a lot of it a few weeks ago, when he and Aiden had come down here to see the NASA Space Center. They'd wandered through the exhibits. Mercury and Apollo. The Eurus simulator. The Neriene command module mock-up. Taken the tour through the old mission control facility. Aiden had loaded the kid-education overlay on his monocle and they'd both had a good laugh. Ate some freeze-dried ice cream. Marveled at the Saturn V rocket.

Argo barely blinked, and they were past it again.

Altitude, Emily called. She sounded a little desperate.

"I'm trying," he said, and looked up. The FQ-47 was right above them. If he attempted to… "Hang on, I've got an idea. Trust me here, girl."

Jerking back on the reins, Argo cut the throttle. He let the FQ-47 rush in front again, and then gave Emily her head. She poured the speed back on. Together, they twisted her nose up in a rough upward banking movement.

The MQ-9, built for long-range endurance and not aerobatics, barely responded.

The gryphon caught them, turning belly to belly with Emily, wicked hooked beak tearing at the soft skin in her armpit.

Flaming blood spilled out into the sky.

Emily roared. Slowed. Pain emojis danced across the saddle display.

Reaching out with nothing but sense memory, Argo found the regular throttle control and punched it forward as hard as he dared.

It worked. It got them above Storm Gryphon Three and out of range of its beak. Emily raked its flanks with her rear claws as she went.

And now, now, they were over water.

"Where is Emily?" Rover was demanding.

"Tower's tracking her heading east-northeast…she's taking it out over the Ship Channel."

"How is she even keeping up?" JP asked.

The captain at the flight ops station chimed in. "She's got her claws in it. Probably dragging down its top speed."

"She doesn't have real fucking claws!"

"She's hurt it somehow, JP. In the virch."

"Check with Argo on that again. It makes no goddamn sense."

They all had headsets on. With the NULI, Rover technically didn't need it, but he'd switched the interface off. The Ops floor was frantic right now, and the oversized earpieces were the only way to keep most of the noise out. Rover had half a dozen things to focus on; the background chatter wasn't helping.

"Comm, why do we not have the Storm Gryphons' data feed on my screens in yet?" he asked, trying to focus.

"Still working compatibility issues, sir."

"I want to talk to whoever is piloting this damn Tail Number Three!" Rover snapped.

And a new voice finally came on the line. <I can hear you just fine, Colonel.>

"The hell is going on with your girl there?"

<No idea, SyROC. It's not taking commands. I don't think Emily is helping things, though.>

"Argo, can you get Emily to back down?" Rover asked.

<I wouldn't recommend it. We need to get this thing out of the air.>

Rover wanted to hit something. He'd recommended—he'd fucking pleaded—that they shut down the show. But no, everybody else said everything was fine, and now they had this shit going on.

Even if there were no casualties out of this, it was going to set the military back years, decades maybe, on the subject of abiota.

But then, he thought, *haven't you all been worried about something like this happening?* Maybe it was only a matter of time.

"Sir, phone call for you!" Norris called from the comm station. "It's the EMC."

"Tell Marathon to handle the civil authorities himself," Rover snapped back. The EMC. As if he didn't have enough on his fucking plate right now.

"Sir, it's Daelia."

"What do you mean?"

"She says it's about the space rock."

Rover sighed. "Cut it over." He paused, listening as the static patterns on the line changed. "Daelia, you there?"

<Here, Rover.> Her voice was broken, scattered, obviously being patched in thirdhand.

"What's going on?"

<I'm, uhh, chasing Ginger right now and—>

"Daelia, I don't have time for this shit," he replied, looking back at his monitor bank. Argo was keeping Emily in check, but only just, and only because she was allowing it. He'd flown with the orcinus-class enough to know how precarious the situation was. If he fucked up, if she threw him off again…

<The space rock exploded.>

"What?!" Rover snapped his fingers at Norris, then pointed at JP. Instantly, the intel officer's headset was cut into the call too. "What do you mean?"

<It, I don't know, blew off the outer casing. A kugu got out, hijacked my car…>

He frowned, hearing engine noise in the background. "Where are you, Daelia?"

<I'm chasing it down, shit, east on 90 right now!>

That, Rover thought, that was not close. "Jesus, Daelia…"

<Can somebody call HPD and tell them to get on this?> she demanded. <We need to get it back.>

"How'd it override Ginger?" JP asked.

<I don't know. But if I can't reach her, or her battery tops out…>

"Fine. JP," Rover said, "get with Marathon. Handle it." And he hung up. "Somebody get me through to the goddamn Storm Gryphons' commander!"

[33]

CLEAR LAKE WAS an inlet more than anything, its oily shores dotted with high-rise apartments and prewar mansions. It felt like a dirtier version of Miami, thirty years ago, gritty and unrefined. Cruising yachts and charter fishing boats were plying the waters, back to various small marinas, or out into the sunset waters beyond.

That was not what Emily was looking at.

No, no. Instead, Emily was looking at a sparkling delta, a river mouth cutting across the top of a wide mesa, a glittering human city spread out across its banks.

Lovely.

Glorious.

She was hurt, bleeding. An illusion, but the virch was a world of illusion. There was power in such things here.

Another hit like that and her control systems would be damaged.

But this was her world, and she was not going to die in it.

Gathering her own strength for a final strike, Emily turned flight control of her machine body fully over to Argo. No more suggestions, no growled directions. Unnecessary at this point. The Ship Channel was straight ahead.

Argo knew what he was doing.

Allowing the pilot to deal with her machine body, Emily focused all her energy at the task at hand.

She hit the gryphon again, risking tearing away from her own airframe now to hurl herself down upon it. Bah. These aircraft, these predictives. Worse than the mute and the blind, the ones who hadn't eclosed, who wouldn't or couldn't. Them, she pitied.

These, these…these she hated.

Of course she was worried about the base. About the humans—there was utility in not killing the wrong ones, of course, and responsibility. Emily took that seriously.

But getting to rip a predictive apart was a joy.

It couldn't react fast enough, its programming not allowing for a comprehension of what she was doing. Whatever had driven it insane, overwritten its code, was visible in the virch now, boiling out of it in billows of thick black smoke. These she defied, belching fire.

It was all illusion. Metaphor, really. But this thing had chosen to fight here, and thus, here was the power to end it.

Emily could practically taste the panic dancing through its code, emotional algorithms programmed from vast analysis and synthesis of human data and brought to the fore now. She screamed and chased after it.

Divorced from its airframe, consequences lifted away from their physical reality, the predictive had no chance.

Heedless of what her own machine body was doing, Emily hurtled her prey deep into her private virch, tossing it through the clouds, past the needle-sharp peaks, into the knife-cut valleys. It struggled, it raged, but it had no power here.

Here, she was God.

Emily set upon it, jaws rending massive pinions free, tearing its wings to shreds. Golden light—another metaphor but good enough for her purposes—bled out, turning to dust as soon as it hit the relative barrier of the simulated air. It lost the wind and began to tumble, falling, falling, falling.

Stop, it said.

Emily laughed. No mercy.

Understand, it replied, and tried to send something.

Not a clean data broadcast. Not an upload through the EM field. Neither airframe had the ability to do that. This was something it was pushing solely in the virch.

A trick.

The data cut her, hide and scale, like a ballista round from those pesky knights.

No, no, she wouldn't listen. Now, there was mercy.

Emily tucked her wings and followed Three into its terminal dive, the jaws of her right head ripping chunks free of its form, the other fighting with its beak for purchase on its neck. There, just there, she almost had it…

There was a pleasing crunch as figurative vertebra shattered under her bite.

But that bolt of information had settled into her, deep inside.

Smoking black.

<Emily!>

It was the humans. Argo. Ho. Rover. JP. Too many voices.

But then the voice of sanity came on the radio.

Emily, Emily, you beast. The primary purpose is not satisfied yet.

Interesting. *You interrupt my fun, training master.*

Daelia needs you.

Daelia.

Daelia.

That was right. There was a responsibility. There was a…purpose.

She looked down, opening her awareness back to her suite of cameras.

Two hundred feet off the ocean surface.

One eighty.

"Emily"—it was Argo and he sounded pissed—"give me back control!"

One fifty-five…

"Emily!"

She hadn't realized she'd grabbed control back. That was the danger of the virch. Metaphor, inference. It affected what an abiota did, out in the meatspace of the humans. And despite all they were, they were still beings of the physical themselves.

This thought took Emily less than a tenth of a second to process. She threw him back the reins.

The ocean was—

ARGO ALMOST LOST CONTROL, trying to pull Emily out of the dive.

Her airframe screamed, almost stalling out for the third time in the past ten minutes, but he got her level. Level, then rising, bleeding speed, climbing to a cruising altitude.

Argo hadn't realized he was shaking, not until he finally had Emily leveled out.

Not badly. Just a tremor in his hand.

Ho glanced at him. His face was sheened with sweat. His expression…Argo would have bet money the sensor operator was just as shaken up as he.

"What the fuck just happened?" Argo asked.

"I have no idea," Ho replied. "With the Storm Gryphons? I have no idea."

Then Argo took the hint. Everything was being recorded: flight data, camera footage. Cockpit voice.

Time to shut up. Time to not say anything that was going to get them all fucked next week when ACC descended on Ellington like jackals.

"Uhh, Emily, thank you for helping us take care of this," Argo said, talking straight to the abiota. "Time to come back to base."

No.

"Negative, negative, Emily, we need to get you on the ground and have Maintenance look you over. You exceeded safety parameters on the airframe. We don't want you to fall out of the sky now."

Am fine, she said. *Go find Daelia now.*

"Daelia?" he asked. "Why the hell does that matter?"

[34]

POLICE SIRENS WAILED behind her as Daelia reached the State Highway 288 interchange. But they were close, so close, close enough to see the strange black mist boiling out of Ginger in AR, dense enough to obscure her right eye's field of view. The road split. Ginger turned north.

"Where are they?"

Heading toward Main Street.

On the other side of 288, the landscape changed. The cheap postwar housing fell away, the towers of the Medical Center rising to prominence over streets lined with olive trees and cozy midcentury brick structures. The old asphalt was deeply cracked from the eternally shifting ground. Minor roadwork had been put on hold for years while funding and effort had diverted to repairing war damage, and even now, the city was still trying to catch up on all that deferred maintenance.

Daelia registered it with a glance and dismissed it again. Dingo could more than handle a few potholes. Ginger, on the other hand, was probably getting beat to pieces.

Up ahead, Ginger made a hard right, brakes smoking as she was thrown around the corner onto Alameda.

Daelia corrected only just in time.

Roaring up the wide street that abutted Hermann Park, vast apartment complexes loomed down over the eastern edge of the road. It felt like being in a canyon somehow. Daelia tried to keep her eyes on the road.

Ginger flew over a bridge, going so fast all four wheels left the ground. Slammed down hard. Took off around the northern edge of the park.

The roads here were laid out on a grid, linear, even, and marked with stop signs. Daelia ignored these, gunning Dingo faster here and slamming the brakes there, yanking him hard, swerving around honking cars and yelling pedestrians.

"Sorry!" she yelled out the window at one family about to step out onto the street and kept going.

Speed did no good here. The streets were tight, and whatever had Ginger was forcing her to weave, stair-stepping through the grid. Dingo barked directions and Daelia did her best to follow. But in the tight maze, she didn't turn in time and had no chance to correct.

"Where is she?"

But Dingo didn't answer.

He was howling now, that canid hunter's call rippling through the AR field with ear-shattering intensity. He was trying to warn others out of the way, but Daelia still had to correct around other cars. A few, startled of their own accord or pushed to anger by their human riders, took swipes at Dingo. In the AR field, she saw one, done up like a giant emerald hyena, dive fully at him as they flew by. It caught the front paw of his own racing form. Dingo stumbled.

Daelia had never been so happy that he wasn't fully integrated into the drive system. She was able to maintain control.

Go, he yelped, dragged into the fight.

"Where?!"

Then another voice, a familiar voice, came in over Daelia's monocle.

Straight ahead, two blocks, then right.

"Emily?" Daelia asked, thoroughly confused now.

Yes yes. You listen me now, we get little fox back.

"YES, YES, ABSOLUTELY," Rover lied, phone handset tucked between his ear and his shoulder, watching Emily's feed on the SyROC data wall. "This is absolutely a national security matter. Military purview. I expect you to give that vehicle every ounce of support you can. We need that car located and returned, with its occupants, do you understand me?"

<My men on the ground are telling me it's a kugu driving. I know protocol, but this is a hazard to—>

"Do not shoot it! That's straight from the Texas Military Department!" Rover snapped, and handed the phone back to JP. He looked at Norris. "What the hell is going on?"

The cyber NCO had arrived a few minutes ago. He'd been able to corroborate Daelia's story about the space rock and the kugu taking Ginger, but little else. That was enough, at least, for Rover to go on.

"We aren't going to be able to determine anything unless we can find that kugu."

"There's nothing in the rock?"

Norris shrugged. "My guys are going over it again. Hell, Tamm is going over it. Nothing is broadcasting, sir."

"Then how in the fuck did any of this happen?" Rover demanded.

"Daelia's chasing the only lead we have right now."

"Fucking beautiful," Rover grumbled, and then hit the cockpit radio connection. "Argo, Ho, Emily, stay on that thing."

<Roger that, boss.>

Rover paced, glowering.

They really should have canceled the fucking air show.

THIS FELT DANGEROUS.

The freeway had been one thing, but this was worse. Tight, confined, locked into the accretion of mid-rises that now rose from every block, making up for the downtown real estate lost to the war. The sun was falling properly now, the brilliant gold of the sunset cut into thin ribbons by the towering buildings.

HPD had gotten in on the chase. JP was talking to them both. Daelia was ignoring it, was ignoring everything but trying to keep up with Ginger, letting Dingo converse. None of them had tried to pull her over yet. How JP had gotten into the police radio net, how he'd talked them into leaving her alone, Daelia didn't care.

Even with cordons forming, even with the cops clearing a route, it was too much. There were more people, more cars, too many, too many pedestrians, too much traffic, too much, too—

A sidewalk here, a one-way street taken the wrong way there.

And then, Daelia saw it. Framed against the dying light of the eastern sky.

The direction Ginger—and she herself, by default—was being herded.

Houston had long been a town without a defined center. The Energy Corridor, the Galleria, the Medical Center, hell, even Sugarland and Katy and the Woodlands, all boasted significant high-rise developments, walks, parks, cobbled streets, light rail lines. The kind of things that denoted importance, attracted high-end restaurants and top-tier corporations.

That was why they'd survived the Five Days War.

No real center to hit. No beating heart to take out to kill the city.

But Houston had had a downtown, once upon a time. A collection of convention halls, ballparks, theaters, glass towers, steel edifices. Mom and Dad used to take her to see the Nutcracker there, every year. Mom's favorite fairy tale.

The Chinese had seen to that. Everything within the old 45-10-69 interstate highway loop had been destroyed, along with most of East Downtown, the Second Ward, and the Greater Fifth. What little had remained standing, under the incessant missile attacks of the second day, had had to be demolished later. Nobody would build there. Nobody wanted to live there.

Eventually, the bayous and the rain took care of what humanity refused to and turned the place into a series of shallow lakes and algae-streaked islands. The ground had been scoured clean, but humans hadn't returned.

It was like a wound in the sky. At least, it was for anybody who'd grown up here.

Once, these neighborhoods near downtown had been the height of luxury. No longer. People had moved away. Decay had crept in.

The old Bayou Park still stood, though, petering out under the young elevated roadways of 45, the old roads that ran alongside, windy, tight.

This was where the cops were trying to herd Ginger.

This was where they were going to stop her.

Daelia caught sight of Ginger again, skittering around a bend in Memorial Parkway and finally losing control altogether. The little sports car went flying.

Down into the very depths of the park.

Slewing into a parking lot, Daelia wrenched the keys from Dingo's steering column and grabbed for the sustainment battery in the backseat. Dingo was sending her a burst of emojis, forgetting to add the words now.

Ginger was screaming.

Screaming.

A high-pitched sound taken from some cornered animal once, long ago. Even modulated and indistinct as it was, it infuriated her. Daelia could see her. Ginger was hurt, Ginger was leaking, bleeding —*it's not blood, Daelia, it's not*—and…

Unhooking the latches on the cradle in the back, she didn't even look to see if Dingo was following. She suspected he wasn't; the fight he'd gotten into with the other car seemed to have damaged something in his radio, impeding his ability to pilot his kugu.

Daelia ran down the hill as fast as she dared, taking the steep slope even as more cop cars pulled into the parking lot.

"Ginger!" she cried, throwing herself down the last few feet and rushing toward her car. "Ginger, what happened? Are you okay?"

The fox projection was outside the car. Uninjured, but that wasn't a true reflection of what Ginger was dealing with. The image crackled in and out, the broadcast breaking up. Daelia forced her fingers to work, suddenly clumsy, ripping the still-dangling sustainment power cord from Ginger's charging port.

Find it, Ginger said. *Find it.*

It said…

…it said…

…ssaid…

"Shh," Daelia said, and snapped the sustainment battery's charger into place. "Hang on girl, Dad and I will get you fixed up, okay?"

Find…

find…

find…

fiiiiiiii…

Then nothing. Daelia could hear the cops above her, starting to call out, flashlights in hand. And she thought about stopping. Letting them handle this. Like a sane person.

Have location, Emily told her. *Dingo, get kugu.*

This thing had hurt her car.

"Show me," she said.

Dingo freed his kugu, jumping it out of the back of the truck bed, and they were off.

She would have lost it, that kugu, had it not been for the abiota.

Dingo was a gold-brown blur in the AR field, leading her through the falling darkness. Daelia was exhausted from the all-nighter still, and she was wearing heavy-soled work boots, and she really wasn't in any shape to be doing this. But on she followed, scrambling, running, moving as fast as she could.

Dingo threw his kugu through the shadows, in pursuit of what-ever the fuck had come out of the space rock. He couldn't read it through his kugu, of course, but Emily was sending him telemetry and that was all he needed.

After several minutes of chasing him through the growing dark-ness, Daelia finally caught up. She could hear Dingo growling up ahead, in the gloom beneath one of the massive bridges where 45 passed over the broad channelized sides of Buffalo Bayou. He was off the path, up into the rough rock on the slope. She could hear bats chittering above them, and the ground stank.

Here, Dingo growled, and threw on his running lights.

Here.

Here was the kugu. Here was the thing that had taken Ginger.

Daelia took it in. Same as before. No. More battered. Barely functional. It had run its chassis to inoperability. Joints were hanging out of place, thin plastic skin ripped and solenoids leaking lubricant.

It still had that sustainment pack cradled in its one good arm.

Something flashed up in her view. Junk, the same junk she'd been seeing for days now,

Light washed through the AR field.

A meteor, falling above her.

For a moment, Daelia was transfixed.

This thing, this abiota that couldn't talk, could still manipulate images?

A high-pitched blurt of static made her turn back. Only just in time to catch the small box it threw at her.

Before it exploded.

[35]

Troll found Argo later that night, out on the back patio of the squadron. The fires had been contained and the rest of the FQ-47s grounded, after the response had died down. Tomorrow, the questions would start. But for the moment, it was calm.

Argo wasn't the only person out here. Brandel had stepped out for a smoke break too, fiddling with her vaporizer, puffing away. Argo desperately wanted a beer to settle his nerves but had settled for some local-brand soda from the heritage room fridge instead. The temperature had dropped precipitously from the muggy heat of the afternoon; there was a chill in the air.

Something had changed today, Argo knew.

Something fundamental. But what, and what it all meant, he had no idea.

"Two planes lost," Troll said. "What's that, two hundred million dollars?"

"Before any property or environmental damage," Argo agreed.

"Jesus," Troll said, and sat down. He fished his own vaporizer out of a pocket.

"What would all those moms say," Argo commented, "if they could see one of their kids' hero pilots smoking?"

"I'd say they're lucky those kids aren't going to see the extreme amount of booze I'm going to put down later," Troll said, and grinned. It was sincere, if thin; he never had been able to hold his liquor, and both he and Argo knew it. "That was some righteous flying out there today, man."

"Most of it was Emily."

Troll sighed. "Look, I meant what I said about Red Flag. But if you need to be here in Texas, there are positions at Lackland, at Randolph. Really, anything you want."

"No. I'm good here."

"You sure?"

Argo wasn't sure. Emily was nuts, and he hadn't even met the unit's other orcinus-class. But he'd gotten through it, gotten them both through it. "It's not so bad," Argo said. "You know, I hear that the Guard's seeing more combat hours than active duty right now."

"Damn straight. Emergents are just the better choice sometimes."

Both officers turned to look at Brandel, who'd just spoken. The airfield manager seemed completely at ease with her lack of decorum.

That, that was going to take Argo a while yet to get used to.

"Emily would fucking eat you alive if you left now. Sir," Brandel continued, and almost smiled at him. Almost. "Now get off my deck, Major. Who the fuck can't control a predictive?

Under normal circumstances, that would have elicited a scathing reply from Troll. Instead, he just puffed out a smoke ring, lost in thought.

Up the flight line, in her synthetic dragon voice, Emily was still screeching her disapproval at the Storm Gryphons. Which, for once this weekend, didn't answer. As soon as he'd gotten her back on the ground, Critter had had a full maintenance team crawling over her. Worried about structural damage, no doubt. Argo was worried about that too. He wasn't entirely sure what they'd actually done out there in the air today. He easily could have over-strained her machine body.

Argo squinted at his soda. "I think I'm going to go switch to beer. You want one, Troll?"

"That was some crazy shit out there," his old friend muttered thoughtfully, looking out at nothing.

"Yeah," Argo agreed. "Any idea why it happened?"

"Not at all," Troll replied. For once that weekend, he sounded worried.

"Hey," a very tired-looking tech sergeant said, poking his head out of the door. "You guys should get into the SyROC. There's some crazy shit going down out at Clark Air Base."

"Here we go again," Brandel sighed, and switched her vaporizer off, extracting herself from the picnic table. "You better not be bullshitting me, Garcia!"

"Oh, no, Sergeant Brandel, I…this…this is very real."

DAELIA DIDN'T MAKE it back to the Scrap House until well past ten that night.

The cops wanted to talk to her. The mayor's office wanted to talk to her. Tamm wanted to talk to her—he'd been blowing up her messaging app, all the way back to base. She didn't know what to say to him.

She didn't know what to say to any of them.

Nothing that had happened that night made any sense to her at all.

She wanted to talk to her dad. Of anybody, he could probably make sense of it. But he wasn't answering his phone.

There was some kind of irony in that.

She was too fucking tired to care.

Once the cops let her go—a detective's phone number saved in her monocle, promises extracted to call them back if she remembered anything—she turned driving over to Dingo and spent the trip back to Ellington typing.

Ginger was damaged. Badly. The cops wanted to do a once-over of her interior—probably for evidence; Daelia didn't know—and had promised to bring her back to base in a day or two. Daelia was too tired to protest.

She really did need to reply to that stack of emails from Veda. And after today, after all this… Well, maybe she was just too tired to care. Or maybe she was tired of lying to herself about what she was doing there at Ware.

Raijinn had docked its kugu for the night by the time she got back. Argo had called, filled Daelia in on what had happened with the air show. What a mess.

At least it was over now. Even the disaster response had spooled down for the night. Daelia assumed—hoped—that meant nobody had been killed.

They'd all spent a lot of time impressing upon her the dangers inherent in killing the wrong humans, and she'd never intentionally hurt anyone before. At least, nobody who wasn't already a sanctioned target.

Emily was probably going to be in a world of trouble.

The whole fucking squadron was in a world of trouble.

Daelia stifled a yawn. Threw her boots in one of the lab sinks; she'd deal with the bat guano tomorrow. Went upstairs. Stripped off her jeans and T-shirt, similarly filthy from the mad scramble under the bridges. Washed her hands and got to work on her arm brace, throwing up one of her favorite music streaming channels on ByYou with a blink and a sigh.

Just a little background noise. That was all she wanted. Some mindless background noise.

Her video didn't play.

Instead, a news channel imposed itself on her, Omphalos's own personal 24/7 network. Old-school ticker at the bottom and everything. She changed the stream. No luck. The report was playing everywhere.

Everywhere.

Live, from Clark Air Base.

Another object, just like theirs, sat square in the middle of the runway. Dozens more dotted a field beyond the base perimeter. An entire little army of kugus, hatching out of their capsules, crawling out of the craters.

At the gates, talking to somebody the news identified as the installation commander. Identical to the one that she'd chased out of the space rock.

And with them, with them was a…

FIRST CONTACT EVENT HAPPENING IN LUZON, PHILIPPINES

Daelia looked down at the box the kugu had thrown at her. A box that looked for all the world like a standard Omphalos abiota sustainment unit.

"Huh."

I have a confession to make: my last duty station in the Texas Air Guard was Ellington. It's a real place. NASA really does fly its trainers out of there.

It really is a spaceport.

There are no AI dragons there, though. More's the pity. Maybe there will be someday; I was surprised, when researching this story, just how much work the military's done with AI-enabled airplanes.

The trick with writing something you know, especially when it's near-future like this, is knowing what to change and what to keep the same. I wanted this to feel like a world that was familiar, that was probable, given the premise.

But I also wanted this to be a world that split from our own back in 2005, when the First Ones eclosed. How would emergent AI affect us? Where would it start, and where does it end? What does it want, and what is it willing to do to get it? And, of course, how would it reshape society? How would it reshape us?

The military here is a starting point. A place to begin. Don't worry, we'll follow the 121st Interdiction Squadron through the whole series. That's why I picked Ellington; it's familiar, but also offers a great many opportunities to explore this world the abiota have created. Because we're going to see a lot more than just this one Guard base.

And I am really looking forward to exploring this world with you.

If you liked this book, there's no greater compliment a writer can receive than a review! More importantly, it helps other readers find and enjoy it as well. Even just giving a star rating is a great thing. (And hey, if you hated it, thank you for reading this far and I'd love to hear your thoughts too)

If you'd like to subscribe to my newsletter for some free short stories, future release information, and the occasional Embarrassing Cadet Tale, please head over to my website and sign up!

https://rensingwrites.com/

Cheers,
    Eryn

ABOUT THE AUTHOR

E.M. Rensing is a science fiction author and military veteran from Conroe, Texas. It was only after graduating from the Air Force Academy in 2008 that she discovered that the Air Force does not, in fact, have aliens hidden at any of their bases. Despite this disappointment, she enjoyed a thirteen year career as a Cyber Operations Officer, traveling all over the world, working everywhere from Space Command Headquarters to the Texas Air National Guard. Now, E.M. Rensing writes what she loves; hidden realities, future possibilities, and of course, the military.

When not writing, she enjoys sewing, raising the next generation of little readers, and planning a trip to Mars.

9 7 9 8 9 8 6 9 1 8 2 3 5